Meteors
in
August

Meteors in August

A NOVEL BY

Melanie Rae Thon

RANDOM HOUSE

NEW YORK

Library of Congress Cataloging-in-Publication Data

Thon, Melanie Rae.
Meteors in August : a novel / by Melanie Rae Thon.
p.   cm.
ISBN 0-394-57664-0
I. Title.
PS3570.H6474M4   1990
813'.54—dc20   89-43436

Manufactured in the United States of America
2 4 6 8 9 7 5 3
First Edition

for my mother and father

Weep not for him who is dead, nor bemoan him;
but weep bitterly for him who goes away,
for he shall return no more
to see his native land.

JEREMIAH 22:10

Meteors
in
August

I

I WAS seven years old the night my father chased Red Elk out of the valley. Afterward he sat huddled at the kitchen table with a pack of men, their boots caked with mud, their whiskey bottle amber in the light. My sister, Nina, and I crouched on the stairs, shivering in our thin nightgowns. Voices slurred until the men all sounded the same.

"We drove that red-skinned trash out of town once and for all."

"I would've killed him with my own hands."

"Damn dogs."

"Hardly worth the trouble to kill an Indian."

"Well, it would've been worth *my* trouble."

"She's just one of Harley Furey's girls—let him have her, and that bastard boy too."

These men worked at the lumbermill with my father. Vern and Ralph Foot were a hulking pair, with black beards and scraggly mustaches that covered their mouths. I could tell them apart only when they laughed. Vern had no front teeth ever since the night he fell on his face on Main Street and didn't stand up till morning. The third man was Dwight Carson; he was burly, but his pale, pinkish skin made him look exposed and weak despite his size. Father was their foreman and had little use for them when he was sober. During lunch breaks, he was glad to take their money at poker: that was the extent of the pleasure he found in their company. Except tonight. Tonight they had a single purpose.

"Don't matter who she is," Vern said. "Sets a bad example."

Ralph agreed: "Nothing but white scum."

"Stupid mutts," my father muttered. "We almost had him."

"Here's to the next time." Dwight Carson raised his drink. All four glasses clinked together. "To the next time."

They downed their whiskeys and poured another round.

MAMA CAUGHT me and Nina on the stairs. Nina took the brunt of the scolding because she was going on fifteen and was supposed to know better. "Fine thing for you to let Lizzie see," Mama said. "Well, I hope you both remember it. I hope you remember the way men look when they're full of hate and liquor, so full of their failure to kill a man that they'd shoot their own dogs and leave them in the woods to rot. You take a good look at your daddy, then you get your butts back upstairs. And don't let me ever hear you talking about what you saw in this house tonight."

We did look at our father, his face slack from whiskey, his hair matted flat to his scalp, his brow cut with dark creases even when he laughed. Blood spattered his pant legs and we knew Mama spoke the truth. The dogs were dead. The dogs were lying up there in the woods with their tongues hanging out of their mouths and all their yellow teeth showing.

We scurried up to our room, but we didn't sleep. Later, when the men were gone, we heard Daddy pounding at Mama's door.

She'd locked herself in the bedroom where her own mother had died the year I was born. He started out yelling and ended up crying. We knew he was on his knees.

It was almost dawn when he came to our room. The air was gray and watery, a sticky film. He leaned over our beds, watching us while we pretended to sleep. I wanted him to go away. I didn't know where. I wanted him to burn his clothes in the woods so I could stop thinking about the blood on his pants and the mud on his boots. I wanted him to bury those dogs so that I wouldn't find their bones someday, so that I wouldn't stumble on their carcasses and remember.

Nina sat up and rubbed her eyes. "It's okay, Daddy," she said. He turned and disappeared so fast I wondered if he'd been there at all. I was hoping he hadn't. I was hoping this whole night was just something I'd dreamed.

WHEN WE woke again, hours later, Daddy was already dressed in his black suit and white shirt, ready for church. He stood in our doorway, acting as if he were a different man than he was the night before. But his eyes looked sore, and his hair had not been combed. He didn't have to tell us to hurry.

At the Lutheran church, Mother sat between my father and me, her back rigid, her eyes on the pulpit. I looked at Daddy's big hands as he cradled the hymn book; he still had dirt under his nails.

Nina sang in the choir. Her golden hair made her shine, and I believed I heard her pure strain above all others, a solitary soprano, sweet and clear.

Reverend Piggott rose slowly so that we had time to anticipate the seriousness of today's business. He warned that we must be prepared to meet our Maker at any time. He was a bald, bony man who trembled when he spoke: "Would you want to face your Heavenly Father stumbling drunk and muttering obscenities? Would you want to hear His call while you lay in the bed of a woman who was not your wife or with your hands in another man's pocket, your fingers on his last dollar? And what if God should send His angels down to earth just as you raised your gun to take the life of one you despise? What if you blinked and found yourself before the Lord, with your barrel aimed between *His* eyes? Pity the man who dies with murder on his mind. Pray for the man who lives with lust in his heart or a belly full of rage."

I don't know if the reverend had heard of the night's escapades, or if he had chosen the day's topic by chance. Whatever the case, my father took it personally: he tugged at his pant legs as if his clothes were suddenly too tight.

During the minutes of silent prayer, Daddy clasped his hands together with a violence that made me think he believed the left one could keep the right from doing evil. Mother bowed her head and closed her eyes. I'm sure she did not pray.

I hoped that Father was asking God to purge the hatred from his heart so that he might love his red brother as himself, so that he might never again raise his hand in anger against another man. As we said the Lord's Prayer in unison, Mother's lips barely moved, but my father's voice was low and fervent. I thought his eyes brimmed with tears of repentance, but now I wonder: perhaps they only stung from whiskey and lack of sleep.

I imagined he had made a bargain with God, agreed on the terms of atonement. I had to trust Father's sincerity and God's mercy. My own salvation depended on it. From Reverend Piggott I had learned that I was born wicked, tainted by original sin, my father's and my mother's crimes of knowledge. I prayed that I would be spared the burden of Daddy's latest transgression. I had been blessed and baptized, but somehow this protection seemed far too slight to save me from the stain of murderous intentions.

Years later I would realize that my father did not regret what he'd done to Red Elk. He did not long to change his ways or expunge the wrath from his soul. He'd lived with rage so long he could not even imagine himself free of it. So he asked only to be forgiven. Should he die that day, he wanted to enter Heaven in a state of grace. And should he live till evening, he wanted to enter my mother's bed without an argument.

God might have been willing to give Daddy another chance, but Mother was not so easily fooled. She refused to slip her hand around his elbow as we left the dark church. As much as I wanted to believe in my father's enlightenment, I couldn't trust the man Mama spurned. He tried to take my hand, but I pulled away from him, clutching Mother instead.

Nina ran to join us. She looped her arm through Father's and kissed his cheek before he asked. I thought she must have forgotten what we'd seen the night before. I envied her for her laughter, her easy faith. Mother and I dropped behind, and I watched Nina bounce along beside Daddy. Her hair glistened. Her beauty and her simple joy filled me with jealousy. If Father and I had died that day, neither one of us would have been in a state of grace.

Mother squeezed my hand too tightly. I felt an unbearable weight that filled my shoes like stones until I could barely walk. When I was old enough to explain it, I realized this weight was my mother's doubt: she did not believe God had the power to save my father.

I wanted to skip ahead, to feel Daddy's huge, callused hand around my own. But I kept remembering him at the table with those men. I saw the blood on his pants. I thought about the dogs in the woods.

Soon Nina and my father were a block ahead of us. Mama clung to me as if she thought I might charge in front of a car to tease her. She didn't know that I was just as scared as she was.

When I was as old as Nina was that day, I found myself trying to understand why she had to leave us. I kept thinking of the look on Daddy's face when he said he would have killed the big Indian with his own hands. That was before he even knew what was going to become of Nina. But no matter how far back I went, I could never quite see how it all started, and I still haven't figured out why Nina, who loved Daddy and always forgave him, was the one who had to go, while I was the one who stayed.

TWO MONTHS later Mama caught Nina in the shed with Rafe Carson, the son of one of the men in Father's gang. I'd been spying on the two of them for a good half hour, peering through a knothole in the side of the shed. Rafe's hand was stuck down Nina's bra, so Mama had time to give him one good swat on the head before he pulled himself free. He made a run for it and hit a stack of wood in the dark. Sprawled on the ground, he was an easy shot. But Mother had already forgotten him. She backed Nina into a corner, pinned her to the wall with one hand and slapped her with the other, four times, hard across the face, slaps that stung just to hear them. Mother who never struck, who only threatened us with Father's fury, our mother waled on Nina, her blows all the more cruel because they were so unexpected, and so rare.

Mama got her voice back in time to say, "Aren't things bad enough? Your daddy ever catches you like that, he'll be a murderer for sure."

Rafe Carson was on his feet again. He didn't need to hear anything more.

Nina crumpled in the corner, sobbing, and Mama just left her that way. I sneaked into the shed and tried to comfort my sister, but she couldn't stop crying. Her whole body heaved. I curled up, close as I could. I was small and warm. That's all I had to offer. I stroked her blond hair with my clumsy hands. It was snarled from rolling around with that boy, and my fingers snagged in the knots. I kissed her wet cheeks, licking at the salt because it tasted good. But everything I did only made her shake harder.

Finally she shivered and fell asleep, all of a sudden, as if she'd cried herself to death. I felt her shallow breath and knew she was still alive. Her blouse was unbuttoned and one breast had been pulled free of her bra. Her chest flushed, speckled with a heat rash. I touched her skin, lightly, with just the tips of my fingers. She didn't wake.

2

DAYS PASSED slowly in Willis, Montana, when I was a child. We had one movie theater and a musty library. The dust on the shelves revealed how seldom books were borrowed. Sunday service at the Lutheran church was the social event of the week. When the reverend had finally worn himself down and let us go, we gathered outside to catch up on the news. Women admired one another's hats in false, girlish voices, then drew into tight clusters to whisper about daughters who stole their sleeping pills or husbands who stayed out all night and never explained. They touched their friends' arms or their own mouths as they talked. The men stood in larger groups and maintained a dignified distance from one another as they debated the merits of clearcutting or the best bait for rainbow trout. Now and then they eyed their wives impatiently, wondering why women always had so much to say.

Willis sprang up in the shadow of the Rockies. A glacier cut this valley, moving mountains by inches through the years, leaving everything in its path forever changed. But even the greatest force cannot escape time: the frozen blue sea turned to muddy water and seeped slowly into the earth.

The first white men slashed through the underbrush with the glint of silver in their eyes. They crouched in the forest, squatting like old men beneath the bristling pines. By instinct, they climbed toward the timberline, where the dwarf trees clung to brittle rock, wrapping their roots around the stony soil, growing twisted and gray, no taller than children.

When the men stood at last on bare rock and saw below them green slopes and glacial pools, glistening jade and turquoise under a blazing sun, they must have thought they were little gods. Not one of them could imagine the disappointments of the future: the shallow veins of silver, the barren mines closing, all the big-shouldered men condemned to labor among the trees, giving up their dreams of sudden wealth to lumber in the hills and live as mortals.

The town of Willis never boomed, but Main Street got busy enough to hang a traffic light in November of 1966. Our Main Street was actually a highway: anyone going to or from Canada had to pass through Willis; now they had to stop. The light was set to change so fast that almost no one could sneak through town without slamming on his brakes and taking a good look at the Last Chance Bar and the Lutheran church. A person on his way to the border wouldn't realize, of course, that two years before we had a light this very corner had been the scene of one of the town's most bitter disputes.

I was almost nine the summer Elliot Foot cleared out the shelves of Pike's Grocery and replaced them with barstools. The Saturday afternoon he raised his sign, the men, women and children of Willis were split into two groups: on one side of the street, a rowdy band cheered on Elliot Foot and his two brothers;

on the other side, an inspired mob shouted that a bar facing a church was an affront to God, and we were certain to bear His vengeance.

I preferred the excitement of the joyful crowd, but I watched the frenzy of the Lutherans and their leader, Freda Graves. I knew Mrs. Graves the way I knew most people in Willis. It wasn't a town where a person could be a stranger, unless you were an Indian and folks made a deliberate effort not to learn your name or mind what you were doing.

Now I think that was the day Freda Graves got a hold on me. At the time, she seemed like a crazy woman. If not for her desperation, she would have looked just plain foolish. But later, when everything she said came true, I started thinking about her more and more, remembering how she saw the future. And I came to believe she was the one person in Willis who might help me understand what had happened to Nina, and to me.

Reverend Piggott was nowhere in sight. He couldn't afford to get folks riled. The same ones who drank themselves silly on Saturday night might drop an extra dollar in the collection plate on Sunday morning. So he left Freda Graves to do his dirty work. She was the Lutheran church's most active member. She pounded the organ with a passion that shook the rafters; she sang with the tremor of the saved. I had seen her at least once a month my whole life, but I had never seen her like this. She feared Elliot Foot would steal her thunder by securing his sign before dawn, so she'd slept all night on the steps of the church, beneath the great white arch of the door. Her hair was matted flat to one side of her head and stuck out in a sharp peak on the other. She rose to her full six feet, her chest swelling, her wide nostrils flaring.

Elliot Foot had no intention of raising his sign in the weak light before sunrise. He wanted an audience. He longed for the fierce glare of noon. Freda Graves was doing a fine job of whipping up more business.

By eleven-fifteen the crowd began to grumble, fretting about the heat. Women pushed their noses against the smoke-tinted windows, trying to catch a glimpse of the Foot brothers. Several of the men muttered about popping the damn lock and helping themselves. When Sheriff Wolfe caught wind of that idea, he brought their nonsense to a halt. He could change a man's mind with a glance. I trusted the sheriff to do his job and hoped he'd never have reason to come after me. Other than the Indians, Caleb Wolfe was the darkest man in Willis. No one dared say anything outright, but in private people questioned the purity of his blood, the skin of his grandfather and the morals of his grandmother.

As I grew older I understood that our tolerance for the sheriff depended on the fact that he had never married. Over the years, plenty of Indians drifted through Willis, hoping to find work at the mill. They lived at the foot of the hills on the west side of town. Their houses were abandoned trailers and plywood shacks. When one family moved out, another moved in. Most disappeared within the month, and few of their children ever attended our school. Children from the reservation had to be tested. They rarely passed, of course. Many of us wouldn't have passed either; but as far as I knew, no one ever suggested the tests might be unfair. Thirteen-year-olds were placed in fourth grade. Humiliation kept them home. Occasionally administrators slipped: One year a light-skinned woman came to the school alone to register her three sons. The last name was a French one; no questions were asked, no tests demanded. But there were plenty of complaints when teachers discovered the Champeaux brothers favored their red father rather than their fair mother.

Daddy said Indians were born lazy, that they turned tail at the first sign of trouble and headed back to the reservation, where they got a government check every month for doing nothing but sitting on their hind ends.

I watched Caleb Wolfe hold back the crowd and remembered the trouble Father had caused a certain Indian just a year before. I thought about the dogs in the woods and the mud on my father's boots.

As we waited on the hot street no one dared to cross Sheriff Wolfe—despite the color of his skin. He was short and bow-legged. His stomach hung over his belt, but his fat was hard, not sloppy, the kind of fat a man can use like muscle: for weight and force. The people who'd been talking about busting locks were suddenly nowhere to be seen.

The white light of noon stripped us, left us without shadow or weight. A dangerous fervor swelled through the crowd and threatened to pull us off the ground, a hundred helium balloons cut free. Gwen Holler stood next to me, poking my ribs with her elbow every time light wavered in the glass. I told her to stop, but she didn't hear me, so I jabbed her back and she got the idea. My cousin Jesse darted through the crowd, pinching girls' butts so they jumped and squealed. The air was full of their little pig cries. He gave my bum a squeeze and I whirled, smacked him up the side of the head hard as I could. Jesse only laughed at me.

At precisely three minutes after twelve, according to Freda Graves—"Oh Lord, let us remember this hour"—we heard the dull click of the lock being released, like a trigger hitting an empty chamber. Gwen gripped my hand, squashing all my fingers together. The door creaked open slowly. Inside, the bar was dark as a cave, and I realized how quiet the street was all of a sudden.

Elliot's two younger brothers, Vern and Ralph, appeared. They hadn't changed since the last time I'd seen them; their beards were still long and matted, their mouths still hidden by hair. They lumbered through the doorway, carrying a long blue sign with bright red letters. The crowd took a single breath as if they'd seen a beautiful thing.

Freda Graves shook with the force of her own words. Her huge bony hands drew pictures in the air, scooped out lakes of fire, scattered the valleys with our bleached and numberless bones. "This is the eve of destruction," she shouted, "opening a house of sin to face the House of the Lord." From the bottom of the steps, Myron Evans shouted, "Amen, sister."

Ralph and Vern each slipped a heavy loop of rope around the sign, preparing to hoist it, then ducked inside the dark bar again. "Mark my words well," said Mrs. Graves, "this is the day of our downfall." She sucked hard at the air, filled her lungs, and seemed to grow before our eyes, her shoulders square and broad as a man's, her legs thick as old pines. "We are leading our brothers and sisters into temptation. We walk in the valley of the shadow of death, and I fear evil."

"Amen!" Myron yelled again. His support wasn't helping Freda's cause. He blinked too much when he talked. It made me nervous just to watch him, as if I had to run to the bathroom. Pale, game-legged Myron Evans, a grown man who still lived with his mother and never learned to drive a car, was not generally admired by the people of Willis.

The brothers emerged with a pair of silver ladders. They propped the ladders against the building, giving them a jerk and a shove to be sure they were steady. Elliot waited inside the bar. Mrs. Graves's audience waned now that the action had started; a few of the good Lutherans had strayed to our side of the street. Still she was undaunted. She called out to her meager band of followers. "Come stand beside me, Minnie Hathaway," she shouted. This renewed our curiosity for a moment. We all knew

Minnie. We could smell her in the heat. She doused herself with perfume, a daily reminder of her dear father's funeral, of his coffin drowned in gardenias. She wore white gloves, every day of her life, through all the blistering days of summer and all the brutal days of winter.

Minnie minced up the steps toward Mrs. Graves. She was a bird woman with no wings, brittle-boned and light enough to fly if she'd had some way to get off the ground. "Minnie Hathaway is our beloved sister," Freda said, gripping Minnie to her breast. "And we all know of her struggles." We certainly did. Early in the day Minnie Hathaway was a perfect gentlewoman, so proper and elegant you almost forgot she lived at the rooming house and shared a bathroom with three men and the Fat Lady. But when Minnie got a few drinks in her, she flew into fits that twisted her cracked face and made her cuss in ways that were embarrassing even to men. "Bad as an Indian with liquor," folks said. I was warned not to listen to nasty talk. "Don't judge what you can't understand," Mother often told me. I tried not to judge. What did I know? I was only nine years old. But nothing Mother told me could have stopped me from listening to what people said. If nasty talk was bad for me, I was already poisoned.

At last Elliot appeared in the bright street. The crowd cheered and clapped when they saw him, hero of the day. He was the runt of the family: a small, jittery man with a full beard and a serious lack of hair. He nodded to his brothers. Ralph and Vern each grabbed a line of rope and started up the twin ladders.

They braced themselves on the ledge and slowly pulled the sign toward them. "Is it fair?" Mrs. Graves bellowed. "Is it fair to tempt our own sister this way? Is it just to remind her of her sorrow each time she leaves this holy place?"

"Tell her to leave by the back door," Vern yelled. The crowd hooted.

"Forgive them," Freda Graves moaned, raising her hands to Heaven, "for they know not what they do."

The sign caught the lip of the ledge; the crowd gasped and stepped back, a single being with a single mind. Elliot was the only one who didn't budge. He stood his ground, ready to accept his fate if the sign crashed on his head. Vern and Ralph each gave their end a jiggle and counted: "One, two, three . . . heave!" The sign was up and the mob whooped. In a matter of minutes the wires were attached and the red letters blinked on and off: LAST CHANCE, LAST CHANCE.

Mrs. Graves made a futile attempt to sway the throng as the Foot brothers riveted the sign in place. "Repent, O ye sinners. Turn and be forgiven, Elliot Foot." But Elliot didn't turn; he held the door open while his first customers streamed inside the cool bar. "I see you on a darkening path," Freda warned. "O Lord, the way is dim. A tear disappears in a well. A soul shrivels in Hell."

Gwen and I sneaked up to the door with everyone else. Inside the bar the light was murky, the air already clouded with smoke. We had just poked our heads over the threshold when I felt a swat on my behind. I whirled to face my attacker. It was Nina, my sixteen-year-old sister. "Lizzie Macon, you better get your little ass home if you want to have any butt left to sit on," she said. "Daddy would skin you like a rabbit if he saw you here." She glared at Gwen. "You too, Gwen Holler. Children got no business hanging around a bar."

Gwen said, "You're not my sister. I don't have to listen to you." Then she stuck out the tip of her pointed tongue and darted inside.

I don't know who made me madder: my sister for spoiling our fun, or Gwen for going inside without me. But Gwen was already out of sight and Nina was right in front of me. When she took hold of my arm, I shook her loose and said, "I wish you'd leave me alone. I wish I didn't have a sister."

THE NEXT summer, my cruel wish became a curse. Nina disappeared. When you live in Willis, Montana, you know there aren't too many places to run where they won't find you within the hour and drag you back to your own front door. But my sister found a place, and it was a long time before any of us saw her again.

Before Nina vanished, she dug through the shoe box Mom kept stashed in the hall closet and carefully cut her own head out of each photograph. She didn't want to see posters of herself stuck on every telephone pole for a hundred miles. She left the rest of us intact, so we're still there, grinning stupidly at the camera. I see Nina's legs and Nina's pink dress, the one I yearned for but never wore. I see Nina's hands clasped in front of her, and I recognize her wrists as easily as I would recognize her face. My sister.

In the photographs I am a skinny child with big knees. I keep my hands in my pockets or behind my back. I always thought my arms were too long. Whatever the year, my hair is chopped off short. Mother had a fear of ticks and lice and believed in prevention. She said I didn't take care of myself. I look like a freckled boy forced to wear a dress. My eyes are pale and surprised, as if the flash frightens me every time.

One of my parents is always missing from the picture, but I feel them behind the camera, creating us again and again. Mother has a tiny waist and thin hands. Though I am still a child, I can see the startling ways I will outgrow her. My hidden hands are monstrous. She wears faded dresses, but the cloth is good. Her shoes have chunky heels and tight laces. She is a sensible woman.

The pictures have no colors, only shades of gray, but I remember. Mother's hair had a red glow when she stood in sunlight. Every morning she drew it back into a perfect knot, held fast with half a dozen invisible hairpins.

There are deep lines at the corners of Father's eyes. No matter what the season or time of day, he seems to be squinting into the sun. I see him squeeze Nina's headless shoulders. He is blond, like her, the handsome father of a beautiful girl. His nose is too big, his brows too dark for his fair hair. By afternoon his stubble makes his face look dirty. These imperfections save him. He cannot stop grinning. He pats my head, but he is thinking only of my sister. I scowl. He stoops to kiss her cheek, and she's not there.

3

THE FIRST year Nina was gone I kept telling myself she'd be back any day. The second year my mother cleaned out Nina's drawers and closet. She took the clothes to the Salvation Army in Rovato Falls and stopped at the dump on the way home to heave a garbage bag into the pit. The bag split before it touched the ground. Makeup and perfume, tarnished jewelry and barrettes, tattered romance novels and ticket stubs with boys' names on the back spun and fluttered toward the rotting heaps of strangers' refuse, toward the junked cars and the decaying corpses of the rats that young boys had shot with their fathers' rifles.

After that day Nina began to fade. I couldn't open the closet and catch a whiff of her, lingering on all her clothes; I couldn't see her leaning close to the mirror, worrying over one tiny pimple on the side of her nose.

Nina had always protected me. She saved me from a thrashing that day at the Last Chance Bar, which made my outburst all the more unbearable. She knew Father was apt to strike first and ask questions later. Better to punish unjustly than to let a child escape without rebuke. If I wasn't guilty of that crime, surely I had done something else, something unknown. I deserved every blow. But Father never touched Nina, not until the night she left. She could tease him out of anger, cajole him with laughter, leave him helpless with her smiles.

As I grew older I learned to fool Daddy but not to charm him. Four years after Nina disappeared I still longed for her to leap to my defense, to shelter me and speak for me. I remembered the last winter she was with us. Late one afternoon in early December my cousin Jesse and I pegged snowballs at the Lutheran church. Jesse had shaggy light hair and his teeth were too big for his mouth. He was always in trouble, but the snowballs were my idea. How were we to guess that Reverend Piggott would be at church on Wednesday? How were we to know that the thud of snow would jar him from his prayers and turn the frail minister into a raving prophet, a man with a vision of our imminent doom?

Reverend Piggott believed in the evil of children; he depended on it. Twisting our ears, he dragged us inside and made us stare at the crucifix above the altar, the image of our Lord. I wasn't afraid of God. I couldn't imagine He'd plunge me and Jesse into the fires of hell for throwing a few snowballs, and I thought Reverend Piggott was a bit of a fool to suggest God might be so petty. But I didn't argue. The reverend kept a ruler beside his Bible at the pulpit; I had seen him use it in the heat of a sermon, slapping wood on wood, creating his own thunder. As we stood before the pained Jesus, Reverend Piggott took the stick to our palms, those wicked hands that had packed the snow hard and hurled it at God's holy house. Jesus hung. His palms bled. My eyes burned. Jesse kicked Reverend Piggott in the shin and ran, and I took a second licking for his sake.

"Ask Jesus to forgive you," Reverend Piggott hissed. And I did, but the wooden Jesus did not speak or raise his head.

At home, Nina helped me hide my wounds. Father would have given me a set of marks on my butt to match my palms if he knew what I'd done. Mother would have marched down to the Lutheran church and told Reverend Piggott she'd have him arrested if he ever laid a hand on one of her children again. I didn't want another whipping, but I feared I didn't deserve Mother's fierce defense. Only Nina could save me, my sister who hid me and kissed my palms. *There, baby,* she whispered, *all better.*

The fourth year Nina was gone I discovered I still wished for her protection, and the need rose in me like a living thing. It had to do with Gwen Holler.

Gwen and I ran wild in the summer of 1969. We were full of the sudden knowledge that bloomed from the changes in our bodies, or, at least, the changes in her body. Gwen had taken on the shape of a tiny woman. She was already fourteen, a few months older than I was, as she often reminded me. In her basement, she unbuttoned her blouse to show me the swell of her breasts, the dark circles around her nipples. I thought of Nina in the woodshed with Rafe Carson; I heard Mother's hard slaps. I longed to touch her again, to soothe her, just as I longed to touch Gwen Holler. I wanted to have something to show Gwen, some womanly change that would surprise her, but my arms were still too long, my knees too big. I had nothing to reveal, yet I felt sure that what was happening to her must be happening to me too.

For two weeks, we prowled the gully, a deep gorge at the east side of town. We stalked Gwen's brother, Zachary, and his friend Coe Carson, Rafe's younger brother. They weren't difficult to track: in their wake they left a trail of dead birds and wounded rusty tin cans. Zack and Coe raised their BB guns for any flicker in the woods. If they couldn't find a squirrel or crow, the sun glinting off a shiny thing was enough to spark a volley.

Zack Holler was tough. He had solid thighs, a bit of hair on his chest. He had never learned to compromise because his fists were fast and his head was hard. Red-haired Coe Carson, gangly and too loose in the joints to be quick, straggled after Zachary. The boys didn't know that Gwen and I were creeping through the ravine, just beyond their range, shaking bushes and imitating birdcalls to draw their fire. Often we took refuge in a rickety tree house, where we could watch them cutting through the under-brush.

In the middle of June, Zack and Coe took summer jobs at the mill and gave up their exploits in the gully. Boredom led Gwen and me to become hunters ourselves; our goal was to catch Myron Evans in the act. We pricked our fingers, rubbed them together and swore a pact in blood.

Myron Evans lived three blocks from me in a house bordered by two vacant lots. The old gray body of the building blistered in the sun, and the untended garden grew into a tangle of roses and milkweed. The frail pillars of the porch sagged, allowing the overhang to lurch at a dangerous angle. The endless footfalls of Myron and his mother had beaten the front steps bare. They lived alone in the three-story house. People said that when one room got dirty, when the stacks of newspapers piled too high, and they couldn't find the cats' litter box to change it, Myron and his mother locked the door and moved to another room. Of course, no one knew this for a fact; they hadn't invited any of their neighbors inside for a cup of afternoon tea since 1937.

My aunt Arlen said Mrs. Evans was pretty once, before she had a crippled son, before her husband disappeared into the green edge of twilight. This former beauty was difficult to imagine. Now her left eyelid drooped over her eye and made her half blind. She always turned her head to look at you, to stare you down with her one good eye, bloodshot from overuse, yellow as an old egg where it should have been white.

Mom said Mr. Evans died of pneumonia in the spring of '38, but Aunt Arlen told me Mr. Evans went out to get a beer one warm evening in June and never came home. "What a pity," Arlen said, "and Myron just a boy. No wonder that poor child turned out the way he did, no wonder at all."

Arlen sipped at her coffee, contemplating misfortune and misery. "And then there was that nasty business with Myron's teacher."

"Nothing but a rumor," my mother said.

"Eugene Thornton had to leave town. Myron quit school—never went back after fifth grade. Proof enough for me."

"He quit school because people in this town talk too much, and even little children turn mean."

I knew the children Mother meant. They were men now; they were married with sons of their own. Boys loathe the weakest among them, just as a pack loathes a sick animal. Wolves will hound a crippled cub to death. On the playground, more than twenty years before, three boys had pinned Myron to the dirt. They ran their fingers through his hair, called him Darling and Dear One, My Sweetheart, the names the teacher had given him, alone, after school.

He didn't cry or buck. He pulled his head up and then bashed it on the gravel: once, twice, a third time, until his eyes seemed to float in his skull. He moaned and smiled, knowing he made his own pain, knowing no one could take that away from him.

The boys scattered, leaving Myron sprawled on the ground, blood in his hair.

"Poor Myron," Arlen said again, just to herself.

Yes, poor Myron, everyone in town said so. But people's sympathy didn't keep them from warning their kids not to go near the Evans place after dusk. Rumor had it that Myron was apt to pop out of the bushes and reveal more than a child should see. That's what Gwen and I meant to find out for ourselves.

Some folks said he was retarded and some said he was crazy or just plain evil, but most everyone agreed he should be put away to keep him from annoying decent citizens.

ON A warm night in July, Gwen and I camped outside in my backyard. She'd shaved her legs. "Feel my stubble," she said, and I ran my fingertips over the short, stiff hairs along her shin. Then I felt my own legs. They were neither prickly nor smooth. My legs were covered with fine down, a fuzz I wished to ignore as long as I could.

I knew this was the night we'd catch Myron. My skin was already hot. I wondered what he'd do if he caught us spying. I imagined his pretty white fingers clutched around my throat, his hair flopping forward and back as he lifted me off the ground. And what would we say if we caught him in the bushes doing what people said he did? He was no kid. We weren't going to swat his behind, tell him to zip up his pants and get on home. A boy who could bash his own head on gravel, not once but three times, a child who could beat himself bloody, was frightening in ways I couldn't explain. Now Myron Evans was a grown man; I was scared of what I might have to do if he got hold of my wrist.

Nina had seen him. Nina said she looked out our window one night after I was asleep and saw Myron Evans perched up in our maple tree just looking at her. If anything, I thought this proved Myron was just like any other man in town. Before Nina ran away, boys flocked in our driveway day after day, popping wheelies on their bikes, doing handstands—trying to make her turn her head. Her silky yellow hair fell straight to the middle of her back. She had our mother's fine nose and pale skin, flushed cheeks, and eyes like no other eyes I've seen, green eyes flecked with gold fires. I remembered hearing, more than one time, the ping of a stone hitting our window long after dark and Nina saying to me, "Hush, baby, it's nothing." That last summer, I saw boys in the trees and boys in the grass. Often, the pained, surprised coo of an owl made Nina stop stroking my head and go to the window. If Myron Evans was one of those owls, who could blame him?

At two o'clock Gwen and I stuffed our pillows into our bags. As we crept down the alley toward the Evans place, we got sidetracked by the sweet smell of strawberries in Joanna Foot's garden. Kids who stole from Mrs. Foot risked a double thrashing: one from her and one from their parents when she called them at two-thirty in the morning to come fetch their thieving hoodlums. She'd been in one foul mood ever since her husband Elliot had left her. Freda Graves had been vindicated; her warnings about the evils of alcohol came true in ways we'd never dreamed. Elliot Foot fell prey to temptation when Olivia Jeanne Woodruff came to work at his bar. She was barely nineteen years old, and she didn't wait till her daddy was cold in the ground before she sold his house and bought herself a Winnebago. She wanted her home on wheels, wanted to be ready to roll. She was ready, all right, and she rolled out of town with Elliot Foot.

Elliot left the week before Christmas, and by summer Joanna was talking about planting a headstone in the family plot. Catching kids stealing berries was Joanna Foot's primary delight these days. Zachary Holler had been dragged out of her strawberry patch by his hair and beaten with a willow switch in her kitchen. She stood barely five feet but weighed close to two hundred. Her bottom was a solid pack of shifting flesh, her neck a roll of lumpy fat. Even Zack Holler had to drop his pants and take his licking; there was no arguing with a woman like that.

Luck was with me and Gwen that night. We gorged ourselves, lifted every leaf, plucked each berry, ripe or not. We left our footprints from one end of that garden to the other and laughed as we ran away, thinking of all the days Joanna Foot would curse any kid who dared to pass her house.

We'd almost reached the high hedges of the Evans place when we spotted two men in the vacant lot. The smaller one was easy to recognize, the curve of his spine unmistakable from any distance, even in the dark. "Who's that with Myron?" I said.

"It's my brother," Gwen whispered. I knew we had the same thought: neither of us understood what Zack was doing hanging out with Myron Evans in the middle of the night.

They seemed to be talking, but it didn't last long. Zachary's knee came up so hard that we heard the dull smack all the way across the field. Myron clutched himself and fell to his knees, voiceless, his face lifted to Heaven as if in sudden prayer. The only night sound was wind through grass. Zack's arm twitched; I thought he'd slap Myron, but instead he spit on the ground and ran, afraid of something we couldn't see. Gwen and I zigzagged through back alleys, chasing Zachary until he collapsed on the Hollers' front lawn.

"Zack," Gwen hissed.

He cussed when he realized it was only his sister.

"What'd you do to Myron?" Gwen said.

"I kicked the fucker in the balls."

"Stupid bully."

"Don't call me that. You know I hate it when you call me that."

"Stupid," Gwen said, jabbing his shoulder. "Stupid bully."

I thought she'd get worse than Myron did if she kept it up,

but Zack just sat on the grass, hanging his head, a bad dog who loved his mistress.

"I had to," Zack said at last.

"What'd he do to you?" Gwen said.

"Nothing."

"That's a good reason."

"He tried to give me money."

I'd never known Zack Holler to refuse money. Most things he'd do for free. When Gwen and I dared him to pelt Joanna Foot's car with eggs, he bought the eggs himself.

"So?" Gwen said.

"He wanted me to let him do something."

"What?"

"I can't say."

"Liar."

"I'm not." Zack was whining now.

I suspected he had kicked Myron for the pure pleasure of it. I lay down a few feet from Zack and Gwen and gazed at the crowd of stars. The night was so black they seemed to sink closer and closer to the earth. If I closed my eyes, I thought stars might fall on my face. I'd almost drifted off to sleep when Zack blurted it out: "That damn queer wanted to give me a blow job, said he'd pay me five bucks for the honor."

On the way back to my house, I asked Gwen what a blow job was, and she told me that was when one guy blew on another guy's dick till it tickled him so much he peed all over. I still didn't get it. No one, not even Myron Evans, would pay somebody five dollars just to see him piss.

Even before the gate creaked and we saw our sleeping bags torn open and our pillows crumpled on the grass, I knew something was wrong. That heat was in the air. I had just enough time to see the red-hot end of a cigarette fly from someone's hand to the ground before I was pushed to my knees.

"Where the hell have you been?" my father said. I didn't answer, and he whacked me. My ears buzzed. "I'm talkin' to you, girl." His hand came at me again, but I ducked the blow.

"I forgot something at my house," Gwen said. "We had to get it."

"Don't lie to me, you little smartass."

He grabbed a clump of my hair and yanked me to my feet. "Clean up this mess and get in the house."

He left us, and I knew I had about two minutes before he'd be back to haul me up the steps. My cheeks stung and my head hurt where Daddy had pulled my hair. Gwen said, "He's a pig," and I told her to shut her damn mouth.

MY FATHER worked seven to three at the mill, so he was gone long before I woke. Mother waited in the kitchen for me. I would have preferred Daddy's slaps to her silence. She looked in her cup of coffee for some kind of answer, sad as she'd been the day the president was shot. The tiny lines around her lips betrayed her, revealing every one of her forty-seven years, and more: they were the words unspoken, the truth sucked back.

She said, "Let me see your shoes, Lizzie."

"What?"

"Let me see your damn shoes. Someone stole every single one of Joanna Foot's strawberries last night." She made me turn around and lift one foot at a time. All our running around had destroyed the evidence; no dark soil clung to my shoes, just the pale dust of the alley. Of course it would have been a simple matter for Mom to take one of my shoes, press it into a footprint in Joanna's garden, and see it was a perfect fit. But she was above that. Punishment was a private matter in our house. She wouldn't humiliate either one of us by allowing Mrs. Foot to take her willow switch to me.

"You gave your father a scare," she said. "It nearly killed him when your sister left. You know that, don't you? You could break his heart, Lizzie, and you wouldn't have to do anything close to what she did. You could finish that man off with one tiny nudge. You don't want to do that, do you?"

"No." I barely heard myself.

"Then watch yourself."

I nodded, but I thought it was unfair that I should have to make up for what my sister had done.

LATER THAT morning, I rode my bike past Myron Evans's house. He sat on his porch steps, rocking back and forth, holding something pressed to his chest. I was bold with knowledge, unafraid of him now that I knew what he'd asked of Zack.

I called out, but he didn't answer. I came halfway up the sidewalk. "Whatcha got there?" I said, straddling my bike. Then I saw the black cat. He lifted it toward me, an offering, raised it tenderly, as if it might still feel pain, or love.

The half-grown cat had white paws. Its head hung limp. "Dog get it?" I said. Myron shook his head. "He did." I knew who he meant without asking. Zachary Holler had killed Myron's cat; Zachary Holler had twisted that fragile neck until it snapped. I wanted to tell Myron I was sorry, but I couldn't. I was too ashamed, thinking Gwen and I were to blame, chasing Myron the way we did, waiting for something bad to happen.

4

FOR A month I was forbidden to see Gwen Holler, forbidden to leave the yard after dark. After dinner one night, in the third week of my sentence, I sat in the kitchen with Mom and Aunt Arlen. Arlen lived across the alley. She was Dad's sister and Mom's best friend. "Would you mind asking Dean not to play cards with my husband," she said. "Les lost twenty dollars at lunch yesterday."

"I'll mention it," Mom said, but I knew she wouldn't. There was no sense trying to talk Dad out of gambling, especially when he was on a streak.

My aunt pawed through her purse. "I thought Elliot Foot would be back by now," she said, "whimpering like a dog and begging for another chance. That young girl is gonna wear him down. Mark my words. A man that age will get tired of being loved so much. He'll either come back to Joanna or drop dead, that's what I think." She found her cigarettes and stuffed one in her mouth. Her straight, light hair was chopped off unevenly just below her jaw. I knew she cut her hair herself, just as my father did.

"I thought you gave up on cigarettes," Mom said.

"I did. Lasted a whole week."

"The first week is the hardest. Why'd you start up again?"

"I'd like to see you try living with Lester Munter without something to take the edge off your nerves."

"You think it's any easier living with your brother than it is living with Les?"

Arlen clucked. "No, dear Evelyn, I know for a fact it's not. You have to put up with Dean, and he's not pretty sometimes, but at least you don't have four of his brats besides. Excuse me, three brats. Lucy is an angel, a blessing, youngest child always is. She saves me. But Les and the boys are enough to drive a woman to the state home. All day long I run like a slave—washing clothes, scrubbing sinks, digging up potatoes—and Les comes crashing in the door stinking of sweat and railing at me because supper isn't on the table. 'Why don't you wash up?' I say, sweet as syrup. 'Supper'll be ready when you are.' He yells, 'I'm ready now, woman,' screams it like he has to make up for being so short." She sucked on her cigarette. "And the boys have all picked up his fine personal habits. Someday I swear I'm gonna tell them the slop bucket's out in the yard, and if they smell like pigs, they'll eat like pigs. Just last week Les went off fishing with Justin and Marshall, and all three of them dumped their fish in the sink when they got home, proud as can be, and not one of those fish was clean. Woman's work, they can't be bothered. Then Justin has the gall to say, 'I'm starving, Ma. Can you fry up some bacon and eggs for me?' Lucky for him I didn't have a knife in my hand right then. I would have stuck him, I swear. That boy should be married and out of the house, twenty-five years old and still drinking his mama's milk, but I wouldn't wish him on any girl."

Mom nodded. When Arlen got on a roll it was best to hear her out.

"I thank God," Arlen said, "that two of my babies had the good sense not to wake up in this world. Lord, what would I do if I had six instead of four? Or seven, counting Jesse?"

"Arlen!"

"Oh, don't try to hush me. I know it must be some kind of evil to stop grieving for a boy who drowned, or to be glad your babies were stillborn, but I am glad—well, not glad, but relieved." Arlen didn't stop long enough to see my mother's eyes turn watery, or to notice how she twisted her napkin till it tore. "And I'm more than glad this spring has gone dry, and I don't have to worry about any accidents. Not that I'd have to worry much anyway—Les hardly *looks* at me in a friendly way anymore. I think he's got a girl. Fine by me. Only thing is there isn't much choice in this town and I'm afraid he might be banging the Fat Lady; he's bound to get the clap from her sooner or later. She even takes the Indians. I shouldn't care about that either, I guess. Of course it'd be just my luck for him to get the notion to climb on top of me some night and I'd be stuck with it too."

"Arlen, please," Mom said, "Lizzie."

"She don't know what this is all about, do you, honey?"

I shook my head. The idea of flabby Uncle Lester forcing himself on Aunt Arlen struck me as ridiculous.

I didn't think Uncle Les was so bad. He wasn't as rough as my father. When he rubbed my scalp, it didn't burn, and when he kissed my cheek, his whiskers didn't scratch my face. He knew a couple of tricks. At church picnics, he'd pull nickels and sticks of Beeman's gum out of the ears of all the children who talked to him. Uncle Les looked soft and harmless when he stood beside hard-angled Aunt Arlen. If he took advantage of her, Arlen would have to be halfway agreeable.

My aunt stayed an hour too long. She didn't notice—or didn't mind—that Mother kept popping up to wash one more cup, to scrub at grease on the stove, or to wipe the counter that was already clean.

Finally Arlen stretched and said, "Better be off before Lester comes looking for me." Mom and I stepped out on the back steps with her. "Come here and give your old aunt a kiss good-night, Lizzie," she said. Her strong fingers dug into my back. She bussed me, a loud, wet smooch, and whispered, "If you ever want to know the truth about men, you come see me, honey." I thought of the kinds of things Arlen said about men, that they were helpless as children and smelly as goats. I knew she could never answer the questions I had, the ones that would help me understand why Nina ran away.

Arlen's chickens squawked when she opened her gate. I had no affection for these creatures. The stink of them wafted through our kitchen door on summer nights. They lived petty, brutal lives, were stupid enough to hold their noses in the air and drown in the rain, cruel enough to pluck each other's butt bald. After a thunderstorm the shells of their eggs were so soft they broke in your hand; the slimy white and brilliant yolk oozed through your fingers. Even when a chicken was a handful of fluff, even when you couldn't resist holding it, stroking it with one finger, the ungrateful thing was still likely to shit in your palm.

Mother pulled me back in the house. "Don't trust everything Arlen says," she told me. "And whatever you do, don't *repeat* anything she says."

Who would I tell? I thought. Mother was always reminding me to be careful: Don't talk about your sister. Don't show anyone your grades. Don't let on your daddy got a raise.

I didn't like having so many secrets. They heaped in my head; my brain was full of things I wasn't supposed to say. I dragged our stories behind me, a bag full of bones and dirty rags. I tried to forget my load, to leave it behind, but with a word or a touch my mother could remind me: *pick it up, pick it up.* And when I did, I never failed to see my sister, to hear the spray of gravel against our bedroom window, and feel myself jolt up in bed.

I was nine years old again. Nina put her cool hand on my forehead and told me it was nothing, nothing, a branch scraping the glass. I pretended to sleep. She slid out of bed and dressed, standing in the square of icy moonlight that fell on our floor. I heard her tiptoe down the stairs, her feet bare. I knelt on the bed to look outside and there was Nina, running across the front lawn, her shimmering hair flying behind her. Someone stepped out of the shadows near the hedge and I almost yelped to warn her, but he grabbed her, and she wasn't afraid. She hugged him so tight I thought she wanted him to stop breathing in her arms.

They lay their hands on each other's face, as tenderly as God must touch the souls of unborn children, the ones called back before they fell to earth, the ones too dear for human life.

In the morning Nina nestled next to me in bed. "I saw you leave," I said.

And she whispered, "No, baby, I've been right here all night. It was just a dream."

Now, looking back at that night, I recognized this boy in my memory: tall and black-haired, slim as a shadow—even at midnight Billy Elk was unmistakable. I had always known him, the son of the big Indian and that Furey woman.

So many boys loved Nina that summer. He didn't steal her or tie her hands. I saw how she flung herself in his arms. She chose. She wanted him. The others she teased or ignored. If she could have loved someone else, a good boy, the right kind, perhaps she would have married him instead of running away, but I would have lost her all the same.

*

I TOSSED from side to side in the hot dark, thinking about what Aunt Arlen had said, that she was glad she ended up with four children instead of seven. Maybe she was relieved when those two babies were born dead. I wasn't there. But I saw her the day Jesse drowned, and I saw Jesse too, and there was nothing peaceful about either one of them. We were all swimming at Moon Lake. It was the summer Nina left, but she was still with us that day in July. Jesse splashed me in the face and swam away. That was the last I saw of him. At first we thought he was playing a joke on us, hiding up in the woods; that would be just like Jesse, doing something mean that he thought was funny. We called and called. The sun was white, burning all the color out of the sky. Arlen wailed at the water, glittering and green, and at the white hot sun too, as if they could tell her. We dove again and again, a hundred places, a thousand. Then we sat on the beach shivering in the heat.

Jesse was hiding—but not in the woods. He hid where we were forbidden to swim, where we didn't bother to look because we all obeyed, except Jesse that day in July. He didn't come out till he was good and ready, till his swim trunks had ripped in the place that they'd snagged, till the lake had stilled, its surface turned to glass, hard and imperturbable, God's great blind eye, a perfect mirror of a cloudless sky.

Only then did Jesse come out, his body bobbing to the surface at the end of the dock. Justin and Uncle Les pulled him from Moon Lake, and the boy hung in their arms. Mother tried to hold me back, but I saw everything: the ripped trunks that had held him fast beneath the rotting planks; the long, bloodless scratch down his back; the gaping mouth, his surprise: his eyes flung open, blue, blue, the water, the sky, Jesse's eyes, the wide, open eyes of the unexpected dead.

Nina fell on him, pounded his chest until the water spurted

out of his violet mouth, breathed into him and yelled at his face: *Wake up, damn you, wake up.* But our Jesse was cruel and cold and did not answer. Still, he was not as cruel as Nina, not cruel enough to take even his body away and leave us to wonder, and imagine.

IF I'D gone to Aunt Arlen looking for that advice she'd offered about men, she probably would have told me they were all as selfish as Jesse. She was still mad at him for leaving her the way he did, as if he'd done it just to punish her, with no thought at all for his own sacrifice.

That's what she thought of all her boys. Everything they did was just another way of getting back at her. "What did I ever do but love them?" she often said. "Well, that's how a mother's rewarded for giving too much of herself."

Arlen was already pounding at our door by eight o'clock the next morning. "Will you come look at this?" she said. Mom and I followed her through the backyard. She pointed at the truck in the driveway. "Now, what do you suppose happened here?"

My cousin Marshall lay sprawled on the seat between two black-haired girls with smeared mouths. Marshall's pants were unzipped and his neck was covered with red blotches. Both girls had flung their lavender sweaters on the floor. They spilled out of their bras, and I swore I saw fingerprints on their breasts, pale purple bruises, the size of Marshall's thick fingers. One of the girls woke and rubbed her eyes. She laughed when she saw us, and made no effort to cover herself. Her teeth were small and sharp. Her turned-up nose looked like a plug on her fleshy face.

"Justin's upstairs," Arlen said, "facedown on his bed with his boots on. I don't know what I'm gonna do with my boys. Some night one of them's gonna mess with the wrong woman and wake up with a knife in his butt."

The girl with the pig nose unrolled her window. "Mornin'," she said. "I don't s'pose I could use your bathroom, could I?"

Mom was pulling on my sleeve.

"You s'pose right," said Arlen.

"Mighty unfriendly of you to feel that way."

"Come on, Lizzie," Mom said.

The girl opened the door and jumped out of the cab. I was letting Mom tug me home, but I wasn't moving fast. "Last chance," the girl said.

Arlen crossed her arms over her chest and shook her head.

"Have it your way." The girl with no shirt wriggled out of her pants and squatted. Mom was behind me now, shoving me toward the house. I thought, *I've already seen it all. What good does it do to drag me away?*

"You filthy scum," Arlen screamed, flailing at the girl's head. The big-bottomed stranger rolled in the grass, laughing, her pants bunched down around her knees, her thighs quivering. Mom hustled me inside and slammed the door behind us.

A few days later I learned how my cousins' evening had begun. Mother gave me permission to go for a bike ride with Gwen Holler—as long as I promised to beat Daddy home. She thought I'd been punished long enough but saw no sense in starting another argument.

I met Gwen at the corner, and we headed out to Ike's Truck-stop to visit her mom. When Ruby Holler was working, we got fries and Cokes for half price.

Ike's sat on a treeless lot north of town. Out here, the wind was always blowing; dust foamed from the eighteen-wheelers hauling up to the pumps, and diesel fumes hung in the air. Even the truckers coughed when they leaped out of their rigs.

Standing on this stretch of scrabby earth, I realized how close the mountains were. In July the snow still hadn't melted off the highest peaks. By late August a fresh dusting of powder appeared. Strangers said the mountains made them feel trapped, but the Rockies sheltered the people of Willis. Hidden in this valley, we were protected from the whimsical Chinook winds that whipped down the eastern slopes, raising the temperature by 40 degrees in a single hour. We knew that if you climbed in these mountains, you would find only more peaks and clear pools that reflected hard sky and bare rock, pools that held the fine glacial silt in perfect suspension, turning the water unbelievable shades of blue and green. An avalanche of snow could bury a man for a hundred years. A sharp thaw could flood the valley, rip houses from foundations and send cows and children swirling toward Moon Lake.

We accepted these dangers and learned not to walk on the ice fields in spring when the snow is heavy, sodden and dense, when a man's footsteps can shake a hillside loose. Tourists died in our mountains: boisterous skiers plunged to early deaths and hikers sank into blissful hypothermic sleep. But we survived. We knew the simple truth: a mountain is greater than a man.

I wasn't worrying about avalanches that day. I was thinking about a plate of salty fries dripping with ketchup. I was thinking how good it was to be free to ride my bike with Gwen Holler.

Gwen's mother seemed almost glad to see us. "Haven't had a

customer for an hour," she said. Ruby didn't need to wait for our order. "Drop a pair of fries," she yelled to Ike as she pulled two Cokes from the cooler. When we had our food, Ruby Holler leaned over the counter and whispered, "Your cousins nearly lost their noses out here the other day."

According to Ruby, the boys had stirred up some trouble with the Furey woman. They were Mary Louise's last customers and she was in no mood to chat. "I was here to take over," Ruby said, "but I had ten minutes to spare, so I made myself an iced tea. I don't owe that woman any favors.

"I recognized Marshall Munter right off. He was grinning at Mary Louise and I knew he was looking for a little excitement." My cousin Marshall had big hands and a flat belly. Grown men with firm stomachs were rare in Willis. He wore his jeans tight and liked his own smell after a day at work. I could just see him, running his fingers through his hair, trying to tame his cowlicks. "That cousin of yours has a way with women," Ruby Holler said. "He talks nice and slow. Makes me think he might know how to take his time when it really mattered." She winked at me and Gwen. There wasn't much about Marshall that appealed to me, but Gwen grinned as she stuffed three fat french fries in her mouth. She knew just what her mother meant.

"So your handsome cousin points to his pie and says, 'Hey, Mary Louise, this here's a nice piece. You cooked this pie up just right.'

"He may be pretty," Ruby said, "but he ain't so smart.

" 'Ike does the pies,' Mary Louise told him, and he says, 'Don't you like to cook?'

"I knew she was aggravated, so I told her I'd fix my face and be right out. I left the bathroom door open just a crack to keep one eye on the activities.

"I heard your other cousin, the short ugly one—what's his name?"

"Justin."

"Yeah, I heard Justin say, 'Why, Mary Louise, I bet you're a *fine* cook.'

"Then Marshall pipes up again, 'I hear you're a regular hot potato, Miz Furey.' " Ruby whistled through her teeth. "He's got a streak—I can see it." She smiled as if this vein of nastiness was to his credit.

"Mary Louise ducked in the kitchen; I expect she hoped I'd be out before the boys needed refills. I couldn't stall any longer."

I pictured Ruby Holler, teetering on heels that would make her spine ache by the end of the night. She'd have to walk barefoot through the parking lot after her shift, but she wouldn't mind. Her hair flamed under the fluorescent lights, a false red, teased half a foot above her scalp. Her nostrils looked pinched, as if something in this place always smelled bad to her. She was the kind of woman men liked and other women didn't. Truckers caressed their mugs of coffee while they told her about the loads of lettuce in their rigs and the wonders of refrigerated trucks. Sometimes they described the pocked skin of oranges, and sometimes they whispered to her about the smell of hogs. But no matter what they said, Ruby Holler always seemed amazed, as if she were hearing this story for the first time. Aunt Arlen said that was the sole source of her charm. "Men love a woman who listens," Arlen told me.

I knew she'd leaned over the counter toward my cousins, letting the Munter boys get a good peek down her dress, letting them glimpse her pushed-up breasts, her leathery skin. I'd watched her do the same for other men. "Why, you boys are *empty,*" she crooned. "Hasn't Mary Louise been taking care of you?" Ruby Holler couldn't stand the Furey woman. She had no sympathy for anyone who could do what she'd done. "If I had my way," Ruby said to me, "I wouldn't even give an Indian a cup of coffee, never mind giving him what Mary Louise Furey did. But Ike says his girls have to serve anyone who walks through that door with money in his pocket. Yeah, I have to serve them, but I don't have to like it." All my mother's warnings about keeping our affairs private seemed to pay off. I didn't think Ruby knew for sure which boy had taken Nina.

Gwen finished her fries and started on mine. Something about her mother's story had made her unusually hungry.

"Mary Louise brushed past me on her way out the door. 'Whatever those boys leave is yours,' she hisses in my ear. I bet they wouldn't have left her two cents."

Gwen shoved her empty bottle at her mother. "How about another Coke?" she said, just as if she were some regular customer who was paying for her drinks and might leave a nickel tip besides.

"In a minute," said Ruby. "I'm talkin'."

"Of course the boys forgot about the tip altogether," Ruby admitted. "They went after Mary Louise." Her brow wrinkled. "Come to think of it, they never paid for the pie and coffee either."

I understood my cousins. Marshall Munter wasn't accustomed to being resisted or refused, and Justin thought that an ugly woman had no right to rebuff anyone—even him.

"I have to say I started to get a little nervous when they followed her to the parking lot," Ruby said, "so I headed outside too. Ike was in the back hacking up rib-eyes. If the situation called for a man with a cleaver to calm things down, I was ready to yell.

"Marshall shouts, 'Hey, Mary Louise, you sure you wouldn't enjoy a little home cookin'?'

" 'Must get mighty lonely up there on the river,' says the other one.

" 'All by yourself in that shack.'

"Mary Louise turned to face the boys. They were right on her tail. 'Go fry your asses,' she says, but they inched closer, thumbs in their pockets. Her car was only a foot behind her. They knew she couldn't get away without a fight.

" 'Maybe you only do it with Indians,' Marshall says.

" 'Maybe you got a taste for dark meat,' says Justin.

" 'Any woman who'd do it with an Indian would do it with a dog.'

"Mary Louise spat on the ground. 'You're less than dogs.'

"That's when the short one lunged for her throat. But she was too quick for him—I saw the blade flash. 'One more inch,' she says, 'one more inch and you'll be missing a nose as well as a chin.' "

Ruby said Marshall was having a hoot, slapping his thigh and snorting. " 'Laugh it up, pretty boy,' Mary Louise tells him. 'I could do some work on you too, and you wouldn't look so fine.'

"I could see the fun was over, but the Munter boys didn't know how to back off without sticking their tails between their legs."

"Why didn't you yell for Ike?" I asked Ruby.

"I was thinking on it," she said, "but just then a car rolled up behind them and Sheriff Wolfe leaned out the window.

"He says, 'These boys causing you any trouble, Mary Louise?'

" 'Just a misunderstanding,' Mary Louise said.

"Justin and Marshall gave the sheriff a wave and hopped into their truck. That's the last I saw of them."

Afterward, my cousins must have decided to go to the Blue Moon to cool down with a few beers. That was the only place near town where you could find girls like the ones they brought home. It was a good drive just for a drink, fifteen miles. I don't know what time they got lucky and met the two girls with the big bottoms and heavy thighs, the black-haired twins in their lavender sweaters. They must have had one apiece to start out, but somehow Marshall ended up with more than he could handle, and Justin ended up with nothing at all.

6

EVEN FATHER agreed to allow me a single night of freedom before school started. He didn't know Mother had helped me cheat on him for the past week. Gwen's parents kept an old silver camping trailer in their backyard. Daddy wouldn't trust me to sleep outside on the grass, but for some reason he believed we'd be safe in that tin box.

Gwen waited for me on her porch, rocking back and forth, using her thick ponytail to flick flies from her neck. She massaged her own thighs, singing to herself, high and off-key. The summer had changed her. I felt jittery, too glad to see her, like a kid come to pester some older girl. She wore a tight pink top and cutoffs with four inches of skin left bare in between. The dizzy girl had the slow eyes of a lazy woman now, and I caught a vision of her as a fat wife, sitting on the steps with her lemonade while a horde of dirty children squabbled in the yard, stamping the last life out of the yellow grass.

She promised to show me something secret if I'd go to the gully with her.

"What?" I said.

"The pond."

"I've seen it." The beavers had built a dam across the stream and the water backed up into a marshy pool.

"Everybody's seen it, but you haven't seen this. Trust me."

We scrambled down the steep slope of the ravine. Pricker plants and weeds grew thick and dry; they scraped our hands and our bare legs, leaving white lines that slowly filled with dots of blood. Mosquitoes buzzed around my head and I told Gwen this had better be worth it.

Gwen turned as we approached the pond, holding one finger in front of her mouth. I wondered what she'd found: a band of mountain people setting up camp in the gully for the winter? A small tribe of Indians bent on reclaiming sacred ground? A dead body so bloated and black that no one would ever know who it was? Nothing less could surprise or interest me, so I was disappointed when we crouched in the tall reeds and I discovered Gwen had led me through the brambles just to get a good look at her brother and Coe Carson taking an evening dip.

I'd seen plenty of naked boys—down at Moon Lake the summer before Jesse drowned; all four of Arlen's boys stripped and plunged. Nina giggled and Daddy threatened to smack her across the mouth, told her to sit in the car till we were ready to go, and stuck to his word. He wouldn't let us go back for a whole month after that. He got it in his head that Moon Lake was a dangerous place, deeper than we knew, with gaping trenches that could swallow a body and never give it back; he said that in those crevasses too deep for light sturgeon grew bigger than men. But we learned that the deep water was safe and still, and a boy could drown in the bright shallows.

I didn't think there was anything wonderful about seeing boys without their clothes. I thought they looked funny, especially when they came out of the water shivering and shrunken, but

Gwen wasn't laughing. She was pushing the reeds apart to get a better look.

Coe Carson wavered, a pale ghost beneath the surface. He turned tail up to make a dive, exposing his skinny white ass before vanishing, sucked down by the murky pool. Zack slapped at the water, shattering a reflection of trees and clouds. When Coe came up behind him, Zack leaped and yelled, "I'll get you for that, you sonuvabitch." Then Zack was the one to disappear and Coe was the one to squawk.

I couldn't see what they were doing to each other and I didn't care. The mosquitoes were eating me alive. The last yellow light filtered through the trees, a golden haze; Gwen's face gleamed with sweat. I wanted to go back to her house and lie in the grass. I wanted to start a story and let Gwen finish it, the way we always had. I tugged at her arm, but she batted my hand away. My feet sank into the soft wet ground. Muck oozed into my shoes.

Zack jumped Coe and shoved his head below the surface, let him up, dunked again. The third time, Coe came out sputtering. Zack sprinted toward land, arms slicing, legs a furious flutter. He crawled up on the slick grass while Coe slogged through the thick water. Zachary did a jig, taunting Coe, his penis flopping up and down as he whooped and pranced. Gwen giggled, then clamped her hand over her mouth. I should have told her how Zachary killed Myron's cat, how he snapped its neck and left it for Myron to find. Maybe she would have understood why I didn't find her brother so amusing.

Grabbing at the slippery weeds, Coe tried to pull himself out of the pond. Zack called him a wimp and a wussie, kicking at his chin. When Coe finally struggled to his feet, he lunged and laid Zack out flat. But he had no chance. Zachary arched and heaved. They rolled in the mud, arms clutching each other, legs entwined. At last Zack twisted free, straddling his friend. Coe's scrawny legs jabbed at the air. Zack laughed, shaking his wet curls, splattering Coe's face.

"Give up," said Zack.

"I give up," Coe wailed.

"Say, 'You're the master.' "

"You're the master."

"Master of all masters."

Coe squirmed and stayed silent.

"Say it, pussy breath. I can keep you here all night." Zachary bore down on Coe with his full weight and Coe groaned. "Say it."

"Bastard of all bastards."

Zack clutched Coe between his legs and Coe yelped. This time the force of his kick threw Zachary, and they lay there, panting in the grass, dirty boys streaked with mud and torn leaves.

Zack wiped his nose with the back of his hand and punched Coe's arm. "Fucker," Zack said. "You gave me a bloody nose."

"Come on," said Gwen, "before they get dressed."

Zachary Holler would pummel us both if he caught us spying on him. Or worse, he'd wait for some unexpected chance and pay us back in a way I couldn't imagine—some heartless way, like the way he paid Myron Evans.

I took one last look. I never understood why Nina took to boys the way she did. Something bad lurked in Zachary Holler, something threatening in his sunburned neck and hard thighs. As he grew older and his chest thickened I could see meanness blooming up in him, a living thing. And Coe, mild Coe, must have had an empty place inside his ribs, a place that could only be filled by Zachary's cruelty. Nina would have found Zack handsome: she liked dark-eyed boys with strong arms, and she would have brought out a kindness in him, false and fleeting. I saw Zack's turned-up nose. I saw his horrible hands, hands that could break the neck of a cat. To me he was half imp, half monster; but to Nina, he would have been just another pretty boy. I knew exactly what she'd think of Coe Carson too, because I knew how she treated his brother, Rafe, after that day Mother caught him with his hand stuck down Nina's bra. He became one of the boys who squatted behind bushes or climbed high in trees to call her name. She called him by his real name—Raphael— made him speechless so she was free to tease and tempt him.

Still, Rafe Carson found a way to redeem himself. He achieved a mythic status in 1964, when he managed to get himself locked up for trying to rob a gas station down in Rovato Falls. He was the only boy we knew who'd been sent to the detention school in Miles City, though many fathers had threatened their sons with such a fate. Nina and her girlfriends talked of it in whispers and hushed if they caught me listening. His name was their chant: Raphael, Raphael, my prisoner, my love. I imagined my sister and her two friends, their hands clasped, dancing. Trapped in their circle, I saw Rafe Carson, his wrists tied with the pink and yellow ribbons from their hair. *Prisoner,* they whispered, *love.* Years later I heard Rafe Carson got himself in real trouble over in Washington, but no one knew for sure and Coe wasn't talking.

"Didn't I tell you?" Gwen said as we climbed up the hill. "Didn't I tell you there was something to see?"

I shrugged. "I didn't think it was so great."

"That's because you're sweet on Myron Evans. He's the only one you want to see with his pants down."

I refused to answer. Catching Myron didn't interest me in the least, not since I'd seen him press his face in the fur of his dead cat.

At the crest of the gully, Gwen grabbed my arm. "Have you

ever kissed a boy, Liz?" I shook my head. She knew damn well I hadn't, unless you wanted to count the time Jesse cornered me on the playground in second grade and licked me from my chin to my nose. I could still feel his rough tongue, the slobber I couldn't wipe away fast enough. I was almost in tears, too surprised to slap him. He flipped my dress to expose my underwear to a gang of boys. Jesse ran and the boys scattered. Later I learned it was a dare. My cousin earned half a dozen nickels by making a fool of me.

"What do you think it's like?" Gwen said.

"Nothing special." I realized that most boys didn't kiss like Jesse. I had seen women swoon in movies; I had seen them surface from a deep kiss, gasping for air but not displeased.

"Do you think that if I kissed you and pretended you were a boy that it would be the same as really kissing a boy?"

"I s'pose." I figured it would be a lot like kissing Aunt Arlen on the cheek, only wetter and probably worse. It still hadn't occurred to me that Gwen actually intended to try it out.

"Well?"

"Well, what?"

"Let's see."

Kissing was kissing. I had no idea why Gwen had to go to the trouble of pretending I was a boy, not that it took much imagination: I was already five foot six, bony as Aunt Arlen, flat-chested as Coe Carson.

"Be Gil Harding."

"I won't," I said. "Anyone but him." In my opinion, Gil Harding was a greaser; his hair was hard and shiny, combed into a tail in back, and all his pants fit too tight. Gwen liked him because he was two years older, because he wouldn't even look at her. "Just for a minute," Gwen said, "just for me."

"He's got rotten teeth," I said.

"You've never been close enough to Gil Harding to see his teeth."

"Don't have to see 'em to know."

She kicked at the dirt. "Are you ready?" she said.

"I'm ready." I puckered my lips and closed my eyes.

"No, stupid. You're the boy. You have to come after me." I bent toward her; her breath in my face was grassy and sweet. She opened one eye. "Don't you know anything? You're supposed to put your arms around me."

I thought of my cousin Marshall, his hand gripping the bare breast of the girl who peed on Arlen's lawn. I saw the bruises from his rough fingers, the girl's smeared mouth, lipstick rubbed all the way up to her nostrils and halfway down her chin. This was as much as I knew about kissing.

Olivia Jeanne Woodruff, that strong young woman, lured Elliot Foot off in her Winnebago. Was she wearing him down like Arlen said? Was she kissing him to death?

Nina flung herself into the arms of Billy Elk. Nina threw herself on Jesse and tried to save him with her own breath. This was all I knew of love and mercy. The line blurred. Passion and salvation seemed like the same thing, like something I'd wanted my whole life.

I lurched forward and clutched Gwen's waist, gave her a fast moist smooch on the mouth—almost on the mouth. My aim took me high and I ended up getting more of her nose than her lips. She wiped her face with the back of her hand and spit on the ground. I was as sloppy as Jesse. She turned and ran. I stood, stupidly staring at the red scar of the setting sun. My eyes burned. I was nothing but a stand-in, a ridiculous failure. *Let me try again,* I thought. But I was sure she never would.

I watched Gwen's hair swing from side to side as she sprinted down the road, so you couldn't help thinking of a horse's tail, an animal's rump. Yes, she could have Gil Harding if she wanted. She could have any boy when she was ready. Soon she wouldn't have to bother with me and my false, clumsy kisses.

I ran after her. It was almost dusk, but she wanted to walk downtown. Boys in trucks and souped-up Mustangs dragged Main. They hung their heads out their windows, whistled at every girl they saw. They didn't care if she was fat or old, pimple-faced or bowlegged. Anything female was worth a blast of the horn. Gwen didn't seem to notice their lack of discrimination. She grinned every time they hooted, certain that each call was for her alone.

Later, we lay on our sleeping bags in the trailer. I said, "This is our cabin. We live alone in the woods."

"I'd be glad to live alone and be rid of my parents," said Gwen. "Ruby doesn't do shit now that she's working four to midnight. She's a slug all day and gives me hell if I don't do the laundry and clean up after Zack and Dad. She says it's high time I learned to do a woman's job. A woman's job? Christ. I'm no genius, she tells me, I've gotta be able to do something." Gwen kicked off her shoes and stripped down to her underwear. "Fourteen years old and my mother wants to get me *trained* so I can marry some fat slob like my dad and wipe up his muddy footprints off the floor when he comes home from hunting and throws a bundle of dead ducks in my sink." We unzipped our sleeping bags so we could have one underneath us and one on top. "Not this girl," Gwen said, draping her warm leg over mine, "no sirree. This girl's going to have a good time before she thinks of promising to love, cherish and obey. Obey? Who thinks up this shit anyway?" She rubbed her leg up and down against mine, and I felt the rough stubble of her shaved calf. I tried to forget our miserable kiss, tried to pretend nothing had happened and nothing had changed.

I stared out the window, watching the sky. "My parents sure as hell don't obey one another," Gwen said. "Dad's been on her back ever since she got the night shift. She says it's twice the money, and he says, 'What're my wages—chopped liver?' Same conversation, five times a week. She wants her own money, never tells him what she makes. She's stashing it and I know where. Makes her feel free to have it. I think she's getting me *trained* so she can split. Like hell. If she screws, I'll be right behind her."

I gazed past Gwen. She nudged me. "What're you looking at?" she said.

"The sky."

"What for?"

"I'm waiting for the first star."

"Tell me the rest of the story," she said, "about our cabin in the woods."

"A crazy trapper built a shack in these parts too."

"Why's he crazy?"

"He married an Indian girl. They lived near the timberline, but her three brothers found them. They tied the trapper to his own stove and kidnapped their sister."

"Where'd you hear this story?"

"Everybody's heard this story. The trapper struggled for a week. The fire burned out. The wind roared through the cracks of the log cabin and the trapper dreamed he was falling down a crevasse in a glacier."

I kept looking out the window as I talked. Already the sky had gone from blue to black, filling with stars that disappeared behind the ragged ridge of the Rockies. "The ropes cut his wrists and thighs, but he was too numb to feel his own blood," I said.

"I heard this story before. You're not telling it right."

"I'm telling the truth. If you don't want to hear it, I'll think the rest to myself."

"No, go on."

"He fell asleep. He would have frozen to death, but he cried out from a dream, and a pair of wolves heard him, and knew his voice. Years before, he'd spared the life of the male. The trapper's rifle was aimed at the animal's head, but he heard the she-wolf howling in the hills as if she knew her mate was in danger. He emptied six rounds into the dirt and the wolf ran free."

"Now I remember," Gwen said. "They found that trapper, and he was still tied to the stove, and he was dead. That's what you get for marrying an Indian. My father says Indians should be able to join the union at the mill, just like anyone else. Ruby says that if we let them do that, the next thing you know they'll be wanting to marry our daughters, and the town will be full of women like Mary Louise Furey. Who cares that the trapper died anyway? No one knew him."

"The animals thought they owed the trapper something. They gnawed through the ropes; they slept beside him to keep him warm. And when he woke, he was changed. He couldn't talk like a man; he could only bark and howl. He's still looking for the Indian girl."

Gwen said, "I heard the girl killed herself when she found out the man had frozen to death. Her brothers locked her up in a little hut and she drowned herself in the pail of water they'd left for her. They buried her in the old way, sitting up instead of lying down, like she was expecting company, wearing all her beads and a doeskin dress."

"It's not true," I told her. "They aren't dead; they just can't find each other."

"I don't want to be buried. I want to be burned. I want my

ashes scattered so no one can dig me up later and look at my bones."

"I want to disappear," I said. "I don't want anyone to do anything with my body."

"No one just disappears."

I didn't answer. I knew how wrong she was. I thought of my mother's shoe box hidden in the closet, all the pictures Nina destroyed. I imagined her coming home, carrying an envelope with all the missing pieces. We'd sit on the living-room floor and tape the pictures together. She'd stay long enough for the seams to mend and fade like old scars.

"Do you think the trapper will look for her forever?" Gwen said.

"For the rest of his life. Maybe longer."

"I want someone to love me that much."

"I don't. You have to be dead for someone to love you that much, dead or gone for a long, long time."

Gwen laughed. "It's only a story."

In the square of sky there were too many stars to count. I thought each star was a person who was lost. Their eyes watched the world night after night. They were safe and knew exactly where to find us.

I DON'T remember falling asleep, I only remember waking. The trailer pitched as if the ground had split open beneath it. For years we'd been warned that Willis sat on a fault line. I prayed I would end up in the same hole as my parents. Gwen clawed at my back. "Jesus, somebody's trying to knock the trailer over," she said. Only then did I realize it was the trailer shaking, not the earth. "Damn you and your crazy trapper," she sputtered. She thought that talking about a man could bring him to life. The rocking stopped and the trailer shuddered as it settled back into its ruts.

Gwen said, "Lock the door."

"Why me?"

"You're closest." She gave me a little kick.

I wasn't scared, but I believed the best thing to do at times like these was to screw your eyes shut and pull the covers over your head until the bad thing went away. I slid the bolt in place. "Anyone who can rock this trailer can rip the door right off the hinges," I said.

Gwen jumped out of bed to rummage through the closet. She came up with a broken broom handle and a flashlight. When she flicked it on, I knocked it from her hand and the light blew out. "He'll see us," I said. The trailer swayed again. I tugged the broken broom handle away from Gwen. Its jagged edge gave me a vague idea of how I might use it.

"I bet it's Myron Evans," she said, "that dirty little creep."

In my mind I saw Myron dragging his bad foot. "It can't be Myron," I said. "He's not strong enough."

"It is Myron. Who else but a pervert would try to scare us this way? I'll beat his head with the flashlight if he comes in here. I'll crack his skull, I swear."

Suddenly everything was still. I pulled myself up to the window just in time to see two boys leap the fence and duck down the alley, Gwen's rotten brother and his slow shadow.

"Can you see anything?"

"No, nothing."

"Do you think he's gone?"

"Yes, I think so."

"I bet Myron knows Zack told us what he tried to do. He wants to scare us so we won't talk. They can lock a man up for good for the kind of stuff Myron Evans likes."

Poor Myron. He even got blamed for things he didn't do. I

remembered a time when a gang of us followed Myron home. We hid behind trees and shrubs and called to him: *Myron, oh Myron.* We sang it. *Sweetheart, Dear One.* He twirled in the street, looking for us, nearly stumbling over his lame leg. *Myron, my darling.* And he hobbled away, trying to run. But he was brave, much braver than I was. When he was just a child and those boys pinned him to the ground, he was strong enough to beat his own head bloody.

Gwen said, "Maybe it was the trapper. I bet he saw my hair and thought I was the Indian girl." She was no longer afraid. The trapper was no different from the boys cruising Main, and Gwen was smiling, her teeth wet and shiny in the dark. She whispered, "Do you think he'll keep after me?"

7

WE CALLED ourselves Lutherans, as good as any in the county, but we only made it to church when the mood struck my father. In late September the feeling hit him hard. That's when I heard the story of Freda Graves, how she'd fallen away, possessed by some private passion.

It all began on a Friday night. I'd been in school for only three weeks, and I was already fantasizing about diseases and accidents that might keep me out of class for months at a stretch. Not long after my father got home from work, someone banged at the front door. I thought one of my teachers had discovered I'd stuck Marlene Grosswilder's locker shut with twenty pieces of chewed Super Bubble. I still owed that girl for things that had happened in third grade; I might never be done paying her back.

I opened my door a crack. If Mr. Lippman, the science teacher, was the bearer of bad news, he would take great pleasure in the details, throwing in a few of my other bad habits as long as he was at it.

I sneaked down the stairs and realized I wasn't the one in trouble today. A small woman was slapping at Daddy's chest. He was too surprised to defend himself. She cried, "Look at you, a big brute like you. You nearly broke my Lanfear's arm. You can have your damn twelve dollars." She threw a wad of crumpled bills at his feet. "What do you care if my kids don't eat dinner? It's better to have them go hungry for a week than to have you beat on my husband so he can't work." She was young, her hands tiny as a child's. I'd seen her at church and knew her name— Miriam Deets. She was not a pretty woman, but her skin was smooth and rosy. You knew just by looking at her she'd be sweet to touch. Miriam had married a man twice her age. Lanfear Deets worked under my father, and I'd heard Daddy say he was lazier than an Indian.

Father dropped down to his hands and knees in front of Miriam and plucked the money off the floor. She looked as if she wanted to kick him in the ribs. But she didn't: she just stared at him, seeing some kind of hideous animal too vile to strike, a two-headed calf, an earless dog.

When Daddy got back on his feet, he stuffed the bills in Miriam's fist and told her to get on home. Her mouth was a tight circle of struggle. She was too proud to take it and too poor to hand it back. "Tell your husband the debt's canceled. Tell him not to bet money he don't have to spend. And tell him the one thing that makes me sick to my stomach is a man who sends his woman out to do his talking for him."

The guys at the mill always owed my father. He had to write all his poker winnings down in a little black book just to keep track. I'd never known him to forget a debt or let a single dollar slide, and I wanted to tell Miriam Deets to shoo before he came to his senses.

All evening Father fretted and paced, popping out of his chair every five minutes. Mother must've said, "What is it, Dean?" six or seven times. Even a night's sleep didn't snap him out of it. At breakfast he put four teaspoons of sugar in his coffee and was ready to dump the fifth when Mom said, "What's eating you?"

"You're eating me with all your damn questions." He stomped out the back door. Mom and I watched him tramp across Aunt Arlen's lawn and pound on her window. When she appeared, he gestured toward the chicken coop. Arlen nodded. She doted on her chickens as long as they were alive, but she wasn't sentimental when one's time came.

As Daddy unlatched the door of the coop the chickens sensed his purpose and squawked, fluttering against the cage. In less than a minute he had what he wanted. Holding the chosen one by her scrawny neck, he made straight for Arlen's chopping block. He laid the hen on the stump, grabbed the ax, and swung once. I jumped. The headless chicken twitched.

"Guess he has a craving for fried chicken," Mother said.

He carried it inside and plopped it in the sink. Mom followed him, crouching to wipe up the trail of splattered blood. Daddy didn't say a word: he just started plucking, both hands moving like pistons.

When the hen was bare and pink, he opened her up to clean out the innards. He dropped the dark liver, the heart and kidneys into a plastic bag, scooped the stomach and lungs and tangled bowels into the garbage, then ripped open a paper sack to wrap around the naked chicken. With the bundle in one hand and the giblets in the other, he shouldered past Mother and me and stalked off down the alley.

"Where is he going?" Mom said.

"How would I know?" My voice gave me away.

"Lizzie?"

Traitor or liar, I had to choose. Father or Mother, who loved me best?

"Do you know about this?"

I spilled the story, minus a few details. The look on Mother's face told me I'd done her no favor. Honesty would win me no grace.

DAD SHOOK me awake at eight o'clock Sunday morning and told me to get ready for church. I knew right away he was still suffering over Miriam Deets. She'd called him a brute and for some reason he believed her.

Guilt had driven Father to church as long as I could remember. Grandmother Macon stared at him from a sepia-toned photograph on his dresser. I imagine she was the first thing he saw when he woke that day. She reminded him. Her lips were drawn into a tight line as if she were ready to scold her son for taking money from other men. Her own husband had lost a thousand dollars during the long month before he dropped dead of a heart attack. She believed God struck him down to spare her family more suffering.

She did suffer, though, dying slowly from a cancer of the stomach. Her three daughters all married young to escape her house, but her only son stayed to the end, enduring her scorn. She fumed when he drank and refused to eat if he came home late with a pocketful of money. She berated him even as he carried her to the toilet.

In the photograph she is young and gaunt with lank hair and bony, unforgiving shoulders. Alive or dead, it did not matter. My father faced her daily judgment.

I groped down the hall, eyes half shut. Daddy was already in the bathroom. The door was wide open. He leaned over the sink, his face inches from the mirror while he shaved. He pulled the razor down one side and then the other, his stroke quick and long. He rinsed his face, dabbed at the bloody spots with toilet paper, then went after his head with a pair of scissors. He lifted one clump of hair at a time, snipping close to the scalp. His hair was coarse, the scissors dull: he had to work them hard, and I saw the back of his neck turning redder and redder.

NOBODY LOOKED as if he belonged in church less than my father did. His good suit was worn to a shine at the elbows and the knees, and was too small besides. He kept squirming to find a comfortable way to sit in his pants. Even when he managed to sit still, there was something awkward about the way his big hands fell across his lap and dangled between his knees.

Reverend Piggott rose in his pulpit. His body was little more than a rack to hang his robes, but he had a face full of fire when he said, "Each time a child of God falls away, we all suffer. The day Freda Graves left this church, I felt as if one of my limbs had been torn from my body, as if my own child had been ripped from my womb. Yes, I tell you truly, that is how deeply I grieved. A great fever raged in her for days. I thought, surely *this* will show her the folly of her ways, but it did not, and she cursed the good doctor and sent him from her house with foul words and accusations." I spotted Dr. Ben four rows in front of us; his thin white hair curled over the collar of his black jacket. I imagined his clean, soap-smelling hands on Freda Graves's burning forehead. He watched her as he had watched me while I tossed in the heat of a fever: his gray eyes watery and strangely opaque, his head shaking in a way that made you wonder if you were doomed to pass from this world to the next before the day was done.

"I prayed for two days and two nights, did not sleep or eat or speak to anyone save God. Our sister is possessed of an evil delusion; I hoped our Lord would show me how to carry this lamb back to the fold." The idea of Reverend Piggott, that rail in the wind, trying to shoulder the massive weight of Freda Graves made me cover my mouth. "Freda Graves is practicing a dangerous kind of worship right here in this town."

The reverend scanned the congregation. We held our breath; a single thought pulsed down the pews: *What kind of worship?*

"What kind of worship, you ask? The most tempting of all evils, an evil that wears a holy mask. Freda Graves believes she is a prophet; she has opened the doors of her own house as a church. Every Tuesday night she commits heresy just a few blocks from this hallowed ground. She has lured away the weakest among us; now she will seduce the strong. Her followers claim to speak in tongues. They lay hands on one another. Oh, my friends, I am afraid, for the devil speaks in his own tongue."

Reverend Piggott's bald scalp glistened. He raised his fists to Heaven, and his fragile body stiffened beneath his heavy robes.

"Do not venture near this woman. Even the blessed are not immune to trickery. She preys on the needy; she snatches tired souls. Oh, we cannot afford to rest. Do not stop by the side of the road though your feet are weary. Do not think that you can save her; she is beyond reason. Professionals must handle this matter."

I wondered what he meant by *professionals*. I pictured all the officers of the church dressed in red robes, led by Reverend Piggott in his violet frock. I saw them marching down Main Street, a band on parade without their instruments. They'd cut down Fifth Avenue and stride along Wyoming Way, straight to the steps of Freda Graves's front porch. Those good men of Willis would batter down her door and drag her off to a tower where they could torture her with talk and rebuke her into reason.

But from what I'd seen of Freda Graves, it would take more than human force to stop her. She was the kind of woman who could walk across a flooding river, a child on each shoulder, a newborn calf cradled in her arms. She would be the last person to flee a burning house, and the first to brave a blizzard to search for children who hadn't found their way home.

As we left church I caught sight of Miriam Deets walking arm in arm with her husband, Lanfear. He was a heavy man, soft and thick, with rounded shoulders and stubby hands. He had a simple look: his features small and unfinished, his mouth and eyes like slats in his fleshy face, his nose a mere bump. His hair had no particular color at all, like sand or dust. But Miriam gazed into that face with adoration.

Father watched them, seeing Miriam's simple love for a foolish man. He grabbed Mother's arm roughly. He couldn't get away fast enough.

THE TOWN buzzed with tales of Freda Graves. Reverend Piggott's sermon stirred up a frenzy of curiosity: he won her more converts in a day than she would have been able to snare in a month. Even so, people were afraid. With all that speaking in tongues and laying on of hands, Freda Graves would have as many followers possessed as she had saved.

We heard of candles and wailing, chalices of wine dark as the blood of a lamb. We didn't know what to believe, but one thing was sure: we knew exactly who attended these prayer meetings. A woman doesn't have neighbors for nothing.

Joanna Foot was one of the faithful. Elliot had returned from Arizona. Olivia Jeanne Woodruff rolled her dusty Winnebago into his driveway one day and gave him a boot in the butt. Joanna took him back—on a trial basis. He had to prove he'd mended his wicked ways before he got any idea about slipping his shoes under her bed. She told Elliot he'd have to show her and the Lord and "that holy woman" that he could live as a righteous man. Public humiliation demanded public repentance. She promised that if he could do right by her for a full year, she might *consider* letting him sleep somewhere other than the couch.

Minnie Hathaway belonged body and soul to Freda Graves. Over the years Minnie had lived up to Freda's expectations, trotting across the street after church to wait for Elliot to open the doors of the Last Chance. Once when Elliot dawdled too long, she pounded on the glass so hard it shattered, and Dr. Ben had to put eight stitches in her hand. Now she was on the wagon and drinking down the preaching of Freda Graves for courage.

"That'll never last," Arlen said. And Mother answered, "Give the woman a chance."

Minnie had even talked one of the other boarders at the rooming house into attending the meetings. Lyla Leona, the Fat Lady of Willis, was shaking and praying. For the time being, she was out of business and living on her savings, which accounted for the unusual hostility a certain group of men harbored toward Mrs. Graves.

Myron Evans was among the first converts. "Well, at least we know there's one night a week when we won't have to worry about him jumping out of the bushes," Arlen said.

In all, Freda had fifteen or twenty people coming to her house every Tuesday night, and the crowd swelled each time Reverend Piggott warned of her evil ways. Some loyal Lutherans talked of breaking her windows or setting her garbage on fire. "Jews live in the East and Baptists stay in Mississippi," my father said. "Nothing but Mormons in Salt Lake City. Here in Willis, folks are Lutherans. If they don't like it, they should move." Mother suggested we could tolerate one alternative, especially since Freda Graves had worked some minor miracles: keeping Minnie Hathaway away from the bottle and persuading Lyla Leona to look for another line of work. But Daddy said, "You tolerate one thing and pretty soon you'll be tolerating everything. We'll have the Indians dancing around a buffalo head on a stake in the middle of Main Street if we don't keep a lid on this."

I longed to see for myself what went on at these meetings, but Mother forbade it. Knowing how little she admired Reverend Piggott, I thought she'd be glad to try something else. My mother's father was a minister, and she never forgave him for hearing a call that made him desert his wife and child. I began to suspect she had little use for religion of any kind.

I remembered the time when Nina was chosen to play Mary in the Christmas story. For three days before the performance Nina moved as if in a trance, smiled as if her knowledge and her pain were too great to bear. She barely ate and refused to dirty her hands scrubbing dishes. I did her chores gladly, satisfied with my small sacrifice.

The night of the play, Daddy was so proud he could hardly sit still. He wanted to jump to his feet and applaud till his palms burned. Reverend Piggott laid one hand on Nina's golden hair. "Like an angel," he said, "the vision of the Virgin herself."

Nina was still glowing the morning after her debut, but Mother told her those pious ways didn't wash at home. She made Nina eat her bacon and fried eggs, made her scrape the plates and scour the grease out of the pans.

Later I found my sister thrown across her bed. She sobbed so hard I thought her bones would shatter. "I hate her," she said. "I hate her."

I believed my mother was as good as anyone I knew, better than most, fair and forgiving. I didn't think people could be good unless they feared God—or at least their parents. My mother's folks were dead. If she wasn't afraid of the Lord's retribution, what kept her on the right path? Sometimes I doubted I had the proper respect for God, but I dreaded the punishment of my father and tried to do the right thing most of the time. Trying to understand all of this only made me more curious about Tuesday nights at Freda Graves's. Sooner or later, I knew I had to worship in that house. I thought of myself speaking in tongues, having a private language just between me and God, having a voice so sweet He'd hear every word. My soul billowed up with the joy of it. My heart beat too fast, a flutter like wings in my tight chest.

8

"WELL, I hope this is the end of it," Mom said. It was a Tuesday night, and she was referring to the cherry pie Miriam Deets had just delivered, warm from the oven, to show her appreciation to my father. Miriam had appeared at our back door with her gift just as we finished our supper. Two of her tow-headed toddlers clung to her skirt, bunching the material in their sticky fists, hiding behind her and peeking at us with wide animal eyes.

"The end of what?" Dad said.

"Don't play the fool with me, Dean. I know all about that chicken." We'd already been to church three weeks in a row.

Daddy didn't look at me straight, but caught me with the edge of one eye, a glance that said he'd just as soon rip out my tongue as see my face. "This pie has nothing to do with any damn chicken," he said.

"Then to what, pray tell, do we owe *Mrs.* Deets's gratitude?"

"I got her husband, Lanfear, moved from pulp to planing—another buck an hour." Mother had to ask him to repeat the words, and even then she looked as if she couldn't believe it. "He's been at the mill six years," Dad said, "can't keep a man in one place forever. Anyway, Josh Holler is the one who deserves this pie. He handles all the union business; he arranged everything."

"You talked Josh Holler into this."

"We do agree sometimes."

"I've never heard of a time until this."

"Josh thought it was long overdue."

"How many times have I heard you say Lanfear Deets was the stupidest man you'd ever met? Lazier than an Indian, you said, and as long as you were foreman he wasn't moving up a single rung."

"Changed my mind."

"Why?"

"His work improved."

"When? A couple weeks ago? A Friday night?"

The legs of my father's chair scraped backward across the floor. "I don't have to listen to this," he said. Daddy won every fight because he never stuck around for the end. He barged through the living room. The screen door popped shut with a snap, loud as a firecracker exploding at dusk.

I hoped this was the end of it too, just as Mother said. Surely my father had more than made amends for twisting Lanfear's arm over that twelve-dollar debt.

I had no trouble sneaking out of the house that night. Mom thought I was going to Gwen's. She was too preoccupied to demand more than a white lie. I hopped on my bike and sped toward the west side of town. Here the houses were low to the ground. Shingles peeled off the roofs. The smaller the house, the brighter the paint. These shacks were built quickly to accommodate the modest boom of the lumber business. There wasn't time or money enough to dig foundations or pour concrete. Houses were raised on slabs of rock or piles of brick. Some were slapped together in early spring, with nothing but the frozen earth to support them. Now the homes sank and slipped. Porches leaned, windows sagged, roofs sloped in threatening ways.

Haverton Grosswilder built these houses and sold most of them to his employees. He started the mill but never worked there. He was an old man now, though his daughter, Marlene, was my age, and his son, Drew, was just two years older. People said his young wife was pretty, but she never left the house. She had some kind of terror of the outside world. I thought this was justified. If she walked through the west side of town, her husband's slums, folks might knock her down and steal her shoes.

I ditched my bike in the bushes about a block from Freda Graves's. I didn't aim to go to the front door—I wasn't ready for that.

Her house had been painted white years ago; now the paint blistered, revealing a layer of dirty red. Her backyard was over-grown with dying duck grass and dandelions gone to seed. I crept around one side of the house and then the other, but all the shades were down. Mrs. Graves would have to be an idiot to leave her windows exposed, so anyone who just happened to be passing could get an eyeful of salvation. I was about to give up when I saw she'd been careless after all. I spotted a bright slat. The window was shut, but the blind was a good inch from the sill.

I peered into the room. Freda Graves stood in the center of her flock, head thrown back, eyes closed, arms flung wide to embrace a vision of the Lord only the blind or the blessed could see. She wore a long dark skirt and a gray blouse with a high collar. Her congregation clustered at her feet, open-eyed as children, rocking and swaying to the beat of her words, shouting the word *Amen* in unison whenever there was a pause in her preaching. *Amen.* Mouths opened wide; I saw the word hover in the stale air, but I heard nothing.

The size of Freda Graves amazed me: the sweep of her arms describing Heaven and earth, the mass of gray curls grown full and tangled, the legs so solid that each step looked final, rooted for a thousand years. She seemed too big for her own house. The ceiling hung low, too close to that furious head. Unlike other adults in my world, she did not loom large in memory as she shrank in real life. She was great in the mind and in the flesh.

When she ceased her praying, the crowd stilled. They barely seemed to breathe. Slowly, Freda Graves began to speak again, a pantomime of passion, waving her hands, staring at first one follower and then another. The words came faster and faster. At last her gaze rested on one man. She pointed and said nothing.

She'd chosen Bo Effinger. He stretched out on the floor and the others gathered around him, laying their hands on his thighs and belly, his neck and chest. Bo was six and a half feet tall, with white hair, no eyebrows, and the biggest feet I have ever seen on a human being.

Freda Graves laid her hands over his face and prayed again. The others mumbled too, each one taking a turn. Joanna Foot and Minnie Hathaway, Myron Evans and the Lockwood twins— Eula and Luella—Elliot Foot, Lyla Leona, and half a dozen more. All of a sudden, Bo began to tremble. His fingers twitched and his legs shuddered. The people holding his arms and legs put their weight into him to keep him from thrashing, but Bo Effinger was a big man and the ripples jerking through his wiry muscles nearly lifted him off the floor.

The big man rolled to his stomach, pounding the floor with his fists, beating the rug with the feet of a giant. This is how being born must have been for Bo Effinger. He was a trapped child. His mother gained fifty pounds carrying him. The bones of her brows thickened and her palms grew wide. She swore he was the size of a calf when he finally came, and she kept crying out, "Cut me, cut me," but Dr. Ben wouldn't do it. He took the forceps to Bo's head, pinched and yanked. Mrs. Effinger often told this story to account for Bo's slow ways and missing eyebrows. She said Dr. Ben ripped them clean off her baby's face and they never grew back.

Bo was still flopping, a great fish beached in a storm. One by one the other worshipers pulled away, afraid of his huge hands. Only Freda Graves still touched him, her fingers on his head, her face turned up toward the cracked plaster of the ceiling.

Now everyone spoke at once, praying and weeping in pantomime, each one alone with God. Joanna Foot rolled from side to side, her fat round body rocking, a curled-up ball of flesh. Her husband crouched near a chair. He pushed his glasses up on his forehead and rubbed the bridge of his nose where the wire-rims had made his skin red and sore. His lips barely moved.

The Fat Lady was not as fat as Joanna Foot. She wore a dress of emerald green with huge, loose sleeves. When she raised her arms, the cloth spread like dark wings above her head.

Minnie Hathaway twirled, an old ballerina who'd lost her sense of balance. Her red lips exaggerated each strange word, like secrets whispered to a lover in a crowded room.

I looked for Myron and finally spotted him in the darkest corner of the room, his face turned to the wall, his spine a curve of shame.

Everyone jabbered at God in a private language; I wondered how He could hear them all. The only ones saying the same prayer were the Lockwood twins. Eula was short and dark and Luella large and fair. Once they were identical, but disease had stooped and bent poor Eula, and a one-week marriage had turned Luella's hair white at an early age. But they still thought as one. They wore matching sweaters, pale pink with pearl buttons. Their dresses were always made of real silk, their stockings sheer and gray. Hand in hand, eyes screwed shut, heads together, they spoke in the same tongue, and smiled, eyes still closed, as if they had both heard God answer.

But I don't believe even the Lockwood twins understood each other. No man in that room knew what mysterious force moved in him. No woman recognized her own words. Some were lifted by joy, some stricken by holy pain. One danced, one twitched, one hung his head, but not one fell to his or her knees.

We Lutherans sat in neat rows, bowed our heads, mumbled in unison. Reverend Piggott reminded us of our flaws and failures. But here, in this room, people jumped and shouted, wailed and were forgiven.

Freda Graves surveyed her flock, a smile growing, tears or sweat rolling down her cheeks. All at once her body tightened. She sensed me: a spy at the window. She glared at the unclosed blind, at my gray eyes. She knew me, I was certain. I flattened myself against her house, directly under that window. The blind shot open; light flashed above my head.

I heard her palm hit the glass and felt it like a slap on the inside of my chest. I made a mad leap, hit the alley at a gallop, knocking over her garbage cans as I swung through the gate. The metal cans rolled across the gravel, raising such a clatter that lights popped on all over the neighborhood. People stuck their heads out their windows, shouting at things they couldn't see, banging windows closed, slamming doors, yelling at me and then at one another as if they had been holding back for months.

By the time I reached the place where I'd stashed my bike, I tasted blood in my mouth and realized I'd bitten deep into the inside of my lower lip. I pedaled down the middle of the street where I was safe beneath the yellow glow of the streetlamps.

I got home at ten and found Mother sitting at the kitchen table, her eyes red and swollen. She knew my lies. I saw her sick with worry all these hours, thinking I had run away for some reason neither one of us could fathom, imagining I had disappeared at the edge of town. I was ready to fall on my knees and confess, ready to promise never to tell another lie as long as I lived.

But she didn't scold, and I realized her suffering had nothing to do with me. The house was too quiet. The air had the stillness of rooms inhabited only by women. Then I knew: Daddy wasn't there.

The uncut cherry pie sat in the middle of the table, a mute accusation in the perfect latticework of its crust. I put my hand on my mother's shoulder, lightly, afraid of her sorrow, how it bled from her body into mine. She reached up and squeezed my fingers, denying me my pity. "It's nothing," she said. "You get on up to bed. School tomorrow."

Much later I heard Father fumbling with the lock. He tripped on his way up the stairs and cussed. Mother had locked herself in the room where her own mother had slept and died. Daddy pounded at the door. Minutes after he stopped I heard the sound echoing down the hall.

I lay in bed, thinking of the prayer we used to say at the table before we ate: *Father, we thank thee for these mercies.* I thought of the Lord's Prayer in church, all our voices raised at the same time with the same words, until the chapel hummed with the pulse of a song beyond music, a song strong and low enough to reach the tired, overburdened ears of our Father in Heaven. And I thought of myself as a child and Nina as a child, our little hands folded, our sweet high voices together: *Now I lay me down to sleep, I pray the Lord my soul will keep. . . .*

I was afraid as I had never been afraid because I knew I had no words, I had no voice to talk to God.

9

MY PARENTS lived in silence for the better part of a week. Every day Mother worked in her garden, jabbing her yellow spade into the cracked earth until the whole bed was black and moist. Soon her poppies would blossom, their blooms unfolding, petals drooping. Poppies are more delicate than roses. A hot day destroys them, a hard rain leaves them in tatters. But their stalks are tough as little trees, woody and dull: nothing touches them.

At the dinner table my mother and father spoke only the necessary words: "I need to use the truck tonight," she might say; and he would answer, "Tank's almost empty." Then they both went back to spearing peas, their forks clinking against their plates.

Sooner or later I knew Mother would break down and ask a favor of Daddy. "I wish you'd clean out the garage and take a load to the dump," she might say. This was a dreaded job, neglected through a year of Saturdays. But this time Father would be grateful and comply, buying her pardon with his sweat.

In the meantime Gwen Holler distracted me. I lived by her whims. For days she might ignore me, not returning my phone calls, sitting in her room while I banged on her front door. But when she whistled, I ran; when she smiled, I forgave. And if she spoke to me in a hushed voice, gooseflesh raised the fine hairs on my arms and legs.

If Gwen was in the mood after school, we played our game in the gully, became the trapper and the Indian girl. We added characters, but Gwen always got to be the girl and I had to be everyone else.

We climbed down the ravine one afternoon in October. "Catch me," Gwen said, her voice low and husky, barely a whisper. She darted through the brush. I stumbled, scraping my knee, picked myself up and sprinted after her. We ran a hard quarter mile before I took a flying jump, caught her legs, and brought us both to the ground.

"Did you think I was your Indian girl?" she said.

"The trapper wouldn't mistake any woman for the one he loves. He'd know her, just by her smell."

"If he got crazy enough, he might see her everywhere. He might think every dark-haired girl was the Indian. He might see her in a rabbit or a waterfall. You don't know how far out of his head he got. If you chase someone for a long time, you could see her in anything that moved."

I nodded. Sometimes I saw Nina when I stood by the pond and glimpsed my own reflection. Sometimes on Main Street I spotted a girl with golden hair and ran to catch her; but when she turned, she was too young or much too old, her face was scarred by acne or her eyes were small and dark.

"You be the trapper," Gwen said, "and I'll be the girl. Give me ten minutes, and then come looking for me, okay?"

"No fair turning into a waterfall," I said. "I'll never find you."

I gazed into the woods and began to count the minutes. Fall had come quickly. Already the leaves of maples and willows had turned rust or yellow. In a week, they'd be blown to the ground. The tamaracks were golden, brilliant in the sun, but they looked like dead pines, victims of a beetle kill, and it was difficult to believe those needles would ever be green again.

I saw Gwen from across the pond, her dark hair knotted in two braids and her skin tawny in the afternoon light. When I got to the other side, she'd disappeared. My heart beat so hard that my chest ached, and I thought this must be what it's like to chase someone day after day and never reach her.

I caught sight of the girl again, running along the edge of the creek, with her shoes in her hand. This time I nearly had her, but she splashed to the other side. By the time I got my shoes and socks off, she'd vanished in the woods like a rabbit down a hole.

For an hour or more I pursued her, until my legs throbbed from running and my shirt clung to my sweaty back. I was the trapper, desperate to find this girl I'd been tracking half my life. The crackle of twigs being broken as someone scrambled through the brush made tears well in my eyes. She was close. I crouched, trying to be quiet, patient: *Now you can touch her if you can only wait.* But my breath came in hard gasps and blood rushed in my ears. I smelled my own sweat; she would smell me too and become her own shadow.

I kept falling into the places she'd been. Pockets of air felt hot and still, as if another person had just stopped there to rest, her body flushed; leaves quivered where her shoulders had touched them; footsteps made the earth vibrate. She led me deeper into the woods, away from the pond. The trees grew close and dark; deer moss hung from the low limbs, brushing against my face like hair. Suddenly I knew where she was going. Her thoughts leaped into my head: that's how close we were. I almost laughed out loud, knowing I had no need to hurry now, knowing she'd hide in the tree house. She thought it was a safe place. High in the trees, she could see every finch and squirrel. But the back side had no windows. If I took a wide circle, she wouldn't see me until I made a mad dash for the ladder. The tree house was a trap; she'd have to fly to get free.

I grew calm. It was all so simple in the end. I lay on my stomach behind a rock and watched her climb the rickety ladder. I tasted dirt. I was a skittery lizard, a long snake, all things evil and smart. The tree house swayed with the girl's weight. The silence in the forest was too deep: as if the river had run dry. She knew I was there, just as a sleeping child knows when someone stands over her and stares at her through her dreams.

I waited. I had the rest of my life. She'd have no chance to tumble down the ladder and slip through my hands like water.

She poked her head out the side window. When she ducked inside, I tore down the path and was on the ladder before I heard her squeal. I took two rungs at a time. The dry wood crackled under my heavy feet.

I filled the doorway and she backed into the darkest corner. "Don't be afraid," I said.

"I left you," she answered.

"Your brothers kidnapped you."

"I didn't fight them."

"You couldn't have won."

"I should have fought them until they killed me."

"No," I said, "you should have done anything to stay alive so that I could find you."

"Death is more honorable."

"Death is for the weak."

"Do you forgive me?" she said.

"I never blamed you."

"Then kiss me."

All at once I was no longer the trapper. I was myself and the

Indian girl was Gwen Holler. I remembered how she spit and wiped her mouth the last time we kissed. I didn't want to be the trapper any more than I'd wanted to be that greasehead Gil Harding. She'd tell me I did it wrong and I'd want to jump out the window because climbing down the ladder would take too long.

But I wanted to touch her. I was light-headed from running through the woods, and I knew how good it would feel to lean against her. I wanted my legs to stop shaking. She took a step toward me. I couldn't move away: one step backward would send me hurling out the door.

"Prove that you don't blame me," she said. She was so close I felt her breath on my lips.

I put my arms around her. I kissed her eyebrows and her hair; I stopped to kiss her brown cheeks and her smooth, hot neck, but I didn't even try to kiss her mouth for fear I'd miss again.

At last she was the one to put her hands on my cheeks and pull me toward her. I tried to keep my eyes open, to see her mouth; as she got closer, she seemed to have two mouths and two noses. I closed my eyes and hoped.

Her lips were so soft I almost jerked away, but she held my head tight in her two hands. I felt I touched something no one should touch, something frightening and delicate, a petal that could be torn by a rough finger, a poppy that could be bruised by rain. I wondered: Do my lips feel as fragile to her? I caught a butterfly once, though Nina cried, "Don't touch it, don't touch it." And when I let it go, it couldn't fly.

Gwen opened her mouth and ran her tongue along the ridge of my teeth. Now I was less afraid: her tongue was strong, protecting her lips.

She whispered, "Do you trust me?"

"Yes," I said. I would have told her anything just then.

"I have a surprise for you," she said.

I nodded—*Anything, yes.*

"Close your eyes."

Yes.

"Hold out your hands."

I did. I heard her pull her belt from her pants, the *whush* of leather on denim. She cinched it around one of my wrists. "Keep your eyes closed," she hissed, then softer, "trust me, trust me," a whisper close to my ear, her cool breath on my neck. She tightened the belt around both wrists then forced my hands down so she could loop the tail through my belt. I was cinched up to myself, a manacled prisoner. "Count to ten," she said, and I felt her brush past me, heard her on the ladder.

This was her surprise. She ran now. Dry twigs cracked. Once, she looked over her shoulder and saw me in the doorway, my face crumpled in despair, a stupid man. She laughed her woman's laugh. I knew what it meant. I had heard that laugh before, Aunt Arlen's laugh in the middle of a fight with Uncle Les when both of them were drunk. "I shouldn't have married such a short man," Arlen said. "Mama warned me." The words had some secret meaning that made her snort and spout and finally erupt, throw back her head and laugh from her gut. That sound beat my uncle down. He shrank, hands in pockets, chin on chest; he slouched, neckless, just as I did now.

I struggled but that only tightened the belt. The leather cut into the underside of my wrists. I clawed and wriggled, scratching myself. The belt stayed taut. My fingers tingled, then throbbed; my hands swelled, fat and bloodless. I thought of trying the ladder but saw myself falling through the rungs, breaking both my legs, shattering my knees, lying in the dark as the gully grew cold and silent. Or I would manage it somehow, make it to the ground without splintering my bones, and I would go home, hands still tied. How could I explain? What stranger could I invent who might do this to me?

I sank to my knees. Finally I worked the tail free from my belt, so I could bring my hands to my mouth. I loosened the belt with my teeth, ripped it free so fast the leather burned my arms.

I scrambled down the ladder, my feet slipping, my hands nearly numb, unable to grasp. They felt twice their usual size, dangling huge and useless as I stalked the girl. I was the angry trapper again, the betrayed man.

Avoiding the path, I headed toward the pond, knowing the girl would move toward water to wash her arms and mouth, the places I'd touched. I stopped half a dozen times, hearing echoes of my own steps. A crow squawked above me, its heavy body teetering on the highest bough of a maple. I passed the egg rock. The ravine was strewn with boulders left by the glacier when it finally melted, but this one was bigger than most, its top smooth as shell, one side split open by a jagged crack. In the legend I'd heard, beasts pecked their way out of this egg when the Indian girl loved the white man. The trapper. Me. Each creature grew more horrible than the last. Cats sprouted wings; dogs had razor jaws and rattlesnake venom.

I had to track the girl and lead her to the Sacred Lake, where our sins could be drowned in the moonlight. I found her in the wet reeds near the pond. I meant to save us, to stand in the icy water until it seemed to fill our veins; I wanted to stop the beasts from crawling out of the stone. But she would not go near the water with me.

"Look what you did," I said, showing her my bruised wrists, the raw, burned flesh.

She didn't apologize. Still I could have forgiven her until the moment she said, "That's what you get." She smirked, disgusted with me, just as she was the night I gave her that first wet kiss.

I shoved her backward, pinned her to a scraggly pine. The bark scraped my knuckles but I didn't care. She arched against me, so we stood pressed to the tree, belly to belly, thigh to thigh. I kissed her, hard, smashing our noses together. Poppy petals, butterfly wings, what did I care if I hurt her? My teeth cut the inside of my cheek, and I opened my mouth, trying to force my tongue between her tight lips. She grabbed my face just below the eye, pinched as if she meant to tear the flesh from the bone with her short, jagged fingernails. Still I pushed at her lips, licked her mouth and chin, let my tongue dart up her nostril. She raised her arms and brought both fists down on my kidneys. I reeled, stunned, giving her time to strike the tender place again. My spine buckled; my legs bowed. Gwen tripped me, knocking me to the ground. I lay on the damp grass staring at the sky, all its color drained. I touched the sticky blood where Gwen had scratched my cheek.

The caws of bantering crows stabbed the still dusk, wings flapped as if trapped in a box. The rhythm of their squawking was almost human.

Gwen knelt beside me. "I hate you," she whispered. I didn't know if she spoke as the Indian girl or as Gwen Holler, but I knew who I was: myself. The trapper was dead, just as Gwen had said that night in the trailer. He was tied to his stove, frozen blue; the wolves sniffed at his corpse and would have eaten him but his blood had turned to ice and his flesh was hard as stone. In the spring he'd thaw and rot. By summer he'd be foul, filling the cabin with his putrid black smell. But by the time they found him, he'd be clean, reborn, a bleached white man of bone. They would stand him up straight and say: *He was a tall man.*

"Liz?" Gwen said. "Are you okay?" Then again, *"Liz?"* Yes, my own name. She lay down beside me with her arm across my ribs, kissed my cheek, licked at the drying blood, nuzzled my ear with her nose. Still I couldn't answer. "Forgive me?" she said, the same words the Indian girl had spoken in the tree house before the trapper was dead.

I moved my mouth in the shape of words. The crows railed in a frenzy, their calls so loud and close I thought they would swoop down on us. Suddenly the woods snapped with the sound of stampeding animals: breaking branches, pounding hooves; they burst into the clearing. Zachary Holler and Coe Carson charged us, waving their arms, grunting like pigs.

"Forgive me," Zack squeaked.

Gwen tried to crawl between their legs, but Zack thumped her chest and shoved her toward me.

"Forgive me, forgive me," he whined. "You two like to kiss? Kiss for us. Come on, show us what you like. Hey, le's be friends, okay?" He gave Gwen another swat and she fell on me. Winding a thick clump of her hair around his fist, Zachary forced her face down to mine. "You like girls, little sister? Give Lizzie a big smooch. Come on, I like to watch. Don't you, Coe? Don't you like it?" Gwen's nose rubbed mine, and Zack kept pushing, pressing our dry lips together. He yanked her hair, jerking her head back. "You like that? Wanna do it again?"

Coe said, "Come on, Zack. You've had your fun."

"I'll say when I've had my fun. If you don't like it, get the fuck out of here. I don't need help from any wussies." He cuffed the side of Gwen's head. "Shit," he said, "I'm tired of this anyway. You little queers make me sick. If I ever catch you at it again I swear I'll kill you."

Coe Carson took a step closer, reaching out his hand as if he meant to help us. "What the hell are you doing?" Zack yelled. "Don't touch them. It's like a disease. You want to end up queer?" Coe hopped back and the two of them fled. The woods swallowed their bodies, but their words hung over us, unmovable spirits hovering in the gray light.

I lay on my back with Gwen half on top of me, staring at the sky, afraid to move. Gwen stood, flicking at the mud on her pants. I studied the spots, a dozen places where dirt was ground into blue cloth. "Look what you did," she said, pointing to the splatters of mud. "You and your stupid game. Don't try to follow me. Don't you dare try." I didn't answer. "Do you hear me?" she said. I closed my eyes and nodded. I listened to her splashing water on herself at the pond. She didn't run. Gwen Holler walked away from me.

I don't know how long I lay in the reeds—a minute, a half an hour, a night and another day. My back was wet and cold. The headless trees shook their dark arms at me. It was dinnertime or long past. Mother might be standing on the porch, looking down the empty street, a fear like hunger in her, *not again, not again.* My father might make her sit down and eat without me, pretending the thought didn't rise in him. Imagining my parents' pinched faces, all their fear turned to rage when they saw my filthy clothes, made me want to lie in the cool mud till the snows came. For the first time I believed I understood why my sister never came home.

The gully grew dark. Lying there alone, I thought of the grizzlies that tore young girls from their sleeping bags and dragged them deep into the forest. I saw the sky dark with eagles, saw them dive toward the water to pluck the dying salmon from the river. Bobcats sharpened their claws on our woodpile, left two-inch gashes in the wood, as if a stump of pine was soft as flesh. I had always known these woods were alive with danger.

GWEN HOLLER punished me with a passion more ardent than any affection she'd ever shown. Hardly a week passed before she latched onto Jill Silverlake. Jill was short and too blond; her face and hair blurred to a single shade, like a doll left unpainted. Her popularity depended on the fact that her father owned the Strand, the only movie theater within twenty miles of Willis.

I wasn't easy to ignore. The junior high and high school kids shared one building. Still we numbered less than two hundred in all. I made sure Gwen Holler couldn't avoid walking in front of me a dozen times a day. I spoke to her every chance I got. "I saw a badger in the gully," I said one day. I was sure this would interest her. But she had a way of lifting her chin that made me invisible. Later I tried to pass her a note in class, and she let it drop to the floor. Jill snatched it up, giggling as she read the message: *Meet me at the tree house tonight and I'll show you where he was.*

School was more tedious than usual without Gwen to break the boredom, imitating Mr. Lippman's twitchy excitement as he explained the digestive system of a cow or the reproductive habits of silver salmon. "The cow has four stomachs and often regurgitates its food to chew it a second time." Mr. Lippman offered up his knowledge as if each fact were a small treasure. "Female salmon die soon after they spawn. Their nervous systems accelerate, and they literally swim themselves to death."

I kept hoping Gwen would wait for me someday, that she'd hide at the corner of the building and jump me as I passed. I'd yelp and she'd squeal, delighted that she'd scared me. "They *literally* swim themselves to *death*," she'd say, her voice high and shaky. We'd laugh till our stomachs hurt and walk home arm in arm. But nothing like this ever happened.

On an evening in early December the snow began to fall in soft clusters. I thought of the glaciers, how they'd carved the mountains from each side, leaving a narrow, deadly ridge of stone. At the summit the temperature dropped to 70 below. On the snow fields, the pack was twenty feet deep or more. I prayed for a chill north wind to whip down the canyon of the Rockies so that I could miss one day of school.

Sometime in the middle of the night, without anyone awake to witness, the snow began to swirl, rising off the ground in narrow funnels. By dawn slivers of ice flew sideways and drifted into sharp peaks across the lawns. Trees bent, shrouded in snow, like the stooped ghosts of great men. I thought that God might be listening to me again after all.

I knew my desire was selfish. Blizzards killed stranded travelers and lost cows. I'd heard of an elderly couple whose fire burned out one night. Three days later a neighbor found them frozen in each other's arms. The truth didn't matter: it could have happened; it might still happen. But I was not sorry I'd prayed for the storm.

When I woke at eight, I knew school was canceled. I didn't bother to get dressed. I imagined Daddy getting up for work two hours earlier. I could almost hear him say: *It's not too bad.* If he couldn't back the truck over the drifts in our driveway, he would have walked to the mill.

I scurried down the hallway to crawl in bed with my mother. I'd tell her I was cold and she'd lift up the blankets for me, too sleepy to protest. But she wasn't in the wide bed. I found her in the other room, my grandmother's room. Mother slept there more and more—whenever Daddy kicked or snored, whenever his breath held the faintest whiff of whiskey.

I opened the door slowly. I could never sleep in a dead woman's bed alone, but Mother was unafraid, curled beneath so many blankets I could hardly be sure she was there at all.

This was a woman's room, not like my parents' jumbled bedroom, where the dresser top was always cluttered and half a dozen pairs of shoes lined the wall, where the bed went unmade day after day, and the smell was always Father's smell. Grandmother's room had white curtains with pale pink roses. The bedspread was white too, and on the dresser the silver-handled mirror and brush lay on the blue runner, ready to be used.

From the wall, the grandmother I had never known gazed at me, amused, as if she guessed I would one day stand here and wonder. The artist who tinted the photograph had made her eyes a brilliant blue and her hair a deep chestnut, but I knew these were small lies: her eyes were as pale and colorless as mine, like clouds, Mother said. Her hair should have been lighter too, my color, unruly, fine, an unremarkable brown. The artist thought that darker hair would make her brows look less severe, but Grandmother's confidence defied his efforts.

So she peered out at me through the years, with all the brashness of her youth. She was sixteen and fearless. Her marriage was two years away, so she didn't know that her preacher husband would take her from Chicago to a godforsaken town in Montana.

She didn't know that he'd leave her and the church and their baby daughter, my mother, to answer another call, that he'd move to California to care for an invalid sister, and die there without ever seeing his wife or child again.

This was what was left of him: in her jewelry box a small packet of letters on blue paper, signed: *Your loving husband;* on her finger a wedding ring she could not remove, first because of hope, and later because her knuckles twisted with arthritis; in her heart a bouquet of baby's breath, so dry and fragile it would crumble at the slightest touch.

Often Mother sat alone in this room, taking the letters out of the envelopes, reading them again and again, as if she were looking for some truth, some explanation she'd missed. But she never found an answer she liked. Once I caught her by surprise. "I don't know why my mother kept these letters," she said. And I wondered: Why do *you* keep them? She showed me the ring and told me about Grandmother's twisted hands, though I had heard the story many times. "She made me promise to take the ring off her finger after she died," Mother said, "no matter what it took. I had a devil of a time, but I kept my word." She rubbed her own knuckles. "Poor woman," she whispered.

I closed the door and left my mother drowned in dreams.

Shivering, I ran back to my own bed and hid beneath the covers. I fell into a fitful sleep. I imagined Grandmother's swollen knuckles. I saw her tug at the ring. But the woman in the dream looked like my mother.

Later, I smelled something baking, something sweet and delicious. Mom had hot cornbread waiting for me when I got down to the kitchen. "Thought I'd warm up the house," she said. We each took a steaming golden square big enough for four people. I slathered mine with butter and honey, but we hadn't chewed the first bite before someone rapped on the back door and pressed a pale face against the glass. Mom jumped up to slide the bolt free and let Aunt Arlen inside.

"Are you crazy, woman, coming out in this storm?" Mother said. Aunt Arlen's head was wrapped tight in an old flannel shirt, and she wore a raccoon coat that held the ripe smell of the dead animals. She went straight to the stove to rub her bare hands together over the heat.

Mom offered cornbread and Arlen shook her head. Skinny as she was, I'd never known Arlen to refuse food. She still hadn't said hello. Finally she took the rag off her head and turned to face us. "I'm not going back," she said, "not even if hell *does* freeze over. I mean it this time. I've had it. Right up to here." She slashed the air in front of her throat. "He can just see how he likes it, cooking and cleaning up after those boys. They're half his—or more—I can hardly see my part in them now that they're grown. Maybe Justin and Marshall will think to look for their own place if they don't have a live-in maid. Lester can iron his own shirts and mend the crotch of his own damn jeans instead of throwing them in my lap and asking me what the hell I do all day that I can't get around to the 'few, simple things a man has a right to expect from his wife.' Now that the Fat Lady's shaking for God and speaking in tongues, there's one more 'simple thing' Lester Munter wants from the old wife. All of a sudden this bag of bones don't look too bad. Well, he can hold his breath till he turns blue and falls on his face. He's not laying a finger on this woman. 'Come on, baby, let's get warm,' he says, right in front of the boys—and them sneering, knowing their father's gone to Lyla Leona for years, and they've seen her too, wallowed in her flesh. Pigs, every one of them. I had to get myself out of there before I stabbed my fork right up his nose." She paused long enough to take her first breath.

"Can I stay here, Evelyn? Just until this blizzard's over? I'll look for a place as soon as the weather breaks. Something for me and Lucy—oh, my poor baby; I can't leave her with her brothers for long. They'll turn her into a little slave. Maybe I can get us a room at the boardinghouse, right up there with Minnie Hathaway and Lyla Leona; maybe I can be saved too."

"Don't even think about living in a dump like that," Mom said. "You can stay here long as you want."

I DON'T believe Arlen ever had any intention of looking for another place. She settled into the den off the living room and slept on the lumpy sofa that was three inches shorter than she was.

For two days she watched her own house like a thief. "Look at Lester," she said on the third morning, "fat and happy and late for work." She snorted. "Looks like Justin gave up on that foolish beard. My boy never thought he had enough chin. Maybe that's why he doesn't go out with girls. Maybe that's why Lester did him the favor of taking him to see the Fat Lady when he was sixteen. What a father. Isn't there some law against a man and his son sleeping with the same woman? Well, there should be. Rubs mighty close to incest if you ask me." Arlen didn't mind that I was the only one listening to her.

"Poor Lucy," she said. "Look at her. No hat, no gloves, you'd think one of those boys would see to it she doesn't freeze on her way to school."

Later that morning Arlen sneaked into her empty house and packed enough clothes to stay with us all winter. The whole thing made my father nervous. He asked Mom how long Arlen was staying. "Just a week or so, honey, until this tiff blows over," she said. She never called him "honey," so he must have known we were in deep.

On Sunday, Arlen went to church; she wanted to hear if folks were speculating on her reasons for leaving Lester. She wanted to know if the reverend judged her with mercy or cruelty. Daddy stayed home for the first time in months. He said he wanted to have a word with Mother, but he looked too red to talk. As soon as Arlen was out of the house, he pounded his fist on the kitchen table and said, "She's not staying here another day."

"She's staying as long as she wants," Mother said.

"It's not right, a woman leaving her husband and kids. I won't be any part of it."

"She's your sister, Dean."

"She's Lester Munter's wife, that's what she is, and she belongs in his house, not mine."

"Blood and water."

"What the hell is that supposed to mean?"

"That your sister should mean more to you than Lester Munter."

"What do you think we're running here, a home for wayward women?"

"She's hardly a *wayward woman.*"

"No? Well I think that's a mighty polite name for a woman who deserts her husband. When I think of her harping away about Elliot Foot, I don't know whether to laugh or be sick."

"It's not the same."

"No, of course not. Elliot Foot is a man."

"Elliot Foot ran off to be with another woman. Arlen left to be by herself. Your sister walked across the alley and Elliot took a Winnebago to Arizona."

"I could make her go."

"I'd go with her," Mother said.

"Are you threatening me?"

"I'm stating a fact."

They glared at each other. They were both bluffing, but neither one was willing to force the hand. Finally Daddy said, "I wish she'd just find her own place and keep us out of it."

"You know she hasn't got a dime of her own."

"Whose fault is that?"

"Hers," said Mom. "She should have lifted ten bucks from Lester's wallet every week and stashed it away for herself."

Dad sighed. He didn't have a chance with this kind of reasoning. "If Les ever comes over here and wants to drag her home, I won't stand in his way."

ARLEN STAYED, one week and then another. The third week began. She didn't have much to talk about now that Lester and the boys weren't around to keep her riled, but that didn't stop her. There was a noisiness to her presence, a clamor of confusion. By the time I came home from school, Mother was worn down by Arlen's jabbering. She soon agreed with my father: it was time to send Arlen back to those children who needed her.

Our house seemed smaller in winter. The tiny windows of my attic room leaked light, but by four o'clock the whole house was dark. In the dim hours, my wallpaper turned chaotic. Nina had chosen it, this tangle of green vines and burgundy roses. I dreaded going home but couldn't stand the cold outside. Often, Arlen followed me from room to room, relating every detail of her day. She stayed on my heels as I climbed the stairs. One afternoon she said, "I couldn't decide whether to wear my blue dress or my green one this morning. So I chose the brown slacks instead." This amused her. She muttered a few words under her breath and giggled. I tried to slip into the bathroom and close the door, but she was too quick for me. "I had toast for breakfast—with strawberry jam. Your mother had apple butter." I sat down on the toilet. "No, wait," she said.

"I can't," I answered, but she didn't mean me.

"I think she had marmalade." The confusion concerning Mother's toast perplexed her. She charged out of the bathroom and down the stairs. "Evelyn," I heard her call. "Evelyn, did you have marmalade or apple butter?"

Later, when I thought about what happened to Arlen in our house, I realized anger was the only thing that had kept her strong. She had to fill her head with nonsense; the steady buzz stopped her from thinking about her husband and sons making love to Lyla Leona, kept her safe from the blinding memory of the day they pulled Jesse from the lake.

I learned something that winter: when things go bad, they can always get worse; misfortune has its own momentum. A week before Christmas, a second storm hit. This blizzard took its toll. In the fields beyond the edge of town, snow blew over the frozen bodies of cows and sheep, the ones that didn't make it to the barn before dark.

Two days after the storm my father roared into the drive. He slammed the door so hard it popped open again, so he gave it a kick and stomped into the garage instead of the house. He growled and knocked cans of nails off the shelves, mad as a bear with a bullet in its hind end. Mom and Arlen and I sat in the kitchen, peeling potatoes and carrots for a stew, leaning over the trash barrel as if it held some magic life-giving flame.

Finally Daddy filled the doorway. The cold air hung in the room, a cloud he dragged behind him. "Red Elk's back," he said. Mother dropped her potato in her lap. "Josh Holler hired him back at the mill. He says if there's any trouble this time, the Indian won't be the one to go."

Red Elk, the man my father had tried to drive out of town, had returned at last. I saw Daddy huddled at the kitchen table with those men, their boots thick with muck, their words loud and slurred: *We showed that red devil.* The night I heard that I was only seven years old. I thought they'd driven him down to the swamp, left him to die for the crime of making a white woman want him. But he rose from the sludge, nose broken, eyes full of mud. Now he was back. Red Elk was respectable, a working-man just like my father, no better, no worse.

Daddy had to treat him right or leave the mill, the only job he knew or ever wanted. He had to look this big Indian in the face, a man he despised even before Billy Elk took Nina in his arms and made her disappear.

Arlen looked from Mom to Dad and back again. She pressed one hand to her mouth. I could see she was about to burst into one of her fits. If she got laughing now, there'd be no stopping her. Mother stood, slowly, watching Daddy the whole time as she walked toward him. Arlen said, "Are you—are you gonna kill him, Dean?" Then she broke up, giggling and puffing.

Mom slipped her arm around Daddy's waist. "I don't want to kill him," he whispered.

Arlen quieted herself, but her mouth still had that funny look.

Mother led Daddy to the living room and sat him down. "I don't want to kill him," he said again.

"Of course you don't. Arlen doesn't know what she's saying."

"I did at first, him and the boy too, but it wouldn't change anything, would it?"

"Not now," Mom said, rubbing his red hands.

I glanced at Arlen. She wasn't paying any attention to my parents. She was crying as she chopped the onions.

We never ate dinner that night. I hid in my room, but around nine I got so hungry I had to sneak downstairs and grab a bowl of stew. Arlen sat in the kitchen with the lights off. "Close your eyes," I said. But she didn't, and she blinked hard in the sudden glare of the overhead light.

"Did you eat?" I said.

"I don't remember."

I looked in the sink: there were no dirty dishes. The drainer was empty. "I don't think you did." I dished up a bowl of stew for each of us. The stew was lukewarm and unseasoned, but I was hungry and shoveled it down. Arlen took three bites and stopped.

"What does he look like?" I said.

"Who?"

"Red Elk." I wanted to know this man if I ever met up with him on the street. Aunt Arlen looked at me as if she were going to start hooting again. "Don't you know, honey? Don't you know?" I shook my head. "Then you must be the only one in town who doesn't." She leaned close to me. "Like an Indian," she said, "he looks like a goddamned Indian."

"I know *that.*"

"No, I mean a real Indian—big and dark, no white blood, still wears his hair in a braid down the back, still wears a blanket instead of a coat, still pisses in a hole in the ground." I wondered how she knew. Arlen cocked her head. "Listen," she said. I didn't hear anything. "They've been at it all night."

"Who?"

"Your parents." She clamped her hands over her ears. "How can they?" The sounds of imagined lovemaking echoed in her head. Grandmother's room was above us, and that room had been dead quiet a long time. "I can't stand it," Arlen said. "I can't listen to that." She pushed her chair back and let it fall, ran through the living room to her dark den where she was safe from voices, dreamed or real.

I turned out the lights, moved to Arlen's place and finished her stew.

I couldn't sleep that night. I was thinking about the night nearly seven years before when my father and his gang had chased

Red Elk up the mountain. I could almost hear the joyful barks of the dogs as they caught the Indian's scent.

I stood at the window, my nose touching the cold glass. A new moon cut the hard winter sky. I imagined how tired Red Elk must have been. Perhaps all he'd wanted to do that night was to lie on the cool rocks of the mountain. If it had only been the dogs on his tail, he might have given up. But Red Elk knew the men were close behind, so he kept climbing.

The dogs grew weary and took the men in a circle. Those dogs never made it off the mountain, and Mother told me and Nina what the men had done.

Later we heard how Red Elk went home that night and sat with a rifle across his lap. He hadn't bothered to wipe his bloody nose or change his clothes.

Mary Louise Furey told him she wanted him out of there before Billy woke up. No boy of hers was going to see his daddy like that. She let Ike Turner know she'd made the man leave. She said she pulled the gun off his lap and threatened to shoot off his toes.

"They didn't catch him," Mary Louise said, "but they killed him all the same." She talked to Ike because she knew he was the only man in town who wouldn't be glad the Indian was gone. And she knew Ike couldn't keep a secret. She wanted folks to believe that Red Elk had left her. She was tired of his kind of trouble.

Just before dawn the day the Indian disappeared, Mary Louise Furey heard ten shots. By the time she got out of bed, Red Elk had vanished and there were holes in the porch, one for each toe, a perfect outline. "He must've come damn close," Mary Louise told Ike.

It was strange that the woman was the one to make him go. Red Elk could hold his own against any white man, but the white woman he loved made him hide out for seven years. I didn't understand why Mary Louise blamed him for the sorrow my father and his friends had caused.

I was cold, standing there by the window, so I went back to bed, but I still couldn't keep my eyes closed. I was remembering my father at church the morning after he'd tried to run the Indian out of town. I saw Nina skipping up beside him as we walked home, Nina who could forget so easily, Nina who didn't know enough to be afraid of our father that day. And I saw my mother and myself behind them, looking at Daddy's back, seeing him exactly as he was.

II

STORIES SPREAD about the way Red Elk got his wife to take him back. Mary Louise Furey told Ike Turner she'd been finding gifts on her porch and tracks in the snow for several weeks. There were three skinned rabbits with their eyes gouged out, a venison rump roast, and a string of sausages hanging in front of her door.

Ike Turner was proud of the fact that he was the first person in town to see Red Elk—besides Mary Louise, of course. Every customer who stopped in at the truck stop that day heard about Ike's conversation with the Indian.

He offered Red Elk a job pumping gas, but the man told him working the pumps was a boy's job, and Mary Louise would never stand for it. "I might as well go back to the reservation as come home smelling like gasoline every night," Red Elk said. Ike Turner understood; Mary Louise Furey was no easy woman to please. But when he found out Red Elk meant to go back to the mill, Ike Turner said he wished he believed in God so he could say a prayer for his friend.

The day after Joshua Holler gave Red Elk a job, Daddy didn't come home from work. At seven, Mother called me and Arlen to dinner. Nobody said a word until Arlen blurted, "He's done it. He's gotten into it with the big Indian. He's drinking himself blind or digging himself into a hole to die."

"Shut up, Arlen," Mom said. "Shut your goddamn mouth."

Arlen straightened her back and sat stone-still, holding her breath, waiting for the ill wind to pass. Finally she dabbed both sides of her mouth with her napkin, said "Very well," and waltzed her way out of the kitchen. A moment later Mother got up too, bundled herself in an oversized coat, and slipped out front to sit on the porch swing.

From my bedroom above the porch, I watched the road. When I cracked the window open, I heard the whine of the swing, my mother rocking—rocking slowly to make time pass more slowly. I felt her fear: a stiffness in my joints like old age springing suddenly upon me, and I lay like a shell across my bed, unable to move.

I tried not to think about what might have happened to my father, but I imagined him changing his mind, deciding he wanted Red Elk dead after all. He might have rounded up his old gang, Dwight Carson and the mangy Foot brothers. Perhaps the men waited for the Indian after work. They might jump him in the parking lot, pull a garbage bag over his head and tie it at the knees, heave him into the bed of a pickup and head for the frozen lake. I wondered if my mother was troubled by the same visions.

An hour passed, and still Mother sat outside in the cold, waiting for the moment of my father's return. Somehow I knew he was near; I felt him just as I felt her. I crawled over my bed to the window. A car whizzed by, but the lights were too low, too close to the ground for me to mistake it for my father's truck. Then I saw him at the end of the block, on foot, lurching against a light swirl of snow.

Mother did not rise to meet him. She let him reel and stumble. Fool. She watched him. I thought she must hate him for making her so afraid, for letting her think he might be dead when all the time he was drunk and very much alive.

Now he was at the bottom of the steps, looking up at her. He didn't try to climb onto the porch; he only mouthed her name. "You should be ashamed," she said.

"I am," he whispered.

"Drinking yourself dumb."

But he wasn't drunk. He swore, no, not a drop, "I couldn't." And yet he said, "Who will forgive me?"

She knew him too well to think he lied. Her rage spilled on the steps, useless now, leaving her as weak as he was. She pulled him toward her. It was a long time before he spoke. And it was a long time before she asked.

At last she said, "Tell me"; and he answered, "Lanfear Deets lost his hand. Lanfear Deets cut off his damn hand because I got him promoted."

"You can't blame yourself for doing a man a favor."

"For the wrong reasons."

"He deserved the raise."

"I told the sonuvabitch a thousand times if I told him once, 'Watch what you're doing.' But he wasn't watching. He was gabbing with Vern Foot, clucking like a damn woman. You can't hear a thing in there; the fool was leaning over so far he practically had his nose stuck in Vern's ear. Saw caught his sleeve, Jesus, pulled him halfway onto the table."

"He's to blame."

"I knew he was an idiot. But she, the way she looked at him. She'll never forgive me. She forgave me for twisting his arm to get my twelve dollars out of that worthless weasel, but she won't ever forgive me for cutting off his hand."

"You didn't."

He stared at his callused palms. "Everything I touch," he said.

IN THE morning the sun fell through the blinds of the kitchen window, throwing rails of light on the floor. My father didn't go to work that day or the next, or the one after that. He chopped firewood for three days straight, brought home four truckloads of logs and split them all, then piled them along the side of the house. He rarely rested, and when he did, he didn't eat; he just sat on a stump and smoked. Mother and I watched the stack grow. "At least we won't freeze," she said.

I was sure people would figure out why my father stayed clear of the mill. He wasn't the kind to take a sick day. But of course no one pieced it together. No one blamed him as he blamed himself. Lanfear Deets wasn't the first man to mangle a limb at the Willis mill, and his wounds weren't the worst. "Lucky to have his arm," some folks said. "Lucky to have his head," someone added. And everyone laughed. The only people who weren't laughing lived in my house.

That was the same week Arlen's chickens died and she went home. The night the temperature dropped to 20 below, Lester Munter left the door of Arlen's chicken coop open a crack—an accident, he said. He claimed he flicked off the lamps just by habit. In the calm of morning, Arlen spotted the open door, the wind-drifted snow. She found her chickens this way: rigid, destroyed, blocks of chicken-shaped ice that would be rotten by the time they were thawed enough to bleed. She cleared the snow from a circle in her yard and gathered two armloads of my father's wood, stacked a triangle on the hard earth, and stuffed the holes with newspaper. Two by two, she carried her chickens out by their legs, tossed them on top of the logs until she had a three-foot pile of frozen fluff.

She spent hours fanning the pale flames in the cold, but when the pyre finally caught, the inferno looked as if it would burn for days. Thick smoke rose and hung above the house, a blue cloud that refused to scatter or drift. The stink of singed feathers and scorched skin filled the neighborhood, squeezed under doorframes, seeped along the sills of closed windows.

By nightfall, when the bonfire flickered low, when her precious chickens were nothing but ash and charred bone, Arlen packed her bags and went home. I was glad when she left, glad there was no one else to hear our secrets or our silences.

12

GWEN HOLLER could have rescued me during Christmas break. Running through the gully with her might have made me forget about my father. I could have gone to the gully alone, but when I was by myself, the stripped tamaracks and the crunch of frozen snow under my boots only reminded me of what Daddy had done. I blamed him for Lanfear Deets's hand—not because the poor man had lost it and couldn't work, but because the saw kept whirring in my brain. I saw Lanfear Deets's fingers, fat as sausages, guiding the rough boards. He remembered a joke and looked over his shoulder to tell Vern Foot. And they laughed, too hard; Lanfear jerked his hand away just in time. That was a warning, a little scare before the real thing. I imagined the second joke, minutes later, Lanfear glancing sideways, the unstoppable saw lifting his body onto the table, the bewildered look before the pain, the bad joke untold.

By then I knew that Red Elk had saved Lanfear Deets. He'd ripped the bandanna from his neck and tied a tourniquet at Lanfear's elbow. Blood spurted on Red Elk's hands and thighs, spit all the way to his eye when he cinched the cloth tight—that's

what my father said. When I closed my eyes, I saw Lanfear
Deets's blood spreading on the floor, a giant poppy slowly opening.

I was almost relieved to go back to school. The first Friday,
Mr. Lippman told the class to choose lab partners for our science
project: on Monday, each pair of students would have one frog
to dissect together. I stared at Gwen, but she leaned across the aisle
to tap Jill Silverlake on the arm. They giggled and squeezed each
other's hands as if they'd just agreed to go steady.

The room buzzed and I waited. Finally Mr. Lippman thumped
his desk with his fist and told us to raise our hands if we didn't
have a partner. Only two other hands wagged in the air: the five
dimpled fingers of Marlene Grosswilder and the dark hand of
Claude Champeaux, one of the three Indian brothers who was
brave or foolish enough to come to our school. Mr. Lippman
assigned Marlene to me and took Claude as his own partner. He
didn't want any hysterical mothers calling him in the middle of
the night. He didn't want some hefty mill worker standing at his
door with a rifle, asking where he got the nerve to let a white
girl work with an Indian boy.

"It's a sign," Marlene said, cornering me by my locker. "The
Lord wants us to be friends."

"Bug off, Marlene."

She covered her ears. "I don't hear nasty language."

"How about this," I said, grabbing her collar and pulling her
toward me until our noses nearly touched, "can you hear me
now? Does your God think that after we whack a little frog on
the back of the head, stab a needle in his brain and slit his gut,
we'll be pals for life?"

"Stop it. You're choking me." I let her go. Marlene shook her
finger as she backed away from me. "I'm still praying for you.
I'm praying for you, Lizzie Macon."

I opened my mouth and stuck my fingers inside to show her that the idea of her praying for me made me gag.

"The Lord tells me that you must be suffering in some way."

I kicked my locker shut. "Yeah, I'm suffering, all right. I'm suffering being forced to talk to a stupid cow like you."

"I forgive you for what you just said. And the Lord forgives you too."

Now that she'd swallowed religion, Marlene Grosswilder was impossible to rile. I said, "The Lord has nothing to do with anything that happens between us." Marlene was the only girl in the eighth grade who was as tall as I was. We stood nose to nose and I peered through her thick glasses thinking how strange her eyes looked, magnified twice their natural size.

She sucked in her breath, gathering up the peace that passes understanding. "God sees everything," she said, "whether you believe it or not."

"If He's watching us, why'd He let me choke a good girl like you?"

"He doesn't always interfere. He allows us to be tempted by the evil one. How else can we prove our faith?"

"The evil one must've tempted you a few times."

"When he does, I pray. And I pray for you, Elizabeth."

The idea of Marlene Grosswilder talking about me to God made the muscles in my chest so tight I thought my heart would stop. The only way I could think to relieve the pressure was to knock her flat on her ass. But we were both spared. She waddled off down the hall. I watched her, following her steps from her thick ankles to her pudgy knees up to the wrinkles of her skirt where it bunched and creased to stretch over her broad beam.

My hatred for Marlene was as pure as it was the year she made special valentines with a piece of homemade fudge wrapped in colored foil glued on top for everyone in the class except for three kids—and I was one of them. That was bad enough, but she wouldn't let it lie: she had to make a particular effort to let those kids know what a delicious treat they'd missed; she had to lick her chubby fingers right in front of me. That was in third grade. I never forgot. I guess that made her some kind of superior person to me because she already forgave me for what I said today, and I'd been holding a grudge for six years. She'd left me in some mighty fine company: the only others who didn't get valentines were the Furey brothers. One was supposed to be in fifth grade and one was supposed to be in fourth. Maybe they were Mary Louise's cousins or maybe they were her brothers. When it came to the Furey clan, these distinctions didn't make much difference. They all had too much of the same blood; they all had short necks and small ears. Some of them were born with six toes on each foot, but Harley Furey was scared of that. He said it was the mark of the devil and amputated the evil little growths, leaving several of his sons with nasty scars and a fumbling gait. Sometimes I worried that Nina's relationship with Billy Elk meant that I was connected to all the Fureys, but I didn't think on it too deeply.

Marlene Grosswilder got me another time, in fifth grade. By then the Furey brothers had dropped out of school; I didn't even have the misery of their company. Marlene had a Halloween party with a haunted house and real caramel apples, and everyone talked about it for weeks before it happened. I waited. Right up to the very day of the party, I hoped she'd just forgotten my invitation. Even Gwen got a card with a ghost that popped out of the fold.

I told myself I didn't want to go through her dumb haunted house anyway. I didn't want to be blindfolded and have my hand forced into a bowl of cold spaghetti while someone whispered I was touching a human brain. I had no desire to get my nose full of water bobbing for apples. I said it over and over as I shuffled through dried leaves, taking the long way home.

MR. LIPPMAN heard me talking mean to Marlene by the lockers and kept me after school. That gave me extra time to think about how much fun I was going to have cutting up a frog with that girl. When Mr. Lippman set me free, the sky was woolly in the bleak half-dark. Only one car still squatted in the lot—not Mr. Lippman's; he walked everywhere and was proud of it. This was Gil Harding's brown Duster. It glistened under the yellow lights, all its windows clouded by the hot breath inside.

I'd noticed the Duster in the lot other nights, but I could never see who Gil had pinned to the seat because the windows were steamed. This night I did see. Gil stepped out of the car to take a piss, making no effort to hide himself. He was the only boy I knew who would pee in the middle of an empty parking lot without so much as taking a glance around to be sure he wouldn't scare any old ladies.

The girl in the car sat up, and in the sudden flash of light from the dome I saw the unmistakable flick of the head, the way Gwen Holler tossed her ponytail over her shoulder. She finally had the real thing: Gil Harding's yellow fingers, stained from cigarettes, stroking her face and breasts.

Gil caught me watching him and turned to face me; then he laughed, shaking the last drops of piss from his penis. Gwen leaned out her window to see who was there. Her look was bored, distracted; she wanted Gil to get back in the car. She peered in my direction without a whiff of embarrassment or remorse, turned her head as if I were nothing more than a stray dog. Her indifference drowned me. I wished we were boys so I could wait for her after school some night and pummel her with my fists.

ON MONDAY, we pithed and mutilated our frogs. Marlene got sick and had to run to the bathroom when she saw how complete the creature was, a little man with bowed legs. I had to finish the job alone. This is all I learned: the tiny muscle of the heart felt tough and hard between my fingertips.

I sprinted home that night, my coat open, my scarf flying. The air stung my lungs like slivers of ice. Even in the cold, I could smell my own hands.

13

IN JANUARY and February it seemed winter in Montana would never end. The fog rolled into the valley and sat, unable to rise. In the morning, when the pink light was still trapped behind the mountains, I heard the bare trees groaning in the wind, their black trunks swaying.

The sky was white for days at a time. If the mist broke enough to reveal the foothills, they too were white, and the distant pines were dark and colorless. Along our block, the dry bark of birch trees peeled like paper. Only the willows held a promise of change, their thin orange limbs quavering with the slightest breeze.

By March we had hope. Winter came and went half a dozen times in a single month. The first heavy rain was too cold to wash away the piles of crusty snow. Pools appeared in the yards, and ice lakes spread across the treacherous streets. Every night the ponds froze.

The lakes melted by noon and slowly shrank. Snow piles were splattered with mud and pocked by dog piss. Day by day, the long yellow grass of our lawn was unburied. It lay flat on the ground like an old woman's matted hair, and the pools turned the color of the grass or the rusty color of dead leaves that we hadn't raked before the first snow came.

The first day that the roads were clear enough I pumped up my bicycle tires and pedaled to Moon Lake after school. Haze hovered over the fields, but the sky above had cleared and the light was pale and gold. Clumps of trees and houses rose out of the fog like the ghosts of a deserted town. For a moment I saw the steeple of an abandoned church, but filmy clouds curled around it, and the vision disappeared.

Moon Lake was eighteen miles long and five miles wide, but it was depth that gave this water strength. Mountains plunged straight down to the waterline, and beneath the surface more mountains rose and fell. I thought about the glacier that had chiseled this lake. Two-ton boulders on the beach reminded me of the power of ice, the slow, relentless energy of the frozen river that had towed chunks of mountains in its wake so many centuries ago. I stood on the beach, listening to the frightening sound of ice cracking.

Three days later the surface broke and the thick green waves piled slabs along the shore. The lake looked swollen and green, ready to take anyone who dared to come too near. After that, I stayed on the safe streets of Willis.

I took long walks through town. Neighbors' dogs followed me. They romped in the dirty snow, delighted by the smell of earth oozing up from the softening ground. They leaped at me and left muddy paw prints on my clothes. When I scolded them, they only barked and jumped higher.

By that spring I had promised myself I would give up on Gwen Holler. But I was still trying to make her notice me, and

I wonder if she may have been responsible, in a roundabout way, for what happened between me and her brother Zachary that first warm day in April.

Gwen had begun wearing pantyhose and short skirts. Her lashes were black and thick with mascara; she painted her lids violet one day and amber the next. I thought she might pay attention to me if I followed her example. I had no money for makeup, but I found an old orange lipstick tucked in the back of a drawer in the bathroom, and I borrowed a pair of stockings from my mother—or stole them, depending on how you looked at it. I spent an entire evening shortening a skirt, ripping out my stitches three times before I got the hem close to right.

The next morning I leaned close to the mirror. I'd teased my hair so it didn't look so wispy. My mouth was wide; I reminded myself to smile carefully and not show too many teeth. I powdered my nose to hide my freckles. I had a good nose, not fine like Nina's or my mother's but not too big. It was acceptable. My eyebrows were too dark and thick, but there wasn't time to pluck them.

Of course my efforts were in vain. Gwen didn't take any interest in my sloppy imitation and would not have been flattered if I'd told her I wanted to look like her. I must've lost my head for a minute. I was four inches taller than Gwen. My butt was flat where hers was high and curved. She knew how to cross her legs in a short skirt; my thighs ached at the end of the day from pressing my knees together. I couldn't wait for school to end. I thought sure some smart-mouthed boy would make fun of my outfit before the day was over.

When the final bell rang, I charged for the door and cut down alleys toward Wyoming Way. I'd been taking the long route home since last fall, past Freda Graves's house, never knowing what I expected to see, but always hoping. Today all the shades were drawn tight, and I had the idea that Freda was inside, alone in the dark with God. She had secrets. I believed she saved the best prayers for herself and that she knew her God in ways her small congregation couldn't imagine. Even after people blamed Freda Graves for what happened to Myron Evans and Elliot Foot, a part of me still clung to the possibility that the woman had a special vision. Her God had eyes to watch her and fingers to stroke her hair. She embraced a God I only glimpsed. When she made mistakes, her God shook her so hard she could not stand. And when she couldn't bear it a moment longer, her generous God clutched her to His breast and wept.

I'd just passed Mrs. Graves's house when I realized somebody was on my tail. I whirled once and saw a bush tremble. I spun again and saw the toes of a boy's sneakers poking out behind a tree. On the third try, I caught him and stood face-to-face with Zachary Holler.

I put my fists on my hips and waited.

"You've got scrawny legs," Zack said.

I tried to stare him down, but my short skirt exposed me. I had no defense: my bony knees were an indisputable fact.

Finally Zack said, "But you don't look too bad."

"Thanks a lot."

"I mean you're not too ugly."

"Thanks again."

"I used to think you were."

"So what?"

"So, I was just thinking that since I was walking this way anyway . . ."

"Yeah?"

"I was thinking I'd walk with you."

I reminded myself that I hated Zack Holler. I thought of him strangling Myron Evans's poor cat; I saw him prancing around me and Gwen, making fools of us, making Gwen decide she didn't want to play any more games with me, ever.

"Well, can I?" he said.

"Can you what?"

He snorted and looked at me as if I'd been cheated when they handed out brains. "Can I walk you home?"

"Free country," I said. I turned and he loped after me. I tried to catch a sideways glance at him without letting on I cared that he was there. I thought of him the way I knew Nina would, and I felt proud that a high school boy who played football and baseball was trotting down the street to keep up with me. I hoped someone would see us. I hoped the whole school would hear that Zachary Holler was seen walking with Lizzie Macon.

He grinned—a wide, close-lipped grin that spread across his face so fast I forgot myself long enough to think he looked sweet. But I recovered. I wanted to tell him he'd made my life miserable by doing what he did to me and Gwen, but I couldn't get the words past my tight throat. I gritted my teeth and lunged forward as if I were fighting the force of some old winter wind.

"Hey, slow down," he said, grabbing my arm. "We're gonna get home too fast."

He was almost laughing; he was laughing at me, at my pride. He was walking me home because he knew what a joke it was to be seen with a girl like me. My eyes stung. The last thing in the world I meant to do was give Zack Holler something to snigger about with the boys.

I shook him loose and darted down the block. He must have been stunned because he stood there yelling before he tore after me. Something steered me away from my house. Later I thought it was the devil, but right then I believed my father might be home early. If he saw me being chased down the street by a boy, he'd have me over his knee before I caught a breath.

I headed toward the gully, figuring I could lose Zack in the woods. My skinny legs were good for something—I was fast. The smartest thing I could have done would have been to stop dead in my tracks. Zack would have left me alone if I'd just let him prove he could wear me out. He was like a dog chasing a pack rat. Only a fool dog wants to catch a rat; but once he's after it, no hound will give it up.

Without thinking, I ran straight for the tree house. I didn't realize how stupid I'd been till I swayed in the branches and Zack came scrambling up the ladder. Then I remembered how I'd cornered Gwen that day, how she thought she was so safe and I thought I was so clever, because once you're in the tree house and someone else is at the door, there's no way out except to fly.

Zack Holler jumped me like a wolf on a weasel in the dead of winter. He had a hunger. He nipped at my neck. His teeth tugged my lips. Kissing Zachary was nothing at all like kissing Gwen. His mouth was dry and his tongue filled my mouth till I thought I'd choke.

He pawed and pushed. I didn't have time to worry about what I was supposed to do with my hands before I was falling to the floor and Zack was falling on top of me and my skirt was riding up around my thighs. Zack clawed at my stockings till they ripped from belly to knee. I said *no* a dozen times, but maybe not out loud. My fingernails dug into the flesh of his back. He moved on me faster and faster. His belt buckle cut into my stomach; the stiff denim of his jeans gnawed at my bare skin, and I pleaded with him to slow down, to stop, he was hurting me; I was sure someone would hear us in the tree house, someone would see it rocking and know. But no one came. No one heard Zack cry out, unless my father heard it piercing through his brain above the roar of rough logs being sheared as he left the mill.

Zack collapsed on top of me and drifted off to sleep. My legs felt prickly and hot, like I'd rolled in poison ivy. The smell of us made me giddy, made me think of putting my whole face down in a barrel of apples being pressed into cider.

I liked that smell, though I knew it would be bad soon enough, something sweet turning to vinegar in the warm afternoon. I could have pushed Zack off: he was in no mood to wrestle. But I lay there. In the end, Zack was the first to go.

DADDY SAT on the porch swing. It was past five. He'd been off work for an hour or two, so I knew he'd had time to suck down more than a couple of beers. He spotted me when I was still a block off, and I felt his stare as I dawdled along toward the house. I'd buried Mom's tattered pantyhose in the gully. My naked legs were scratched and dirty, my hair a tangled mat. It was plain my father didn't like what he saw, even at a distance. The idea of turning around and tearing down the street to avoid the whole scene crossed my mind, but I didn't know where to run. Only Nina could fool our father; only Nina knew him well enough to hide forever.

The instant I touched the steps of his house he was on me. He grabbed my wrist and jerked me onto the porch, then shoved me inside the house, giving my behind a sharp jab with his knee as I stumbled through the doorway.

"Where've you been, dressed like that?" he shouted. Mother ran out from the kitchen to see what the ruckus was.

"Calm yourself," she said, trying to wedge between us. My father had already worked himself into a sweat. Mom knew the slapping would start if she didn't do something fast. Daddy pushed her out of his way with one hand and said, "Did you see your daughter leave the house today?" She refused to answer. The beer on his breath smelled sweet and strong and made me remember.

"What have I told you about girls who put that crap all over their faces?" he said to me. "What did I say I'd do if I ever caught you ratting your hair and wearing your skirt halfway up your ass?"

Mom tugged at his arm. "It's just a little makeup, Dean. It doesn't mean anything."

But my father and I knew different. Daddy's eyes were clear and pale, glacial ice reflecting just a hint of blue from the sky. Those eyes saw everywhere. He knew all about me and Zack. He saw us falling. He saw that I almost liked it, that I was already imagining it might happen again.

Damp rings darkened Daddy's T-shirt from his armpits halfway to his waist. I never understood how he knew things about me. Maybe we were too much alike. Maybe at the moment he left the mill a squawking crow flew high above him. As he raised his head to see why she was yammering, she swooped in the direction of the gully and the vision came to my father as clearly as if he had followed Zachary up the rickety ladder of the tree house.

"Go take a shower," he said. "And find a decent dress before you sit down at my table."

I climbed the stairs with all the dignity I could muster, knowing how Father judged me. I remembered the smear of orange lipstick across my swollen mouth and heard Zack say, *You're not too ugly*. But I was.

AT DINNER, Dad wasn't talking to me and Mom wasn't talking to him. It was a four-word meal. Father stopped picking at his beans and chop, stood up, threw his napkin on the table and said, "Damn kitchen's too hot." He was only looking for an excuse to go outside for a smoke.

I went straight to my room after Mom and I did the dishes. I opened my window wide and hoped to hear the first crickets of spring, but they were still months away, hundreds of miles south of Willis. I thought of Zack as he stood to leave the tree house. I had stayed on the floor, staring up at his long legs, at the damp spot in his crotch. He'd grinned in a way that made me think he might put his foot on my chest before he left, lightly, a threat, a joke from his point of view. But he hadn't bothered. And I'd watched his thighs as he squatted, easing himself onto the unreliable ladder. I covered my head with my pillow, but the memory didn't fade.

Later the screen door whined, and I knew Mother had gone out on the porch. I pictured her folding her arms, just waiting for Father to turn around and snarl, "What is it?"

Their two voices rumbled along at first, slow and soft, as if they tried their best to be polite and have a real discussion, giving each other time to think and time to speak. But before long their words jumped on top of one another. Daddy swung so hard in the porch seat that it groaned, and I thought it might fly clean off its hinges. The squabble didn't last long. Father won the quarrel by marching down the road and calling back to Mother, "You drive me to drink, woman."

She sat for less than a minute before she came inside. I heard her on the stairs. I figured she had come to her senses and realized what a troublemaker I was, giving her one more thing to fight about with Daddy. I suspected she was on her way to give me the scolding she wouldn't let my father give me earlier.

She tapped at the door and said, "Lizzie, Lizzie honey, are you awake?"

I told her I was. Only the devil could sleep after doing what I'd done that afternoon. I was no better than Zachary Holler. I was impatient and much too hungry. I remembered how I felt as I shoved Gwen against the tree in the gully, strong and mean, thinking only of what I wanted. I felt my own brutal kiss and tasted blood where my teeth cut the inside of my lip.

"May I come in?" I got nervous when my mother was that polite. "Why are you sitting up here in the dark, baby? Come down and sit on the porch with me. Your father's gone."

I didn't want Mother's company, especially if she was going to be so sweet with me when all the time I knew Daddy was right. Zack Holler never would have given me a second look if my lips weren't orange and my skirt wasn't tight. I would have been invisible, the same Lizzie Macon he'd always known, and nothing would have happened in the tree house.

"I've got something to tell you, Liz." The way she said it gave me no choice, so I followed her downstairs to the porch.

She didn't start talking right away. She was thinking so hard that she didn't see how I watched her as we rocked together in the swing. Most times I kept myself from looking at her this way. Tonight I noticed her fingers were stiff, and she rubbed her knuckles one by one. I thought of Grandmother's hands, crippled by arthritis, her joints so swollen she couldn't remove the ring of the man who had deserted her. I wondered how long it would take before my own mother's hands grew twisted, too weak to hold a pot of soup. I saw her by the stove, saw the handle slip from her grasp.

I wanted to swear no boy would ever steal me away. I would be there to mop the soup off the floor, to chop the vegetables and start another pot. I wanted her to put her head on my lap so I could stroke her hair and face and tell her I'd never be a problem to her again. But I did nothing; it wasn't our way, not since Nina left, not since Nina stuffed all her easy love in a canvas bag and vanished in the dust on the road.

Mom patted my knee with her thin hand. "Your father loves you, Lizzie. I hope you believe that. He's rough with you, I know, but he's afraid. He doesn't want you to end up like Nina.

"He loved that girl too much. Sometimes I think he loved her more than he loves me. Men are strange that way. A wife has flaws and no one knows them better than her husband—but a daughter can be anything he wants to see. She looked like an angel, and that's all your daddy saw. He couldn't bear it when he found out. He couldn't forgive her. He still can't. That's the evil that can come of love."

I saw Nina twirling down the stairs in her pink dress with the crinoline slip that made it float around her legs. She was fourteen, like me. Nina didn't have to tempt boys by painting herself like a bird. She was temptation itself. Everyone saw it, everyone but my father. "My baby," he said, his voice a prayer, "my beautiful girl."

"Do you understand what I'm trying to tell you?" Mom said. "Your father wants you to stay his little girl. He says nasty things he doesn't mean. Promise me you won't be too hard on him."

"I won't," I said. Just an hour before, she'd been railing at my father to go easy on me. Sometimes I thought she wanted me to love him in ways that she couldn't. No wonder her soft cheeks were crossed with tiny lines. No wonder her long hair was streaked with gray.

We moved from the swing to the steps to look at the night sky. Once in a while Mom pointed and said, "Look at that!" Or, "There's another one." But I never saw a shooting star. Maybe she was only pretending, or wishing. Maybe the stars in the blur of tears that swelled slowly in the corners of her eyes seemed to leave a trail in the night.

We sat for an hour or more, until Daddy appeared, swaying down the poorly lit street, his hands in his pockets, the whistling man. Mom gripped my arm. "Don't let him catch us," she said. Even in his stupor he might sense we'd been talking about Nina.

I climbed slowly to my room, our room, Nina's and mine, the room where she had read to me night after night to help me fall asleep. I was restless even then, chased by dogs at the edge of my dreams. I thought of that last summer and how there were so many mornings when I'd wake to find her curled around me in my bed instead of sprawled across her own. She must have known she wouldn't be around that long; she was trying to say good-bye. At night the shadows in the yard were alive, swarming with boys. But I was only nine and didn't understand. I tossed in her arms, kicked the blankets from us both and let her soft kisses fall on me, thinking they would always be as plentiful and constant as the rain.

That night I prayed to a god I barely knew, and I made a bargain. I didn't want to be lost like Nina. We knew nothing of her life. I had no place to root her. In my mind, she drifted in a desert, parched at noon and frozen at midnight. I couldn't stop thinking that what Zack and I had done in the tree house could make what happened to Nina happen to me. I saw the stain in the crotch of Zack's jeans when he rolled away from me. I felt the pressure of his hipbones grinding into mine. Then I saw Daddy slapping Nina so hard I thought her jaw would snap and her teeth would clatter to the floor like the pieces of a broken teacup. I heard him call her those names, names I'd never heard before but understood at once; my father's tone could not be mistaken. I crouched on the stairs. He grabbed her yellow hair, twisting it around his hand. He told her not to show her face in his house again, and she thought he meant it.

I was no purer than my sister, no more virtuous than that

loathsome cruel boy who could snap the neck of a cat. A grin could tempt me, muscled arms could hold me down, a boy's tongue in my mouth could make my hands numb.

That night I promised my new God that if He spared me, just this once, I would devote my life to His work. I'd never give Mother and Father cause for grief again. I would be good enough for two people: my sister and myself.

14

BY THE end of April I knew I'd been spared this time. I wasn't going to end up like Nina, my stomach swelling so I couldn't hide what I'd done. I figured a girl wasn't going to get too many breaks in her life and that I'd better find a way to show God I was grateful. It wasn't easy. Zack took no interest in me, so I had no opportunity to resist temptation.

I kept my eyes on the ground when Father spoke to me. I wore baggy pants and long sweaters so that even I wouldn't notice my body. I set the table before I was asked, scrubbed the kitchen floor on my hands and knees, and scoured the toilet once a week. When I saw Marlene Grosswilder at school, I forced myself to think one kind thought. "That's a pretty dress," I said to her one day. She peered at me through her thick glasses, suspecting some nasty intention, then hurried away without a word. I smiled to myself: virtue was its own reward.

Still, I wasn't satisfied. These were small changes. My knowledge of God's truth was one drop of rain in the river. I didn't want to *do* good things; I wanted to *be* good. The vast difference wasn't lost on me even in my ignorance. I was hungry for the

Lord now that I was sure He'd heard me. He'd let my beautiful sister go to ruin, had cast her into the wasteland, a barren place that was only beautiful when twilight turned the horizon green for half an hour. But He had chosen to pardon me. I began to wonder if I'd been saved for some special mission. A girl like me had little chance of becoming a saint or martyr. I'd have to accept a more ordinary course, without glory or recognition. By chance, Aunt Arlen revealed the simplicity of my calling.

She plunked herself down at our kitchen table. "Dean can stop flogging himself over this Lanfear Deets business," she said. "I saw him this morning pumping gas out at Ike's Truckstop, working every bit as fast as any two-fisted brute I ever saw. Thank God for Ike Turner, always willing to hire an Indian or a cripple. He took Miriam on too; she's waitressing on the morning shift. I have to say, Lanfear looked like a happy man. I believe there's a kind of person who's so common he takes a certain pleasure in being maimed. Sets him off from the rest, know what I mean?"

"That's the craziest thing I've heard you say all month," Mom said.

"The lame shall enter first; says so right in the Bible," said Arlen.

"No one wants to be deformed in a permanent way."

I leaned against the stove, curling my fingers into a stiff claw to see if I could imagine a mangled hand making me feel special.

"Well, anyway," Arlen said, "Dean can stop feeling responsible. Lanfear Deets most certainly is not suffering."

"Dean knows he's not to blame."

"I got eyes, Evelyn. I've never seen my brother so thin. And his drinking is no secret."

"We can't all be fat and happy like Les," Mom said. She made the word *fat* sound vile, something you wouldn't want to touch, but Arlen didn't choose to notice.

"Yes, he is happy, my oh my, don't I know. He gave Justin and Marshall the word—six months and they're out. Collin goes soon as he graduates. Fair warning. Les wants some privacy before we're too dried up to enjoy it." Arlen had become an expert on marital bliss ever since she'd gone back to Lester. I didn't think it would last. I didn't think that loving my uncle would be nearly as satisfying as bitching about him had always been. She turned around to look at me. "You keep that in mind, Lizzie. Find yourself a decent job or a half-decent man when you get out of high school. Give your parents some peace."

"She doesn't have to do anything of the kind," Mom said. "There's room for her in this house as long as she wants to stay, till she's forty if it suits her."

"Oh, Evelyn, *please,*" Arlen said, "I hope you aren't seriously wishing such a thing on your daughter. Look at Myron Evans living in that filthy house with his mother and those awful cats. Look at Eula and Luella Lockwood, the terrible twosome. For all the time they've spent apart they might as well have been joined at the hips since birth. Siamese twins couldn't be more attached than the two of them. No one's invited them to dinner or tea for twenty years. No one can stand it—all that giggling and carrying on; you ask one of them a question and they both answer, same time, same words. They're always poking their heads over the fence, babbling at poor Jack Wright. They got him so rattled the other day he backed his car over his own cat. And I hear they do *everything* together, you know what I mean? One doesn't go to the bathroom without the other one trotting right behind. And they take baths together too—long, hot baths."

"They're lucky to have each other," Mom said.

"You're talking nonsense, woman. No one should live in another person's skin. I don't have to remind you what taking care of her father did to Minnie Hathaway."

"No, you don't."

"Turned her into a lush. And when he died, she had to sell his house to support her drinking. Lives like trash. I hate to think what's going to happen to that woman when the money runs out."

"Me too," Mother whispered.

Arlen stood and kissed the air near my cheek. "Staying with your family too long will warp you, Lizzie," she said. "You just look around this town and you'll see I know what I'm talking about."

As soon as Arlen was out the door, I said, "Mom—"

"Not a word," she said.

I tried again. I wanted to tell her that I wouldn't leave, not until she was ready to have me go. She pressed her knuckles into her eyes. "Not now," she said, "please don't tell me anything now."

I thought of growing old in my parents' house, cooking their dinners, washing their sheets. I imagined Eula and Luella in their bath, soaping each other's back—who cared what anyone else thought? I saw Myron making his mother's tea after dinner so that she could rest her feet. There were so many things he couldn't do, but he was able to do this night after night, and I believed the smallest acts of kindness might save us from God's anger, might allow Him to be merciful in the end.

Now that I believed I saw the answer, the humble path, I was anxious to show God how gladly I would give up my life to His will. To my mind, nothing could be more work than attending the prayer meetings Marlene Grosswilder held in the auditorium every morning before school. But I was God's docile lamb. This was just one small test.

For three mornings in a row I lurked in the back of the room, hoping Marlene and her friends would tell me something I didn't know. I knew the man who was supposed to be my savior had healed lepers and raised men from the dead, but I didn't know how to live like him, selflessly and free of desire. I saw Mary Magdalene on her knees, anointing him with her perfumes, burning her incense, combing his long hair. I wondered how he could resist her.

Marlene's followers spoke of mounting the wings of eagles, and went into a swoon singing a song about love being patient and kind and altogether lacking in envy. I longed to have the patience to love Marlene, but I swiftly failed.

On the fourth day Marlene indulged in a rousing reading of the Twenty-third Psalm. Her flabby thighs shook when she claimed to be walking through the valley of the shadow of death, and she looked straight at me when she said God was preparing a table for her in the presence of her enemies. When she finished her bit, Marlene wiped the sweat from under her nose and marched down the aisle toward the very place where I stood. I looked over my shoulder, but sure enough, I was the only one there. "I'm so glad you've joined us," she said. "I hope you'll sit in front tomorrow and that you'll prepare a reading of your own to share with the others."

I considered Marlene's generosity through the years: the valentines I didn't get, the parties I wasn't asked to attend. "You know," she said, "it's a wonderful thing. We've had our disagreements in the past. We never could be friends before, but now we can be friends in the Lord. Isn't that fine?"

"That's not fine at all," I said. "That's a heap of crap. Either people are friends or they're not." Marlene sputtered but couldn't answer. Swearing was a great sin to her. She had a gift for meanness when she was a kid, but as far as true wickedness was concerned, Marlene Grosswilder was as helpless as a blind woman describing the color red. I was sure no boy had ever chased her through the woods, no dogs had ever bounded across her dreams.

I didn't waste time on guilt. I needed guidance, someone who understood that the depths of my sins went far beyond using a cuss word now and then, someone who would recognize evil at a glance, a woman who wouldn't hesitate to pluck out her own eye if it offended her. I knew just where to find that woman, but I'd have to wait until Tuesday night.

15

I HAD to sin to go to Freda Graves's house. I had to lie to my mother. This was the price God demanded, the rip in my veil of purity, a constant reminder of my inability to escape myself. God kept me humble.

The night I joined Freda Graves's group, people nodded to me as if they'd been expecting me for some time. I spotted Myron Evans, more pale than ever, his hands resting limp on his knees; I had to look away, thinking how he'd offered to pay Zack Holler for something I was beginning to understand. I was ashamed to know, ashamed to be tempted by the same boy. I flushed with the memory of Myron as he cradled his strangled cat, its early death the cost of desire.

Lyla Leona wore a red satin top with spaghetti straps. We'd had a freak spring storm the day before and a fine layer of snow still clung in the shadows near the houses, but Lyla never shivered. Her cheeks burned bright as just-slapped skin. She was a warm woman. Bo Effinger sat squeezed up against her on the loveseat. He pinched his own legs, fighting the urge to lay one of those gigantic paws on Lyla's big thigh. He meant to leave a trail of marks up and down his leg, a reminder to be good. He had to keep hold of himself. Who else would dare to stop a six-and-a-half-foot man with a bulging forehead and no eyebrows? No one. His white hair shot up straight from his skull, fine and sparse, dead grass on a hill, ready to blow away.

Mrs. Graves's congregation had swelled to nearly twenty; I was the youngest but not the furthest astray. Minnie Hathaway motioned to me, patting the empty place beside her on the couch. I couldn't refuse her invitation. Now that Minnie denied herself the calming effects of alcohol, she couldn't keep still. Her head bobbed on her skinny neck; every few minutes her whole body jumped, as if an electric jolt buzzed through her cushion. She tried to pretend nothing had happened. After punching the air with her bony fists, she folded her white-gloved hands over her patent leather purse and smiled at the ceiling. She had tried to paint a beauty mark at the side of her mouth, but a spasm in her palsied hand made the mole look huge and cancerous.

I knew Minnie Hathaway's father had lived too long. That's what Arlen said. He chased every young man from their porch. When he finally had the decency to die, Minnie was already wrinkled and her hands shook in the morning. She couldn't make her coffee fast enough to stop the tremors. After a while she didn't bother to try: whiskey was just as warm and worked twice as fast.

She owed her father her life, that's what she thought. Her mama died the day she was born. "That old fool Dr. Trent told Herman Hathaway his wife was dead before he mentioned his daughter was alive," Arlen told me. "When the poor man heard the baby wail, he thought she'd been born of a dead woman, and no amount of talk could convince him otherwise. He dressed her up so fine, in little wool capes with fur collars, pretty lacy dresses, and patent leather shoes. But he couldn't bear to look at her—

even in the end when she had to feed him from a spoon that old man didn't look her in the eye."

Minnie was only twenty when her father had his first stroke. He never spoke again. He didn't speak but he lived. Fifteen years of silence. Fifteen years of blinks and grimaces. Fifteen years of bedpans and soiled sheets, and oatmeal dribbling down his chin.

I stared at Minnie Hathaway, looking for the girl she had been before she watched her father die so slowly. But that girl was gone; the face I saw was withered beyond salvation, withered even beyond the grace of love. I thought she'd done the right thing, staying with her father all those years, but I saw how she'd paid, and I was afraid.

These were my comrades, Lyla and Bo, Myron Evans and Minnie Hathaway, familiar people I did not know. Just being in their company made me think there must be hope for somebody like me. I wasn't too far gone, not by comparison.

The lights flickered. A blast of cold air moved through the room like a parade of the dead. Freda Graves stood in the entryway, stomping snow off her boots. Her hands were bare, chapped and raw from the cold. She wore layers of scarves and shawls, dark and unwashed, tattered moth-eaten wool and frayed silk. She unwrapped herself quickly, leaving the last shawl draped around her shoulders.

I thought, the face of God himself could not be more fearsome. Her gray curls sprang from her head, thick and impenetrable. Only a steel pick could find its dark way through those unparted strands. Deer moss hanging in the forest was like silken threads next to the hair of Freda Graves. I was sure no smile had ever tainted her lips; no young girl's brazen blush had risen on those bony cheeks; no summer light had ever broken in her eyes. Her eyes burned with the dark fires of redemption. Jesus might be kind, but God and Mrs. Graves were only merciful.

She glided to the center of the room and raised her hands. "Praise the Lord," she said. "Let us bear our suffering on earth. Let us fall to the ground and thank God for testing us. Let us curve our backs to the whip and be grateful." She whispered, "The closer you are to God, the more the devil wants you. You've got to look behind you."

I resisted the temptation to glance over my shoulder to see if the devil hunkered down behind the sofa. Her words were strangely comforting to me: I was still so far from the Lord that the devil couldn't possibly have any interest in snatching my soul, not yet.

"The devil loves attention. He doesn't care if you worship him or curse his name. To the devil, it's all the same. He hears you call and his pitiless heart pumps with pride just knowing he's stolen our thoughts from the Lord. He prances on his goat legs; he sings from his frog throat. But we won't utter his name. No, he won't trumpet and dance in this room. But I warn you—the devil lies in wait for you, for all of you. The God you love will watch with idle hands while His evil brother tries to snare you. God only wants the purest hearts. An untried soul is an empty prize.

"One among us is tested even as I speak. One man in this room has the sweet fruit of evil pressed to his lips. Oh, do not bite that apple, brother. Let your body wither to the bone. The body's life is short, but the soul suffers for all eternity."

No one dared to look around the room. I could almost see the heat jumping off Bo Effinger's skin, fierce and dry. Second by second, I grew more certain he was the one. I thought he'd have to crawl to Freda Graves's feet and beg her to stop him from doing what he wanted to do to Lyla Leona.

But Bo Effinger's soul was not the one Mrs. Graves saw perched on the shore of the lake of fire, not tonight. She turned and lit three candles on the table behind her. "Come to me, Elliot Foot," she said. "Come and stand before the flames."

Elliot rose like a man condemned. A runt in any litter, that's what Aunt Arlen said, a scrawny little man with spectacles. His hair started halfway back his skull, and the unsteady light of the candles made shadows pass like clouds of remorse across the high curve of his forehead. Freda Graves beckoned, forgiving mother, brutal angel.

She stood behind her table and Elliot faced her. The row of candles flared. "Can you hold your hand in the flame?" she said, her voice soft as wind through grass.

Elliot pulled his wire-rims tight around his ears as if to remind her there were certain things you couldn't do to a man wearing glasses.

She waited for an answer, but none came. "Elliot," she said at last, "how close can you bring your finger to the fire?" He shoved his hands in his pockets and settled into himself, shrinking by the second, a boy with a beard.

Joanna Foot squinted so hard her eyes disappeared, and I feared her face might crack. She rocked back and forth, all two hundred pounds of her, silly Humpty Dumpty about to fall. Careful, I thought, careful—there's too much of you to put together again.

"Give me your hands," Mrs. Graves said. She clutched his fingers and pulled them toward the flames, closer and closer, ever so slowly, giving him time to struggle or plead. But the little man was proud. He let her have her way until his knuckles grazed the fire, until we heard a sizzle and smelled the hair burn off the backs of their hands. Elliot jerked free.

"Oh, the flesh is tender," she said, "and the flesh is weak. You who cannot hold your finger to the burning wick would risk plunging your soul into the fiery pits of hell for a few days of pleasure on this earth. Do you fear these pitiful flames? The final conflagration will scorch the face off the earth. Oh, pray that you will be among the chosen, pray that you will be raised in grace before you see the days of our Lord's wrath."

Freda Graves squeezed out the flames, one by one, between her thumb and forefinger.

Elliot sat down beside his fat, grinning wife. Mrs. Graves spoke with the voice of a woman who has crossed the valley of bones and climbed to the mountaintop, her bare feet cut and bleeding. "My children," she said, "didn't Matthew tell us that a man who looks at a woman with lust has already committed adultery in his heart? If your right eye leads you into sin, pluck it out."

She made Elliot confess. "Olivia Jeanne's come back," he said. "Wants to take me on another ride." He wouldn't let her in the door, so she'd parked her Winnebago right in front of the Last Chance Bar. "Says she'll ruin my business if I don't do what she wants." Now I knew I'd seen Miss Olivia Jeanne Woodruff, but I never thought she'd be any man's temptation. Her skin was yellow, and her long eyes had a sleepy, stupid look. Even so, I wondered what a girl as young as Olivia saw in the likes of Elliot Foot.

"Heed the words of Peter," said Mrs. Graves. "She has eyes full of adultery, insatiable for sin. She entices unsteady souls. Her heart is trained in greed. She would steal you from your children."

There was some speculation among us that Olivia Jeanne had been carried back to Willis on the very wings of the devil. This was an interesting topic, and we couldn't help letting our minds wander for a half hour or so—though Mrs. Graves had warned us about giving the devil that kind of attention.

The room was cramped and sticky with the heat of our bodies. There was too much furniture: a heavy green couch, the over-stuffed loveseat, the long table, and a dusty bookshelf that stretched along one wall from floor to ceiling. But Freda Graves kept no books on her huge shelf. I suspected novels were evil in her mind, the work of the devious imagination. History was a lie. There was only one book worth reading.

The bottom shelf was devoted to Christ. She had a dozen crucifixes, variations of suffering. One was a crude wooden carving. Thorns pierced Christ's head and he wept. His twisted body was emaciated. Another was smooth soapstone. This fat Jesus looked blissful as a Buddha, grateful for his pain, as if he had transcended worldly sorrow. In a small painting the Son of God was angry; he had the look of a rabid dog ready to bite the hands of the women who longed to comfort him. I wondered if one image was true, or if Christ had taken all these forms.

We prayed for Elliot to be strong and shun Olivia Jeanne Woodruff, but even as I prayed I thought we might be wrong. What if Olivia was the woman he was meant to love? What if his years with Joanna had been a mistake? Some of the women moaned and sobbed just thinking about the depravity of it all. Eula and Luella Lockwood crooned, arms locked, heads touching. Perhaps they were thinking of Jack Wright; perhaps they tormented their neighbor because they loved him.

Lyla Leona wriggled out of her place—her flesh shook under that flimsy satin; her breasts sagged. She lifted poor Elliot right out of his seat, squished his face into the soft folds of her chest and wailed, "I know, baby, I know how it is. Ain't it awful, baby?"

Elliot's glasses hit the floor, his nose disappeared. That brought Joanna Foot to her senses, and she pulled her husband out of

Lyla's grasp. Bo Effinger wiped his palms on his pant legs, but there was no way to slow the sweat.

I was confused. I thought about Aunt Arlen telling us that Joanna Foot wasn't going to let Elliot touch her for a whole year, that he had to prove his devotion, had to be purified by abstinence. Maybe Joanna was long past loving him in any way that would do him any good. For all Elliot knew, he might never be clean enough for her. The year was only a trial period. Now I couldn't be sure Olivia Jeanne loved Elliot either, but she wanted him—that was plain. If she did love him, I thought that might be stronger than law, even God's law. I didn't dare say it. What did I know? It was my first night. God's mind was wide as Moon Lake and twice as deep. But as I prayed for Elliot Foot I could only bring myself to ask God to show him what was right.

16

ONE OF the high school boys had bought a keg. All day the secret rippled through school in whispers and scribbled notes. At dusk the revelers planned to meet in the gully.

I'd spent three Tuesday nights at Freda Graves's, so I already knew that I had to witness, to take the Word where it had not been heard. Of course I considered alcohol one of the most dangerous temptations, an evil in itself that gave men an excuse to commit other sins. "Jesus walked among the worst of men," Freda Graves said, "and he asks you to do the same." The worst I knew were boys who drank themselves into idiocy. I meant to work my way up from there. I was proud of my knowledge, pitiful as it was.

I'd invented a friendship for myself, with Rita Ditella, to explain my evenings away from home. I hoped Mother wouldn't see Rita's mom at the grocery store and just happen to say, "I'm so pleased our girls are getting on." Mother knew Gwen and I had some kind of rift between us. She felt sorry for me but respected my privacy too much to ask what had happened.

Though I'd never actually spoken with Rita, she came in

handy, and I used her again tonight. I told myself the lie was justified: I was off to do good works. But when Mother said, "Have a nice time," I couldn't quite convince myself I was doing the right thing.

I found the gang near the pond. The woods were shadowy and tempting, full of memories I wished to escape. So I concentrated on my recently acquired wisdom instead. I thought my holiness must be visible, a light around my head. If I unfolded my hands, my palms would glow with the sacred flame protected there. But no one seemed to notice these extraordinary gifts.

Gwen Holler rolled in the grass with Gil Harding. Her blouse was torn open, and Gil clutched at her breast. Jill Silverlake sprawled, facedown in the dirt. Zack Holler turned her over. She groaned. Even Zachary couldn't take advantage of a girl in her condition. She crawled toward the woods on her hands and knees. Her skirt was hiked up around her waist, so everyone saw her underpants, dotted with dozens of red hearts. Jill would be my first convert. I followed her. "Jesus loves you," I said, kneeling beside her. She swatted at the air as if my voice were a pesky mosquito around her head. "You can be saved tonight, right here, if you give your life up to Jesus."

"Fuck off," said Jill.

I stood. Somehow I'd expected my work to be much easier. Perhaps Jill Silverlake wasn't a good choice for a witness as inexperienced as myself. "Come find me if you change your mind," I said.

I returned to the clearing. Rita Ditella danced around the campfire. She was sixteen, already a woman with a large bosom and full hips. Her pants were unzipped, but no one bothered to tell her. She'd squatted behind a rock to pee and had forgotten this last detail. I was glad she wasn't really my friend.

Drew Grosswilder, Marlene's brother, had bought the keg.

Now he sat beside it, filling his cup again and again. Drew's face was smooth and rosy; he was so fat he had little pointed breasts. "Take it off," he yelled to Rita, his voice surprisingly high. Rita ignored him as she pirouetted in the flickering light.

Drew's lack of success with Rita Ditella rankled him, so he looked around for someone he knew he could bully. He didn't have to go far. Lewis Champeaux sat on the other side of the keg, holding an empty cup. Drew rocked forward on his knees to jab the Indian boy in the arm. "Who invited you?" he said.

"No one," Lewis whispered.

"Yeah? Well there's a reason for that, boy. This party's for white people."

Lewis was half as wide as Drew Grosswilder. He inched away from the keg, out of Drew's reach.

Drew filled his cup one more time. "Want a beer?" he said to Lewis. His voice had gone sweet, the closest he could come to making an apology. Lewis leaned closer to take the drink, and Drew laughed, a shrill girlish giggle, then guzzled down the beer himself. "I know what liquor does to Indians," he said. "Once I made a man roll over and play dead just by promising to buy him a pint. I think it might have been your daddy, Lewis."

Lewis Champeaux stood up without a word and walked to the other side of the clearing. I wondered why he stayed at all. Perhaps he considered this some test of patience. I wanted to ask him, but I was afraid he wouldn't care to talk to a white girl after what Drew had said.

I moved toward him, a foot at a time, until I sat beside him. The air around Lewis Champeaux was entirely his own; I was no more important to him than a rock or a cloud. Finally I said, "Why are you here?"

"To watch," he said.

I waited for him to say more. Just watching seemed unkind.

"And you?" he said.

I'd come here to witness, to lead one wayward soul out of the forest. But I'd failed with Jill Silverlake and given up. "The same," I told him.

"Is it true?" Lewis said.

"What?"

"Does liquor make Indians more foolish than white people?"

I looked at Drew—fat, silly Drew who was mean even before he was drunk. "No," I said, "of course not." But I had believed it did all my life.

Slowly, boys and girls paired off and wandered into the forest. Rita Ditella ended up with Zack Holler. I thought they were a good match. Rita was big enough to handle Zack. She wouldn't let him do anything she didn't like. Soon I was the only girl. I sat on a rock, safe in the shadows. I longed to be approached, to be desired so that I could refuse. But the three boys who were left, Drew Grosswilder and his friends Luke Stallard and Albert Cornett, only cared about the keg of beer and the fire that was fading fast. There was a fourth boy. He sat close to me but stayed so still I almost forgot he was there.

Luke and Albert tried to keep the fire torched, but the wood they'd gathered was damp and gave off more smoke than flame. Drew was too drunk to help. He laughed at the other boys. "No more beer for you if you can't get that fire going," he said.

Lewis Champeaux approached the dismal blaze. He pulled smoldering sticks off with his bare hands and rebuilt the stack, breathing on embers, fanning the first flames with his long fingers. He never took his eyes off those flames, as if turning away would be betrayal, as if the fire would know and flicker out.

Soon the fire roared, and Lewis sat back, satisfied and warm. But Drew's two friends didn't like being shown up by a skinny black-haired boy.

"Just an Indian," one muttered.

"Only good for one thing."

"Who asked you here, anyway?"

They poked at his shoulders.

"Speak up, boy."

"Somebody cut out your tongue?"

A knife flashed, glinting with firelight in Albert Cornett's hand. Albert's face was wide and flat, his eyes unusually small, squinty little pig eyes. He looked like a moron when he grinned, a boy born with half a brain. "Somebody will," he said.

"Keg's empty," said Drew.

"Goddamned Indian drank all our beer," Albert said, slashing the air.

I couldn't move. I should have yelled Albert's name to remind him who he was, but I sat, pretending nothing bad was going to happen. I prayed for faith. I told myself God would protect us all if only I could believe.

"Stand up, boy."

"You hear me?"

"That's more like it."

In a minute they'd stop. They'd laugh and slap Lewis on the back. "No harm done," they'd say. I kept praying. God would save us if my trust in Him was pure enough.

"Give me your belt," Luke Stallard said. The fire lit his face. His cheeks were pocked with acne scars, and his big nose made him look like a mad wood rat.

"Mind the man," said Albert.

"Faster, red boy. We don't got all night."

Drew Grosswilder propped himself against the empty keg. He was smiling, enjoying the show.

"That's a nice boy," said Albert.

"Now empty your pockets."

"All of them."

Lewis turned his pockets inside out. A few small coins and a key fell near the fire. He shook the cloth and seemed bewildered, surprised by his own poverty.

"Shit, he ain't got nothin'," said Luke.

"Unzip your pants."

"Now."

"You wanna die?" Albert said, waving the knife under Lewis's nose.

"Unzip them."

"Good boy."

Any second now, I said to myself, any second this will all end.

Albert yanked the Indian's pants down and Luke knocked him to the ground. Lewis scrambled in the dirt, his pants bunched around his ankles. I saw his bare ass, his smooth dark skin. The boys pulled him to his feet.

"Now scat," Luke said.

He was shackled by his own pants.

"You heard the man."

They knocked him down again. I thought this could go on all night, so I shouted and charged. Surely the noise would bring someone from the woods. But no one came. Luke Stallard grabbed my arm and flung me backward. I stumbled over my own feet and fell on my butt. "Mind your business," he said. "Only thing worse than an Indian is an Indian lover." Lewis rolled toward the trees. When he finally got free of his pants, he tried to grab them, but Albert heaved them out of reach. "Get the hell out of here," he said.

It was too late for me to help Lewis. I stayed on the ground, minding my business, just as Luke said. The boys turned to face the fire, bored by their own game. They rubbed their hands up and down their thighs. Their faces glowed.

Lewis Champeaux stood in front of me, staring down at my head for just an instant. He was the only one to really look at me that night. He knew I'd seen everything. He knew I hadn't done a damn thing to help him, not really. My cheeks burned, like the sticks that burst into flame under his gaze. I looked away and still felt his heat all around me. He darted into the trees. The half-naked boy disappeared and left me alone, not to burn but to shiver.

I inched backward to the edge of the woods, waiting a half hour or more for Drew and his friends to forget about the pants and leave them crumpled in the dirt. I gathered them up, a limp bundle, tucked them under my arm and ran, intent on finding Lewis Champeaux. He would see I was better than the rest. I could still redeem myself.

Stumbling in the dark, I climbed out of the gully and headed toward the edge of town, beyond the shambles of the west side, and then another mile to the foot of the hills where the Indians lived. The streets meandered aimlessly; billows of dust rose up with each footstep. There were no streetlights, only the stark glow of bulbs inside unpainted shacks and old trailers.

I'd have to knock on every door until I found Lewis. I was afraid. Anyone could see I didn't belong here. These two-room huts were crowded with people: old women and babies, men without shirts standing at the windows, and girls taking baths, six or seven in a room.

They were the stragglers who passed through Willis, looking for work at the mill. Indians were lucky to get hired at all. Most times they got jobs sweeping up piles of woodchips at the end of the day, earning half a white man's wages. In a month or two the constant hunger of too many children drove most families back to the reservation.

Once in a while an Indian was lucky enough to be hired to

load the trucks. That pay was decent, but there were accidents: a winch left unsecured, a slipped knot, another man who didn't pull his weight. Those Indians left too, crippled in one foot or not quite right in the head.

I'd never thought too much about it until tonight. These people left town before I knew their names or recognized their faces. So I never troubled myself with the circumstances of their rushed departures. Daddy said that as soon as a shack was empty, a new family moved into it. Squatters' rights. "One Indian's the same as another." The only one who mattered was Red Elk. Everybody noticed him because he was fool enough to take up with a white woman, because he was bold enough to demand a real job at the mill. I thought about Red Elk all the time, wondering about his son and my sister, knowing how much my father hated him.

I walked the streets, snooping in windows, a ghost no one could see. I clutched Lewis Champeaux's pants, my one chance to prove myself. He would be grateful. He'd take me in his house. His grandmother would put a fat, dark baby in my lap and I'd hold her close. His mother would kiss me.

Someone hissed from the bushes and I jumped, ready to flee. "Give me those," he said, stepping out of the brush. I held out the pants and the boy snatched them. He put them on right in front of me. What did it matter what I saw now? "Where's my belt?"

"I couldn't find it." I had forgotten the belt. I was too anxious to get on with my good deed to mind with details.

"Shit," he said, "cost me three bucks."

"I'll go back."

"Forget it." He wasn't grateful. He wasn't going to ask me inside. "Get outa here," he said.

Nothing was forgiven. I was a coward, but he knew that already, so I didn't bother to confess.

It was a long walk home. I had plenty of time to think. My prayers were useless. Lewis Champeaux's knees were scraped and his butt was bruised. I hadn't helped him. I had waited too long, expecting God to intervene. I knew people who were brave but not good. Zack Holler had the courage to steal and the strength to fight. That kind of courage was worthless. But what did I have? I believed in the idea of virtue, yet I'd done nothing for Lewis Champeaux. I stood by while Luke Stallard knocked him in the dirt. Without bravery, all my acts would be like this one: puny and meaningless. Such kindness was just another kind of cruelty. My knife was as sharp as Albert Cornett's and did more damage in the end. I reminded Lewis of his humiliation. I reminded him that his kind was not welcome here. I'd shown Lewis Champeaux what he must have always known: a white girl couldn't be trusted.

17

I STARTED thinking about Red Elk more and more after that night with Lewis Champeaux. I was determined to see him for myself. He had the courage I lacked, and I wondered if he looked different from other men. When Lanfear Deets was bleeding on the floor, Red Elk didn't stop to think about the blood. He didn't ask himself if any white man would do the same for him. He simply did what had to be done: he tied a tourniquet and saved a life.

Every afternoon for a week I rode my bike to the mill and waited for the shifts to change. I saw men with thick chests and bulging biceps, men with dark hairy forearms. But I didn't see the man who wore his hair in a single braid down his back.

By Friday I got the idea that a man like Red Elk might leave by the back door to avoid any trouble. I climbed high in a willow near the building and waited, hidden by a thousand tiny leaves. I could see most of the town from my perch. I hadn't been there more than five minutes when a small woman appeared on the road. She walked quickly, looking over her shoulder like a girl who was afraid of being followed in the dark. As she moved closer I recognized Miriam Deets. She looked tired and thin, but no longer childlike.

She was waiting for someone too. This was strange, since Lanfear worked at the truck stop now—Lanfear, the one-handed gas man. So did she. Poor Miriam. I thought of her waking before dawn to drive out to Ike's. I wondered about those hungry children of hers—who watched them in the early hours of the morning?

The sky was dark, yellow with the threat of rain. Miriam glanced at her watch minute by minute. She turned to go, but someone called to her from the doorway and she spun to face him.

The sound of that voice nearly pulled me out of the tree. My father. The wind ruffled his scraggly blond hair. A deep crease cut his forehead down the middle. He pulled something from his pocket and pressed it into her hand. A fat roll of money, I thought, but couldn't be sure. He tried to pull her close, stooping to kiss her cheek, but Miriam, demure or frightened, turned away. He stared at the ground; he couldn't look at her until she took his hand in hers and kissed his palm. She must have knocked the breath out of him with that touch.

For minutes after she was gone, my father slumped against the wall. At last the thunder rumbled and the first drops fell. Father raised his face to the cool fingers of the rain. When he walked toward the road, he was not heading home.

I watched till he was out of sight, then shimmied down to a low limb and dropped to the ground. I rode my bike through puddles and mud, pedaling as fast as I could.

I found my mother in Grandmother's bedroom. She sat by the window, staring down at Arlen's empty chicken coop as the rain pounded its roof. She knew I was in the doorway, but she didn't turn to look at me. My wet clothes clung to my skin; my hair was plastered to my forehead.

"Can you imagine," she said, "leaving your wife and child to take care of a sick woman?"

How did she know? Was he leaving us? "Is she sick?" I said.

"She's dead now."

No, I thought. I looked around the room for the knife, for the stained handkerchief, for splatters of blood on Mother's dress.

"Mama promised he was coming back. Told me that till I was thirteen and knew better." She held up one of the blue letters my grandfather had written. "Listen," she said. The paper was so dry I thought it might crumble in Mother's hands. "*My dearest Rose,* he wrote, this after fifteen years, *Albertine is dead. I'll be home soon, two weeks, a month at the most.* Your grandmother never told me about this letter. She knew what I would have said. 'Tell the bastard he doesn't have a home.' But what does it matter? He didn't come. He died instead. Coward. He let her hope to the very end.

"That's why she told me to marry your father—'He'll always come home,' she said. 'He may be drunk, his nose may be bloody and his fingers broken, but he'll always come home.' She was right about that. And I know he may chase that silly little woman all over town, but he'll sleep in his own bed."

I wondered how long she'd known. I wondered why she didn't try to stop him.

"*He'll* always come home, but one time I thought about driving north as far as I could go and never turning back. I went looking for your sister back in '67. I never told you I did that. I had to hitchhike down to the reservation. I couldn't ask your father for the car without answering his questions.

"It was summer, two years after she left. Maybe it was the

misery of the day that made me go. It was hot, I swear, not a dog on the street. They all were lying up under the porches, playing dead. I walked two miles before I got a lift.

"An Indian woman with three children finally stopped for me. She was drinking whiskey from a pint bottle. 'Take some,' she said, 'it eases the heat.' I told her liquor made me hot. 'That's what I mean,' she said. 'You get a fire going inside, you don't mind the air so much.' I didn't believe in her logic, but I drank. She kept weaving over the center line. I clutched the door. Her two boys poked at the girl baby between them in the backseat, making her squall. I drank some more and she was right. A fever inside makes you stop minding the heat.

"She dropped me at the edge of Arco, the only town on the reservation. I started knocking on doors, but nobody knew a thing about any blond girl. Some folks thought they might have seen her back in '65, but I started to wonder if they really had or if they were just saying what they thought I wanted to hear. I asked about Billy Elk. They said no boy by that name had a white woman in this town. I carried my shoes in my hands. People gave me water if I asked.

"Children ran in the streets. They didn't mind the heat. If you were just driving through, you would've thought no grown-ups lived here, just kids living in shacks they built themselves. A gang of them had circled a skinny dog. They threw stones at its head. I yelled; but when they turned and saw I wasn't one of their mamas, they just laughed.

"I had to find some shade, so I walked down to a little dried-up bit of a creek. I lay down in the rushes and fell asleep so fast I couldn't remember closing my eyes. When I woke, the wind was cool. My teeth felt fuzzy and something was banging behind my eyes.

"I staggered toward the road. I don't know if I was drunk or if I had some kind of sickness from the heat. The dog lay in the ditch. I suppose its eyes were open but I couldn't be sure: they were covered with black flies.

"I knew I didn't have much time. Not many cars pass through the reservation after dark. I imagined calling your father, explaining where I was. I saw myself sitting on the side of the road, waiting for him to pick me up, knowing I'd have to pay him for his trouble.

"But I got lucky. A trucker geared down when he saw me on the side of the road. 'Hop in, pretty woman,' he said, and I knew it was going to be a long drive. I rolled my window down and let the wind beat my face. The trucker had hair growing in his ears and the thickest neck I ever saw. 'What's a lady like you doing on the road alone?' He had to shout to make me hear.

"What was I supposed to say? 'My girl ran off with an Indian boy and I came looking for her'?

" 'Not safe for a woman to be hitching,' he said.

" 'I expect not,' I said.

" 'You're quite a talker,' he said. 'But you sure are pretty.' I suppose I looked all right to a weary trucker who'd been keeping company with Patsy Cline for two days straight, crooning in the dark, drinking coffee and popping speed to stay awake. I told him about the dog and he looked like it mattered. He patted my knee, too hard, but it didn't feel bad. I told him about Nina. I don't know why. He put his arm around me. I cried on his shoulder. I cried for thirty miles, all the way up the edge of the lake. Your father never let me cry for her. He swore when I said her name. When I was alone the tears never came. Maybe I knew I needed somebody's arm around me. Maybe I knew I'd cry till I fell apart if I let myself cry alone. My face would crack. My arms would drop off.

"When I saw the lights of Willis, I wanted to tell him to keep driving. I don't know if he would have taken me. I suppose he would have gotten tired of my sobbing soon enough. But for a whole hour, we were the only two people in the world, and the cab of the truck was my whole life.

"He let me out at Ike's so he could gas up. 'I'd like to buy you a cup of coffee,' he said, just like that, so polite.

" 'Folks know me here,' I told him. For some reason those words made me feel even worse. Yeah, they knew me. They'd recognize my face. They'd tell my husband I had a cup of coffee with another man. They'd understand if Dean gave me a black eye, but there wasn't anyone in this town who would let me cry as long as I wanted.

"I put my head on his chest. He kissed my hair.

"I dreamed of the dog that night. And I was the one to heave the stone that split its skull. The children scattered. They hated me. They returned with sticks. They beat my legs. I woke screaming but I couldn't cry because my eyes were full of flies. Your father snored beside me. Even my yelling didn't wake him. So I had to wonder. Did I make any sound?"

Mother pointed at the window. "Look, there's your daddy now," she said, "just like Mama told me. He'll always come home." She crushed the letter her own father had written so many years ago. It came apart in her fist, crumbled like blue dust. "Well, that's that," she said.

I had seen too much today. I didn't want to know Daddy gave away money we needed. I didn't want to hear that Mother dreamed of abandoning us—not only my father, but her entire past, her memories of Nina, and of me. I was afraid none of that was ever going to change.

*

THREE DAYS later I took a ride on my bike after school. I headed for Ike's Truckstop though I wasn't sure what I'd do when I got there.

All I ordered was a Coke. I sat at the counter; two truckers sat at a window table. We were the only customers. Lanfear Deets was outside, resting against a pump, waiting for a cloud of dust to appear on the road.

Miriam set the bottle of Coke in front of me. "Need a glass?" she said.

I shook my head. Her skin wasn't so pretty anymore; she had a grimy look from working in this place, and I could see why Daddy felt bad about the misery he'd caused her and Lanfear.

Sympathy was getting the best of me, and I almost left without saying anything, but then I got to thinking about my mother and the money Daddy gave to Miriam Deets. She was wiping the counter a few places down. I cleared my throat to get her attention.

When she was close enough for me to talk without the men at the window catching my words, I said, "Miriam, I got something to tell you." Ike called to her from the back and she glanced over her shoulder. I grabbed her wrist. "Don't worry," I said. "This won't take long." She tried to tug free of my grip, but I was much stronger than Miriam Deets.

I said, "My mother hasn't bought herself a new dress in five years. We eat pork fat and beans for three days at the end of every month. There's been a hole in our couch ever since I can remember. I got a box of colored pencils for my birthday last year. That's all." Ike called again. I said, "You hear what I'm telling you?"

Miriam nodded and I let her go. She ran into the kitchen. I wanted to run too, but I didn't. I sauntered past the men at the window, acting casual though my legs were going soft so fast I could barely walk.

I had a hunch that my father paid Miriam once a week. I waited. On Friday I rode out to the mill and climbed the willow. Daddy appeared at the back door several times; he shaded his eyes and scanned the road. But there was no sign of Miriam Deets. I beat Father home by a good hour. When he finally turned into our drive, he sat in the truck for a long time with the windows up. He wasn't smoking; he wasn't doing anything. Mother watched him from the living room. "What's with your father?" she said. I didn't answer. For once, I was smart enough to keep my mouth shut.

18

BY THE middle of June, Montana rivers ran swift and cold, swelled by snow melting off the mountains. One evening, just at twilight, Freda Graves marched us down to a bend in Bear Creek, a place where water caught in the shallows, tripping itself over pebbles and stones, whirling to a white froth. I'd been sneaking off to these meetings for six weeks. For the most part, I'd stayed out of trouble; my worst transgression was that I had to lie to Mother every Tuesday, embellishing my imaginary friendship with Rita Ditella. My thoughts were pure enough, I suppose, but I'd done nothing virtuous, and I was still looking for someone to show me how to be good in ways that mattered.

Lyla Leona led our parade. Close on her heels, all in black, Freda Graves followed. Lyla wore a white bonnet that tied in the folds of her chins, and a white dress that brushed the ground, turning it gray at the hem. She was going to be baptized. Like the rest of us good Lutherans, she'd had water dribbled down her forehead when she was a baby; now she said she needed something more, a true baptism, because she believed she'd been born a second time, and she was afraid she still carried more than the taint of original sin.

Lyla had been a free woman since she was sixteen. She was the first female to live at the rooming house, the only woman in Willis who had money all her own, not her daddy's trust or her husband's goodwill, but solid cash—coins and bills she counted every morning and took to the bank promptly at nine. I'd always admired her independence, her modest fortune, and had never worried myself over the nature of her work.

People remembered her parents. Her mother played the piano. She sang sweetly and off key, with an honest voice. Her father laughed a lot at other men's jokes. Folks liked them and were sorry to see what became of their daughter. But Lyla's parents had been dead for more than ten years. It was too late for her to be a good daughter and go home. Lyla sought salvation for her own sake.

Wind beat the trees along Bear Creek, and I knew how cold the stream was this time of year: cold enough to send a dull ache from your ankles to your thighs. But that didn't stop Freda Graves. She unlaced her dusty boots and led Lyla into the stream. Water swirled up to their knees. Lyla's dress floated around her and lay like a great lily on the water.

Night rose and walked the earth; leaves fluttered like dark wings. The sky was still desperately blue, but the ground sank into shadow. A fast river could knock a grown man's feet from under him, throw him on his face and drag him all the way to Moon Lake. A body in this river wouldn't be found till morning. We all had the same thought. I saw my cousin Jesse's startled face. I wondered how the angels kept their laughter down when they witnessed the surprise of the dead.

Danger gave Lyla Leona a glimpse of glory. She risked her life to be clean in God's eyes. I longed to be pulled under, not merely dunked but immersed. I knew I'd have to wait for the slow water of August for that.

Joanna Foot forgot herself and crushed Elliot's fingers. She was wearing white shorts with huge yellow goldfish. They swam around her full bottom and thick thighs. They bobbed as she waddled to the shore. Eula and Luella Lockwood chanted: *Dunk her in the river, give her to the Giver.* Bo had a blanket ready. At last he'd have his chance to grab hold of Lyla, and even God couldn't disapprove. Only Myron Evans seemed unconcerned. He limped over to the bushes, dragging his heavy shoe. I heard his zipper go down, then a soft spray on grass.

Freda prayed above the rush of Bear Creek. Her lips and hands praised God. "I baptize thee in the name of the Father, Son and Holy Ghost." She pulled a handkerchief from her pocket and stuffed it against Lyla Leona's mouth. Lyla bent at the waist, stuck her head in the black river like a duck going tail up. It was done.

Lyla sputtered and cried as she surfaced. Joanna Foot sobbed too and splashed into the frigid water to take Lyla in her arms. I thought they'd fall for sure, the way they were carrying on, rocking and moaning, their two huge chests heaving. Bo Effinger held the blanket wide, ready to enfold the reborn woman. He paced the shore, impatient, cheated by Joanna Foot.

When Lyla reached the shore, she pulled the blanket from Bo's outstretched arms and wrapped it around herself. She was proud and separate, too holy for anyone to touch, the first among us to be baptized a second time, in the spirit. And she who had never been more pure than anyone meant to hold this moment close as long as she could.

For weeks after that night I didn't see Lyla rub up against any of the men in her casual, accidental way. She stopped wearing red and started going door to door, witnessing. She won no converts, but Freda Graves praised her for her courage and told us the true test was to persist even in the face of defeat. When I first met Lyla, she was always busting into *Amen* and *Sweet Jesus.* She'd sing it out, jumping to her feet and shaking the floor to keep her sides from splitting with the joy. The river had truly changed her. Once, she had danced and shouted for God; now she shuffled. Her serenity gave me hope. I might still be saved.

Lyla Leona was born again, but she kept her old room at the boardinghouse. Now that the days were warm, the long porch was crowded with old men, some who lived there, some who didn't. They smoked pipes and played cribbage. Lyla held her head high when she moved among them, but they failed to see her new dignity. They wheezed and whistled; they said, "Lyla honey, I got ten dollars if you got ten minutes." She told us she ignored their offers, but they were hard of hearing and weren't surprised by silence.

MRS. GRAVES kept reminding us how the devil loved attention, and every Tuesday night we gave him that. We had to be warned before we prayed. Over and over she told us: the closer you are to God, the more the devil wants you. This made no sense to me. I thought of the devil as having every bad trait imaginable, laziness high among them. I thought, Why does he bother with people who are hard to trap when there are so many of us lingering near the borderline ready to be snatched?

The story that scared me the most was the one about Freda Graves's daughter. The devil came after her in a serious way. She was pregnant, and Mrs. Graves was going to be a grandmother for the first time. Just days before the baby was due, Freda Graves heard a crackle of laughter. She felt a flash of heat in her brain. For a moment she went blind; then a voice inside her own head told her she'd have a surprise when she saw her grandchild.

The devil had spoken to her. She knew him. She didn't pray to God to change things; He alone chose the time and place for miracles. No, Freda Graves was humble. If there was something wrong with the baby, she prayed to be strong enough to bear her trial.

After three days of prayer the child was born. A valve in her tiny heart had not closed, and she couldn't breathe without a tube stuck in a hole the doctor cut in her throat. She had a cleft palate and low, unformed ears, shaped in the simple whorls of tiny shells. Oh, the little monster, well loved and taken back to Heaven in a week, she was born to test the fortitude of Freda Graves, a human sacrifice for the soul of another, Jesus born again and again so that we might be spared.

Freda prayed to understand, and God gave her an answer in the night. The child was too dear for earth, the beautiful soul in her ugly body too precious, and God had called her back to be with Him.

I wondered why God let Mrs. Graves's daughter carry this child for nine months. He must have known all along that her soul was too pure for this world. Why didn't He give the woman one of those pretty babies with an imperfect soul and hang on to what He wanted? The wooden Jesus writhed on his cross in the shadows of the bookshelf. I wanted to ask him to explain the reason we had to suffer, the reason he had to die. I didn't know who to fear more—a careless God or a malicious devil.

I NEEDED a glimpse of the Lord's plan, so I came to Freda Graves's house every Tuesday night, hoping to find a way to talk with

Him. But I held back my paltry confessions. My temptations were pitiful things: the strawberries in Joanna Foot's garden, a dream about Zack Holler, the memory of Gwen's kiss in the tree house, my knowledge of my parents' lives.

I believed I was still too far from God for the devil to have any serious interest in me, but Freda Graves thought otherwise. My silence meant I hid my sins. This was a fool's crime; you can't deceive the Lord. My redemption depended on Freda Graves, and she intended to have her glory. On the last Tuesday in June she headed straight for my sullied soul.

Her living room was darker than usual, the windows shut tight and locked. I thought Mrs. Graves wanted to make a point about hell, about gloom and heat and how much of it we could bear before we cried out. I vowed to be the last to complain, but I was worried about some of the others. Minnie Hathaway sat next to me on the sofa. Her head kept rolling back. She tugged at her gloves but wouldn't take them off. I saw her swollen joints through the thin cloth. Her hands were crippled by arthritis. She was ashamed. All those years I thought she wore white gloves to look like a lady. Now I saw the truth. That was happening to me too much lately.

"One among us is afraid to give herself to God," Freda said. "We must help her." I thought of poor Minnie. "The dark one works in many ways. He squats in our hearts. He gives us doubt and keeps us from speaking to our Lord. He tells us our prayers are selfish and that the Father will not listen to our puling pleas. The devil wants to keep you for himself. Silence is the devil's language. God longs to hear our voices raised to Him in exaltation. You will speak, my child. You will speak in the tongue God has chosen for you alone. Come to me, *Elizabeth Macon.*"

The sound of my name jolted my heart into an extra beat. No one called me Elizabeth.

"Come forward, girl," said Mrs. Graves. I had to obey, but I slouched toward my redemption, certain I wasn't ready to be saved.

"Gather around, all of you, gather around our child who is afraid to speak to the God who loves her. Help her open her heart and her mouth to Him. This lost lamb needs our guidance, needs our hands on her. Lie down, Elizabeth, here on the floor before me."

The carpet was prickly, stiff with wine that had spilled and dried. I stretched out in front of those strangers who told their secrets to God while we stood witness. I laid myself before them and let them encircle me.

"Do not be afraid. God has given each one of us a language all our own, a language only He can understand. You cannot say the wrong words if you allow the spirit to enter you. Free His tongue to speak in you. Let your words flow like a river into the bottomless lake of God's great mind. Your heart will know the truth. Do not try to understand. Trust the word of God, and He will raise you in His mighty arms. The Lord will ravish you with sweetness."

I was willing to let her have her way because I still didn't believe that anyone, not even Freda Graves, could make me speak in a language I didn't know. If she failed, I'd be free. I could stop hoping for salvation. I could try to accept my weaknesses and learn to live with my desires.

They laid hands on me, all of them, as they'd done to Bo Effinger the night I watched at the window. Minnie had her hands on my shoulder, and she leaned close enough for me to catch a good whiff of her whiskey breath. No wonder she suffered from the heat. I hoped Freda Graves wouldn't smell what I smelled. I was afraid of how she might punish Minnie.

Mrs. Graves touched my head. On my right thigh, Elliot

Foot's fingers burned through my dress. The man was still in torment. His hands exposed his guilt. Bo Effinger spread his palms across my stomach.

I didn't have to raise my head to see who touched me. Myron's hands gripped my left ankle so tight I thought my foot would go numb. Lyla Leona's soft fingers rested on my hipbone. She rubbed me in a distracted, dreamy way. She led a celibate life but hadn't lost her sense for pleasure. Joanna Foot poked at my knee, and the twins sat arm in arm at my side. For weeks I'd thought of these people as well-acquainted strangers, but now I realized I knew them all from their fingertips to their souls.

Freda said, "Close your eyes, Elizabeth." She pulled on the s's; a buzz hissed through my skull. "These hands on you are not human hands; these hands are the pathways of God's love. Let yourself open wide to Him. Speak to Him in the voice He longs to hear."

She was wrong. The hands on me were human, terrible and human. A dozen pairs rose and fell with the motion of my own breath until I believed my breath depended on those human hands. I thought: *If they press too hard, I'll choke and smother; if they lift their hands too high, I'll take in air until I burst.* My mother leaned against the thick-necked trucker; he laid his hands on her so gently she wept. Father moaned when Miriam pulled her hand away from his palm, the loss of that pressure too painful to bear. Sweat pooled at the backs of my knees and the base of my spine. I wanted to fling their searing hands from my body. Their palms branded my skin. I wanted to buck free and run through the cool night, like Nina running barefoot across the dewy lawn, like Nina running into the cool arms of the Indian boy, the cool arms of the devil. Let them have their fiery God. Let me be mute. I didn't want Him this way.

But I had no will. My body was stiff, muscles clenched so tight

I shook. I told myself I had to wrench free before I shattered, but their hands kept me bound. Their hands, gentle now, light as breath itself, barely touched me but held me fast as chains and shackles.

When I couldn't stand it a second longer, when the sweat beaded on my face and trickled into my ears, when the murmurings above me merged with the endless babble of the dead, the flood of words exploded from my chest, the language I had never learned came to me. Sentences drummed through my brain, inchoate but pure. I cried out to God, honoring Him with every utterance.

The Lord looked at me and smiled. His eyes were blue, light as my father's eyes, but they did not disapprove. He did not raise His finger to wipe the lipstick from my mouth; He did not pull at my teased hair. This father listened and forgave. My tongue fluttered with simple joy.

Slowly the fires flickered out as the hands lifted. Someone opened a window. A cool breeze whipped over my body, and I shivered with delight and was silent.

They all praised God, some in words I knew, some in strange tongues. Minnie curled into a ball and rolled on the floor next to me. Bo Effinger pounded the floor, a giant child on his knees. He stayed mute, but his hands knew another language, his hands beat out his story of desire. Elliot Foot was the only one who hadn't loosened his grasp the moment I began to speak. He alone pinned me to the earth and kept my body from floating free to God. His fingers dug into my thigh, and I thought he'd rip my dress. But the memory of the words sang through me, and I was afraid to make him stop, afraid to defile my lips with an ordinary sound.

19

NOW THAT God was listening, I had to be ready for the devil to test me. I felt him crouched in my heart, about to spring. I thought the gift of tongues would spare me from desire. But instead I longed to touch my own body, to rock myself to sleep. I dreamed of dogs chasing me, nipping at my heels. The only way I could fall asleep was to chant: "In the name of Jesus Christ, I rebuke you, Satan. In the name of Jesus Christ, I rebuke you, Satan."

Mother worried. She said I was too thin, too pale, too quiet. She said I slumped when I walked, I mumbled when I talked. How could I tell her that I was trying to pray without ceasing, that food and conversation got in my way?

Fortunately she couldn't dwell entirely on me. She had to fuss over Daddy. He forgot to shave. His hair grew over his collar. He owned three pairs of jeans and five plaid shirts, one for each day of the week, but he'd started sleeping in his clothes and sometimes wore the same shirt for days in a row.

I felt responsible in a way for my father's unhappiness, depriv-ing him of whatever pleasure or peace of mind he'd had from giving money to Miriam Deets. But I still didn't regret what I'd done. I figured he'd get over it soon enough and we'd all be better off in the end.

After dinner he'd often sit in his chair, rubbing his own ribs as he read the paper. He seemed to have conversations with himself: his lips moved; smiles and scowls flickered across his face. Mom stared until he looked up. "What?" he'd growl. "What is it?"

"You're doing it again," Mom said.

"Doing what?"

"Rubbing your side and grimacing."

"I am not *grimacing*."

"You're rubbing your side."

"Can't a man—"

"Does it hurt?"

"No, it doesn't hurt."

"You look like it hurts."

"Christ, woman, lay off. I've got a little gas, do you mind?"

Mother suspected the pain in his side had something to do with Miriam Deets, though she didn't know what I'd done. I don't think she ever considered the possibility that Daddy's discomfort might be truly physical.

She was sure to ferret out the truth sooner or later, and I knew she'd find me out too: she'd guess where I went Tuesday nights. I was as untrustworthy as my father. We kept our secrets, we told our lies. If Mother left us, we deserved nothing better.

I didn't have to confess. It was a bad night all around and started to go wrong when Myron Evans pissed on Freda Graves's front window. A splatter like rain hit the glass. We knew the night was clear, swirling with stars. Freda pulled the blind and it flapped on its roller. Myron Evans stood in her garden, feet spread and planted, penis aimed at the pane, its stream dwindling.

Mrs. Graves walked to the door, slowly, opened it, slowly, giving Myron plenty of time to dry out. "Come in here, Myron," she said.

"You can't help me," he called. His voice cracked like a boy's. "No one can."

"Don't talk nonsense."

"He took my money and God didn't stop him."

"Myron, come inside."

"I liked it."

"What did you like?"

"And God didn't stop that, either. God closed His eyes."

"God never closes His eyes," Freda said.

"God has no eyes."

"God is all eyes."

Myron looked behind him. "Monster!" he yelled.

"He sees you now, Myron. He sees us all. He wants you to come inside."

"No, there are flames at the door. He won't let me in."

Freda waved her arms. "There are no flames," she said.

But I think she was wrong. Myron tucked himself back in and zipped up his pants. Just before he turned to go, I was sure I saw the reflection of a fire in his eyes. I knew the boy who had taken his money was Zack Holler, and I knew what he'd done to earn Myron's five dollars.

I ran all the way home, talking to God in my private language so I wouldn't have to think about Myron and Zack. But I kept seeing Myron on his knees. I hoped he wouldn't pop out of any bushes tonight. He wanted to piss on us all. I didn't understand, exactly, but I couldn't say I thought he was wrong. I saw Zack Holler grinning, taking the money, zipping up his pants. I wondered what pleasure there was in any of this.

I kept praying, hoping for answers but not knowing enough

to ask the right questions. My house was dark. That was a relief.
I hoped my parents were asleep. I slipped inside, muttering a final
amen as I tiptoed toward the stairs.

"Lizzie," Mom said, "what's that gibberish?"

I had to grab my chest to keep my heart from jumping. It beat
so hard I felt I could almost touch it.

"Lizzie? What're you saying?"

"Nothing," I said.

"I heard you talking crazy."

"You scared me."

"Tell me what you were saying." She kept walking toward
me. I edged backward, inch by inch, until I hit the wall.

"It was only a prayer," I said.

"Where've you been?"

"I told you before I left."

"Tell me again."

"I went to a movie with Rita."

"Don't lie to me." She grabbed my shirt. "Don't you dare lie
to me." She was too weak to hold me, but she kept me cornered.
I had a choice: shove her down or listen. "Never mind," she said.
"I know where you were."

She'd tricked me. I was no longer a liar—I'd been trapped.
I said, "Did you follow me?"

"I didn't have to."

"Then how?"

"Arlen told me."

"I might have known."

"I didn't believe her. I said, 'Lizzie wouldn't lie to me.' But
you showed me to be the fool, didn't you?"

"Mom, that's not why—"

"I wish I could slap some sense into you."

"Why don't you?"

"You're too old." She waved her fingers in my face. "*I'm* too damn old if you want to know the truth." She let her hands drop to her sides. "There," she said, "I hope you're satisfied."

She left me that way, jammed up in the corner, too ashamed to move. I wondered where Daddy was. He'd thrash me and be done with it; he'd forbid me to pray with Freda Graves, tie me to a chair if he had to, lock me in my room on Tuesday nights.

Mother sat alone in the dark living room. I stood at the doorway, the light of the hallway at my back, my face in shadow. I said, "I'm trying to be good."

"Well, that's just it," Mom said. "I hardly know you these days. It makes me wonder what you're learning from that woman." She was only a voice in the unlit room.

"Look at yourself," she whispered. I imagined my silhouette, my scrawny neck, my long arms. "You're almost a woman. How can I keep you from doing whatever it is you want to do? You're my daughter, but you're not *mine*. I know the difference. But I have to speak what's on my mind. I blame myself for what happened to Nina. I blame myself for holding my tongue when I should have been talking. I saw her future, saw her belly swell to bursting in my dreams—this before she was even pregnant, before she even met Billy. Your sister had rocks for brains when it came to boys, like one half of her body shut the other half off. She itched. You could see it plain as a rash rising up on her back. I should have strapped her to her bed, bolted her door, barred her windows till that fever passed. Well, you'd do it for a cat to save its skin. You'd shut a cat in the cellar to keep those Toms away, but my own daughter, I did nothing for her."

"I'm not like Nina," I said. I was still hoping that was true.

"You can go as far one direction as the other. What's that woman teaching you?"

I had to think. We spent our nights discussing sin and temptation. I knew the words the devil whispered; I'd heard the story of a child born with her heart unfinished, her ears unformed, but the mysteries of human kindness had not been revealed to me.

"She's teaching us what's in the Bible," I finally said.

"God didn't write the Bible, Lizzie. God has no hands. Men wrote it. Then more men translated it and even more read it. There's a lot of room for mistakes. You have to trust your own head."

Whoever would have thought the devil would stoop so low as to use my own mother to put doubt in me? Whoever would have thought someone as crazy as the devil would resort to logic to get his way? He was a sly one, but he couldn't fool me. I wasn't tempted. I didn't want any part of Mother's distant God, who couldn't write in stone, her God with no hands, her God with two clean stumps where his wrists should be. He looked like Lanfear Deets, his face smooth and stupid, blank as worn wood. Instead of one hand, he had none. My God had huge hands, to strike down the wicked and raise up the blessed.

If I followed every one of His laws and didn't falter, I surely would be saved. When I woke from death, the keys to the kingdom would already be in my hand. A girl like me needed to be told how to be good. Deciding for myself was too risky. I could blow it anytime. I could piss it all away like Myron Evans, I could start thinking God had no eyes and no hands— then who would stop me? My mother was the most decent person I knew, but I could see what happened when you didn't pay attention to the rules. The devil had crawled right into her ear and was using her to get to me.

"Why do you think your daddy was so hard on Nina?" she said. She didn't wait for an answer. "Because he believed in certain laws. Because he knew a lot about right and wrong, what the Bible and all those good Lutherans had to say about girls who got themselves in trouble. He forgot to think, Lizzie. He forgot to love, and he forgot to forgive—his own child, and he forgot that."

I was afraid. I didn't know enough to argue. Mother's words made terrifying sense. I wanted to save her. I didn't want to be alone in Heaven with Freda Graves and Joanna Foot. I didn't want to spend eternity listening to the Lockwood twins talking in rhyme.

This was my first trial. The real measure of my faith began a week later.

20

THE DAYS of August loomed before me, hot and dead. People seemed to wade down the sidewalks, their bodies waffling at the dizzy height of afternoon. A white sun scorched the grass. In Willis, we gave up on sprinklers, saving our water for the farmers and letting our own lawns go stiff and yellow. The grasshoppers got so mean you couldn't walk through a field barelegged. Their crushed bodies littered the parched streets and stuck in the grille of Daddy's truck. But the dark of evening still pulled a chill down from the mountains, a gust straight off the glaciers.

We sat on the porch one Sunday evening, my mother and father and I, in our after-dinner silence. I hugged myself, thinking I'd have to go inside soon and find a sweatshirt. And when I rose, Mother or Father would say, "Are you cold?" The words would cut between us, and I would have to answer. There would be other words when I returned, polite and ordinary.

A bell clanged. Both my parents stood. Daddy pointed toward the center of town. "There," he said, "looks like it's right on Main." I followed the line of his finger until I saw a curl of smoke in the night sky. Mother had already run inside for the keys to the truck.

Everyone else in town had the same idea we did; no one could get within three blocks of the fire. But as we ran along the street a cry passed from group to group, and we knew the Last Chance Bar was burning.

A block away, the smell in the air was sweet, like the first morning fire of autumn crackling in the fireplace. But as we moved closer, the air grew dense with the stink of things that shouldn't burn: hair singed by a candle flame, a tire doused in gasoline, a wet wool sweater set too close to the open door of the oven.

There wasn't much to see yet, just the flickers in the blackened building. The few men who had been at the bar stood on the street, hacking and choking. They'd tried to stamp out the blaze while it was still small, but an ember hidden in a pile of soiled rags burst into flames and sent them scurrying outside.

Huddled together now, deep in speculation, they looked down the street, counting the minutes until the city fire truck rumbled along the potholed pavement.

The truck pulled up in front of the bar, to a hydrant that hadn't been used since the fire of '42. That winter wildfire charred an entire block. As the men in high black boots and long coats struggled with the crusty plug and heavy hoses, I realized something was missing. Olivia Jeanne Woodruff's Winnebago had disappeared from the front of Elliot Foot's bar. She wasn't in the milling flock of the curious, and I couldn't see her house on wheels anywhere down Main. I thought, So this is how Elliot is repaid for spurning her love. I imagined Olivia Jeanne planting a dozen coals, leaving them to smolder.

Then I saw the man, Elliot Foot himself, standing on the

sidewalk, his arms crossed over his thin chest. He didn't rant or pace or pound the walls; he didn't rush inside to see what he could save. Elliot Foot stood and smiled like a man who had just laid a royal flush on the table.

In a flash I saw the purpose of all this, knew without a doubt that Elliot Foot had torched his own bar to scald the temptation out of his heart. He wanted the Last Chance to burn to the ground. His hands seared my thigh the night I spoke in tongues. He didn't need a match; those fingers were on fire. Others would blame Olivia Jeanne; he counted on that, on the simplicity and logic of the deed. If she had any sense left, she was crossing the border into Canada this very minute. Only a fool would stick around long enough to leave the decision to a judge and jury and newspaper in this town.

Maybe Elliot instilled deeper fears in her that night. Perhaps she loved him well enough to smell the fever of repentance and know that her Winnebago would go next. Parked in front of the bar, she would have felt the first wave of hot air in her face.

At last the hose was hooked to the hydrant. Vern and Ralph yanked it off the truck themselves and shoved their runt of a brother out of the way. He looked delirious, too distracted to wipe the sweat from his forehead.

When we saw the arc of water, the single dirty stream, women cheered and men scrambled to help aim the hose. Elliot Foot stopped grinning, wondering if something might still be saved. A second truck arrived and skidded up to a hydrant around the corner. Hope surged through the crowd.

I lost my parents in the mob. Most everyone in Willis who could walk had gathered in the street to gawk at the fire: it was better than the traveling circus that had come through the valley six years ago, better than the woman with four arms or the pinhead fetus in a jar.

Gangs of kids ran wild. Fire released some native urge, turning children into thugs and thieves. A band of ten-year-olds circled a younger child, demanding his belt and then his shoes. They would have stolen his comb and pocketknife too, but the boy's mother swooped down and dragged her son away by the wrist.

Someone hit me square in the back and I pitched forward. It was Coe Carson and Zachary Holler jabbing at each other's chest behind me. They argued, but I couldn't make out the words. They jostled me again without seeing who I was. Zack Holler, the boy who had changed my life, who had thrown me into the arms of Freda Graves and forced me into weeks of lies, Zack Holler could look right through me without a glimmer of recognition.

I heard him say, "Do what you want. I'm going in. It's free." The veins of his forearms bulged. He lurched through the crowd, knocking people out of the way. In the months since I'd seen him he'd lost his adolescent leanness, and his strong body had begun to reveal its brutality. Full-blown, Zack Holler would crush other men's fingers as he shook their hands; he'd slap their backs too hard and knock them forward. I hoped for a small tragedy, a wound to weaken him. I believed in fate but knew it was wrong to yearn for misfortune, so I was careful not to pray for an accident; instead, I reminded God how I trusted His infinite wisdom.

Zack Holler darted through the doorway of the burning bar before anyone got wise to his plan. Skittery sparks shot across the floor. Through the tinted windows I saw flames lapping at the frame of the storeroom door.

Coe Carson faced me. He still didn't remember who I was, the girl in the gully, the girl on the ground with Zachary's sister, the girl on the tree house floor with Zachary—but Zack Holler wouldn't be proud of that; he'd forget to tell Coe. "Dammit,"

Coe said, "did you see that? He says it's a great time to get free booze. No hassle, he says. He's going into a burning building for a goddamn bottle of tequila. I'd buy him one, you know. I'd buy him one every day from now till Christmas if I had to. You think he cares? 'What fun is that?' he says. He gets off on it. He gets off on scaring the shit out of himself. What kind of crazy person lives that way?"

Before I could answer, Coe Carson shouldered and shoved his way to the bar, Coe, who would never be able to grow a beard or get a real job at the mill, according to my father. I hoped he didn't want to be a hero. His arms were thin as a girl's, smooth and freckled. Going into the bar after the likes of Zack Holler made less sense to me than going after a bottle of tequila. Bravery is a fool's damn luck. But Coe Carson knew himself. He stood in the street where he could watch the doorway.

A siren ripped down Main. People jumped to clear a path. As he hit the intersection of Main and Center streets, Sheriff Caleb Wolfe slammed the brakes and spun into a quarter-circle stop. A big Indian climbed out of the passenger side, a real Indian, not a questionable quarter-blood like Caleb Wolfe himself. This man had a broad face and high round cheeks, the smooth hairless chin of a full-blooded Kootenai. His blue shirt could have fit around two ordinary men, but it wouldn't close over his dark chest. A thin black braid hung halfway down his back.

I didn't need to be told this was Red Elk, the father of the slim boy who stole Nina that summer night long ago, a night much cooler than this one. I saw Billy Elk take Nina in his arms and make her disappear. But he forgot the second part of his magic trick, the part when the girl reappears, when all her scattered molecules are gathered from the air, a fuzzy image, almost transparent, wavering, a body underwater, and then Nina, Nina whole and laughing.

Now I saw the man my father hated, the *red-skinned dog* he tried to drive out of town, the *heathen* he threatened to strangle with his bare hands. No wonder Mother was afraid. Red Elk could crush a man under each foot and keep on walking.

I realized there were no other Indians in the crowd. They bore a history of blame; none dared come close enough to be accused.

The crowd swarmed around the sheriff's car, and it vanished almost as quickly as it had appeared. Caleb Wolfe strutted in front of the bar, pushing the horde back a step each time he passed. His short bowlegs seemed to snap as his feet hit cement. Someone aimed the high beam of a flashlight into his face. He squinted but didn't raise his hand to block the light.

"There's a boy in there," a woman yelled. "Look, can you see him?"

Caleb Wolfe whirled toward the door. An explosion from the storeroom doubled the size of every flame with a single blast. The fountains of water from the hoses seemed futile now, children pissing on a bonfire. Sparks scattered like milkweed, and each spark became the seed of a new flame.

Red Elk opened the door. Thirty feet away, the heat hit us like a wall and we shrank back. Air had turned to smoke inside the bar. But the big Indian stood his ground, as if to see how much he could bear. Then he threw himself into the fiery pit. I gasped; my lungs burned as I watched him, a shadow in flame.

A sound like thunder rocked the building. Flares climbed, finding the driest wood, the pulpy rafters. The thunder roared again, and we saw a beam tear loose and fall, engulfed in a blaze. The fast, brilliant bodies of flames writhed across the floor.

I was sure the Indian and Zack didn't have a chance. I imagined the rafter had fallen on their backs or pinned their legs. I heard their cries above the rush of air on fire. The church bell rang and rang. High in the steeple, its insistent, foolish voice beat out a single tone.

But I was wrong. Red Elk dodged collapsing beams. The Indian had been inside less than a minute when the front window burst, splintering onto the sidewalk in a thousand smoky shards.

He sailed through the jagged opening, a huge man, suspended in this long moment when every mouth opened but no one made a sound. He hit the sidewalk with a thud, suddenly back in the world of gravity. His face was black with soot and his chest heaved. Zachary Holler was slung over his shoulder, draped on his back like a sack of meat.

Caleb Wolfe cleared the clot of people from a circle of cement in the street and helped Red Elk lay the boy down. "Give us air," he yelled. "Give us air!"

Red Elk tilted Zack's head back, put his hands on the boy's chest and leaned forward and back, forward and back—but Zack Holler was as still and stunned as Jesse was when they pulled his pale body out of Moon Lake. The big man breathed into him, put his mouth over Zack's mouth, shared his smoky air with the white boy. But that paltry bit of oxygen was too little for either of them. After a few mouthfuls, Red Elk sat back on his broad haunches, gulping. Caleb Wolfe took over. He pounded Zachary's chest and swore. I think it was the cuss that called Zack Holler back, that pulled his soul down to the gritty street and made his rib cage swell with the first living breath.

"Water!" Caleb cried. "Jesus, his hands."

Coe Carson brought two pails for his friend and lifted Zack's red hands into the water. Coe's knuckles bled from grinding them into the gravel. His lips moved, a plea; tears rolled down his cheeks. I prayed for a miracle that would deliver me from the kind of accident I'd wished upon Zachary.

Dr. Ben hobbled down the street. Stooped, his white head

bobbing, the old man took his time. The doctor saw it this way: if the boy was dead, why should he bust a gut getting there; and if they had him breathing, a minute or two either way wasn't going to change anyone's chances. I hoped that when Dr. Ben lay on his bed, wheezing out his last gasp, he would look down the long tunnel of this night. At the edge of his own dark dream, I hoped he'd see a vision of himself, walking and walking, but never moving closer, never reaching the bed to sit beside himself.

By the time the good doctor crouched beside Zack Holler the sheriff had given the boy his second life.

Father stood across from me in the ring that had formed. He was pressed up close to Miriam Deets. Lanfear was on the other side of his wife, and he and my father spoke a few words to each other over Miriam's head. Lanfear couldn't see what I saw, that Daddy clutched Miriam's hand, the left one, the one Lanfear could no longer hold if he strolled side by side with his wife. Father's eyes looked strange, milky as the eyes of a fish tossed up on the beach, two days dead. He gripped Miriam's fingers, his own fingers clenched as if in pain. She let him hold her. Maybe she was sorry she'd refused his money all these weeks, sorry for his sake as well as her own. I thought her touch was all that saved him, all that kept him from leaping on the big Indian. He'd worked with Red Elk day after day, holding back his anger. Now he saw his chance: Red Elk was down and out of breath. I was afraid my father might sink low enough to jump the man while he was on the ground.

Zack rose into fierce consciousness, wailing. He jerked his hands out of the water, but Caleb Wolfe forced them back down. Dr. Ben filled a syringe and rolled Zack far enough on his side to shove it into his buttocks, right through the thick denim of his jeans. Zack's head dropped before the needle was out.

The doctor began bandaging Zack's hands. They grew large,

snowpaws. I imagined Zack grabbing a bottle of tequila in one hand and a bottle of whiskey in the other. He didn't know how hot they were, that the glass was ready to crack. His touch shattered them, sending slivers of glass into his fingers and palms, splattering alcohol up his forearms and into his face, alcohol that burst into flames, torched by a wild spark.

Joshua Holler clawed and kicked to get to his boy. Seeing him gave me an image of Zack as a grown man: his fingers thick and dirty, good for poking into other men's chests; his jowls and belly slack from all those brews with the boys. I was wrong to wish for Zachary's misfortune: men like this heaped misfortune on themselves.

There was no sign of Zack's mother. Ruby Holler was probably out at Ike's Truckstop, slapping coffee and greasy slabs of beef and gravy in front of thankless truckers on their way to Canada, strangers who didn't give a damn that the center of town was going up in smoke.

I wondered where Gwen was too. I thought of the steamy windows of Gil Harding's Duster in the school parking lot last winter. Tonight they could stay home in Gwen's upstairs bedroom. I imagined them falling onto Gwen's flowered quilt, bouncing and laughing, laughing because this bed was soft, softer than the grass in the park or the vinyl seat in the back of Gil's car, softer by far than the rough boards on the dirty floor of the tree house, the only place I'd ever lain down with a boy, softer than the street where that boy lay now.

Gwen didn't know about any of that. And she wouldn't be sorry when she heard. Her mother wouldn't be sorry either. No, they'd say Zack was to blame, a boy who plays with fire gets burned. But I regretted it all the same because I'd wished for it. I had dreamed this pain into the body of Zack Holler, ached for him to feel one quarter of what I felt.

Late as it was, I dared to hope Gwen and her mother might still come. Their cool hands on Zack's bruised forehead were the only hands that could soothe him in his deep sleep. I scanned the crowd. Miriam Deets stood on her tiptoes to kiss Lanfear on the nose. My father was gone.

Red Elk scooped Zack off the pavement and carried the limp boy to Joshua Holler's truck. The closest hospital was in Rovato Falls, but if Zack was in a bad way, they'd have to take him all the way to Missoula, a hundred and seventy miles south. A lot could go wrong on the way to Missoula.

I thought of Joshua Holler, alone on a dark Montana road. His journey would be endless and silent—unless Zachary woke again. And what could a father do? What was there to do with a wailing boy but thump him on the back of the head and pray you hit him hard enough, but not too hard.

And Joshua Holler might notice, as if for the first time, all the white crosses along the highway, at least one at every curve, the markers of death, reminding him that a car had spun out of control in this very place.

I worked my way back to the alley. The roar was steady now, the fire sure of itself and strong, drowning every other sound like a river surging down a gorge. The firemen had given up on the bar and turned their hoses on Saddles & Studs, the Western clothing store next door. Already its roof smoldered and one wall was sure to go. My uncle Les and his three boys had organized a human chain from the back of the Last Chance, a line of men and women passing buckets, hoping to save something that was clearly destroyed. Arlen joined them. She was proud to see her boys working together, inspired for the first time.

All her life, Arlen had watched the slow, sullen way men work when the job they do has no worth of its own, like the work a man does in the mill, where sawing wood doesn't mean there will be a fresh stack in the shed to get his family through a month of winter. The boards a man measures and cuts only remind him that there will be more wood tomorrow and the next day and the day after that, and none of it will ever find its way to his pile.

I was sad to think of it just then, to think of all the men in this town who worked at the mill, who got their first summer job at sixteen and retired at sixty-five. Their dream of Heaven was an endless plain of sage and sand where nothing grew tall enough to bother chopping it down, where the tumbleweed broke from its own stalk and rolled away.

My cousins worked in vain. The blaze had grown beyond any human desire to control it. It would have to consume itself.

Flames glowed brilliant and orange inside the blackened skeleton, but I could see the fire had eaten a hole in itself and was dying. Flares no longer danced; they only burned, steady and fierce. I walked up and down the street, looking for my mother and father, but I couldn't find them in the crowd.

People were slow to admit it was time to abandon the cause. Caleb Wolfe and Red Elk could barely hold folks back when they realized every hose had been turned on the building next door. Red Elk wore a shiny badge. Sometime in the past half hour he'd been deputized.

Despite the heat, some of the men shoved their way closer to the bar; their voices rose, as if they meant to rip the hoses from the hands of the firemen and aim them back on the bar. Folks took this personally. The Last Chance was the only bar in Willis, the only bar for a good fifteen miles, and everyone dreaded the inconvenience, the long drunken drives along narrow Montana roads, the impossible winter miles.

Myron Evans breathed right in my ear. He was trying to tell

me something. Finally I heard the words: "I wish I'd done it."
He grinned. "Did you see what happened to that boy?" He
grinned. I wasn't the only one with a grudge against Zack Holler.
I felt ashamed for both of us, ashamed of the company I kept.

Minnie Hathaway tottered down the alley, cussing. She hadn't
been on a bender in months, but she'd pickled herself tonight. Her
black hair was damp and tangled. She staggered toward us, falling
into Myron. She pinched his arms. "Wanna dance with me, you
handsome sonuvabitch?" She puckered her red lips and closed her
eyes. Myron stooped, pushing his face up nose to nose with
Minnie. I thought he really meant to kiss that wrinkled mouth,
but instead he spat words in her face: "Get thee behind me,
Satan." She cussed. She was no temptress and no devil, only a
woman who made a man realize how terrible the flowers are at
the end of summer. Myron tossed his head and limped away.

"You're not such a fine piece," Minnie shouted at his back.
"You're not breaking my heart, mister."

The insides of the bar crumbled. The roof collapsed, a slow
fall of flame. It was over. If Olivia Jeanne Woodruff ever dared
return, all she'd find would be a burned-out shell. I saw Bo
Effinger's head half a foot above everyone else's in the crowd.
Lyla Leona clung to his shirt sleeve. In the final heat of it all, Bo
crushed her to his chest and stole a kiss. Sorry for his deed before
it was half done, he tried to pull away, but Lyla grabbed the back
of his neck and held him fast, smashing his nose and his lips into
her face for a minute or more. I watched that kiss, forgetting the
fire for those long seconds, forgetting my father and myself.

Luella Lockwood shook me from my stupor. "Have you seen
my sister?" she said. For an old lady she had quite a grip. She'd
painted her mouth on crooked and had two pairs of overlapping
lips, moving together.

"Don't smirk at me, missy."

"Calm down," I said, "everyone's lost tonight, but she can't be far."

"Don't tell me to calm down. You don't know what it's like."

"How long has she been gone?"

"Ten minutes," Luella said, "maybe more."

"Ten minutes? That's all? I haven't seen my parents for an hour or more."

She squeezed my wrists so hard my hands tingled. She might have held me there all night if Eula hadn't tugged at the back of her sweater just then. They fell into each other's arms as if they'd been separated since birth and searching for their twin all these years. "Isn't it something?" they wheezed with one voice. "I was so worried." They fell apart with giggles, and I walked away, back out to the street.

Two more fire trucks rattled down Main, relief from Alpena and Rovato Falls. They hooked up around the corner and down the block. Dewey's News would be smoking soon if they didn't get the roof of Saddles & Studs cooled down.

I felt my mother next to me. She said, "See what comes of all that praying?" She scared me when she knew things like that. She didn't have to go to Freda Graves's prayer meetings to know the torment of Elliot Foot and guess that he had taken a torch to his own bar. She didn't have to see me thrashing on the floor to know my beliefs were strange and my fear dangerous. I wondered how long it would take other folks to figure it out. The man looked sorry now, his head buried between Joanna's comforting breasts, his body shaking with muffled sobs. Joanna Foot patted her husband's back, satisfied at last that he had paid dearly enough for his sins of the hands and of the heart. The beams of this charred building would crumble and the body of love would lie in a black heap.

I thought Elliot would be relieved if people found him out. A jury of his peers would surely send him to jail for destroying their only drinking hole—even if it was his place. Maybe he wanted that, maybe he longed to be confined and safe, free of Olivia Jeanne and free of his wife's forgiveness. A jail can be a monastery to a simple man, a cave he doesn't have to dig himself, a place to be good.

On that day in 1964 when the Foot brothers raised the sign for the Last Chance Bar, Freda Graves shouted from the steps of the Lutheran church and Elliot Foot, brave and indestructible, shouted back. That was a lifetime ago, for all of us. Elliot was his own man then, not the victim of Olivia Jeanne's temptations or Freda Graves's holy wars. Myron Evans was still skittish as his own cats. That was a time when Gwen Holler and I held hands and tried to get a good look inside this house of sin. Now, alone, I was trying to peer into the gutted bar again, hoping to under-stand, but there was nothing left. Another memory burst into my thoughts. Nina swatted my butt. *Daddy would skin you like a rabbit if he saw you here.* Then I heard my own words: *I wish I didn't have a sister.*

Why did God always hear the wishes I made in haste and anger?

I stared through the shattered window of the Last Chance Bar. There, beyond the ragged opening, dancing on red embers, her golden hair aflame, I saw Nina. She twirled in the light, her hands raised above her head, spinning to a blur. I squinted hard. Smoke stung my eyes. I rubbed them but that made it worse. When I opened them again, my sister had disappeared. *How long has she been lost?* a voice like Luella Lockwood's said inside my skull. I had to count on my fingers. Luella smirked. "Five years," I said out loud. But there was no one to hear my answer, and no one to comfort me. There was only the feverish babble of the mob.

It was in this moment, when the bar was lost and my sister was gone, again, that Freda Graves appeared on the steps of the Lutheran church, just as she had six years before.

She bellowed, "The wrath of the Lord is upon all ye sinners!" Those of us who knew her well couldn't help hearing her voice above all other sounds. The word *sinners* called to our blood and burned our cheeks. I saw Myron and the Lockwood twins, Bo Effinger and Lyla Leona. Even in her daze, Minnie Hathaway managed to teeter toward the church. Only Elliot Foot hung back, the wound of his conscience cleaned and cauterized.

Slowly the word passed through the horde that *she* was here. The swarm turned and inched toward the church. Vern and Ralph Foot headed the pack, bent on revenge. An insidious whisper hissed from person to person. By the time it reached me the words had twisted but the meaning was clear: the throng had found the one it wanted to blame—someone had to pay. If anyone had asked, I would have said, "I don't know her."

Freda Graves was not afraid. "For behold," she said, "the Lord will come in fire, to render His anger in fury, and His rebuke with flames of fire."

Shouts answered her, and then a single cry, shrill and unforgiving. The pack surged forward, a huge animal with many feet and one small mind.

Caleb Wolfe and Red Elk leaped to the front of the mob and jumped the railing of the steps to shield Mrs. Graves. But they were only two men and the crowd was at least a hundred strong. Blinded by the veil of righteousness, Freda Graves shook her mane of gray curls, raised her broad knotted hands toward Heaven and said, "For by fire will the Lord execute judgment." The clot of people pressed closer, and Freda Graves remembered her mortality just in time to slip inside the white arched door of the Lutheran church.

Caleb Wolfe drew his gun and fired a round into the air. Red Elk spread himself across the door. Legs braced, arms outstretched, he seemed to hang in the arch. The sheriff fired another round, and the crowd drew back, almost tamed.

Then I saw my father, slamming his way to the church steps. His hair was singed and his face was covered with soot. He still had that blind glaze, a man with two glass eyes, but he knew where he wanted to go. Soon he stood on the third step of the Lutheran church, and there was no one between him and the two Indians.

He clutched a rock in each hand. "We're not gonna let a couple of Indians keep us from getting what we want, are we?" he yelled. That was all he had to say. The crowd swayed and sang, a chorus of *no*'s. A mob does not demand eloquence of its leader, only that he take the first step. How could these people guess that my father didn't give a damn about their precious bar or the preacher woman? He would have stood by and watched the whole block burn to the ground. It was the big Indian spread across the door that drove him wild. It was Red Elk's hairless face and skinny black braid that turned my father into the leader of a gang of idiots.

Spurred on by his own words, Father flung himself toward Red Elk. He fell against the Indian's massive chest; his knee rammed into the big man's groin. His rage was old. He stood before the man he'd always hated. He saw Nina. He knew what she'd done. He blamed Red Elk for this too, blamed him for having a son.

He tried to pummel the Indian with his stones. But fury clouded his eyes. The rocks rained down on Red Elk's shoulders and arms, a long way from the forehead my father wanted to crush.

Sheriff Wolfe brought a polished stick down hard on the back of Father's knees, then again sharp and swift across each kidney. His aim was perfect and precise; it took only three blows. Daddy crumpled to his knees, then fell in a heap at Red Elk's feet.

The sheriff cuffed my father's hands behind his back. The crowd hummed. Wolfe fired a third round into the dark and waved his nightstick as if to ask if anyone else wanted to take him on. No one moved.

Vern Foot yelled, "You're not on the reservation, Wolfe. You can't run us by tribal law. You'll answer for this!" But it was an idle threat. Even Ralph Foot didn't back his toothless brother. Sheriff Wolfe was not a man to cross on this night of the hot wind.

The big Indian leaned against the white door; the arch came to a point above his head. He rubbed his left shoulder and looked somewhere far beyond us, to the black outline of the hills, to the peaks of the Rockies where the snow never melts.

Together, Red Elk and Caleb Wolfe lifted my father to his feet. He was too weak to walk. They pulled him down the steps, his feet dragging. A path opened as they passed through the crowd. Daddy's fickle followers shrank back. I lost myself among them, listening to the buzz of his name on the lips of the people around me, hoping no one recognized his daughter.

Reverend Timothy Piggott climbed the stairs of his church with a shotgun in his hands. He looked gaunt and ridiculous packing that big rifle, but when he spoke, people had to listen. His was the only voice of reason on a night of impulse. "What evil has possessed you?" he said. "Would you chase a woman into the Lord's house? Would you stone her there while the eyes of Jesus stared down at you from the Cross?"

Maybe he was just protecting his church, saving his carpet from a hundred pairs of sooty soles, saving his pulpit from the scars of bricks and rocks. But I heard something more in his voice, something human and compassionate. He spoke as a man, not a minister, when he said, "Go home. There's been enough trouble for one night."

The fire dwindled to smoke and embers. The show was over. People gave up and started home. As the crowd thinned, I saw that Caleb Wolfe hadn't taken my father to jail. His green Plymouth was still there, parked beneath the stoplight where Main Street crossed Center Street.

My father, his hands locked behind him, sat in the backseat. Wild children cavorted around the car. One tow-headed boy had a pair of shoes dangling from his belt loops, the trophy of a bully. He was the loudest, proud as a cavalryman who'd taken an Indian scalp. He pounded the hood of the car. A dirty-faced girl knocked on the windows, and two small boys flattened their faces to the glass. I saw them from the other side, saw their smashed noses, their cheeks pushed up so high they seemed to have nothing more than slits for eyes.

Father stared at his lap. His chin was cut, and I wondered if he'd fallen or if Caleb Wolfe had punched him in the face. He didn't see the children. He didn't see me. I looked for my mother, the only one who might be brave enough to shoo these little monsters away. I ran in circles, from one end of the street to the other. I sprinted to the place where we'd parked the truck. It was gone. I thought she must not know about any of this.

I raced down the streets. I ran so hard my heels kicked my butt with every step. I wanted to go someplace where nobody knew me. But I couldn't get far enough from home. My father's humiliation was inside me. His anger was mine. I might be a stranger to everyone I met, but I would always know my own name.

Weary drivers leaned on their horns when I darted into the yellow glaze of their headlights. I never stopped.

Gasping for breath, I leaped up the steps of our porch. I heard the whine of the swing, Mother creaking back and forth in the dark. "Daddy," I whispered.

And she answered, "I know."

21

IT WAS already midnight, and Mother had no intention of going to rescue Daddy. "Stew in his own juice," she said.

I told her about the cut on his chin. "He might be hurt," I said.

"He'll live till morning."

I knew she was probably right, but I still thought it was wrong to let him sit in jail. Arlen agreed. She came charging up the steps half an hour after I got home.

"Those heathens are probably beating Dean bloody right this minute," Arlen said. "And here you are sitting on the porch doing nothing to stop them."

"I'm sure the sheriff is too tired to beat on anyone," Mom said.

But Arlen wouldn't let up, so we headed downtown to pay Daddy's bail and haul him home. The streets were already deserted, and the air was thick with smoke.

Sheriff Wolfe said my father was asleep, and that he'd be better off staying right where he was for the night. "Let sleeping dogs lie," he muttered, which got Arlen on her high horse.

"You listen here, mister," she said, "we've got a right. You tell us the bail. We pay it. We take him home. Right, Wolfe?" He didn't budge even when the spit started flying with the words.

"No bail till we see a judge." He said it slow; he had all night.

"Well, that's that," Mom said.

Arlen looked at Mother the way you'd look at a woman drowning a litter of newborn kittens in the toilet. "What kind of woman . . . ?" Arlen said, and my mother answered, "A tired woman."

I wanted to take him home now, while the streets were still dark and empty.

Arlen glared at Caleb Wolfe. Sooner or later she'd have to blink. "And just when will you be seeing this judge?" she said. The sheriff wasn't coming up with any answer quick enough for Arlen, so she repeated each word, nice and slow, talking to the sheriff as if he were some kind of full-grown moron.

"No judge comes through Willis unless I call him," Wolfe said.

Arlen ripped the phone from his desk and shoved the receiver up against his ear. "Then call him," she hissed.

"You don't call a judge in the middle of the night, ma'am."

Arlen flicked the receiver as if she meant to whack him across the jaw. "What's the number, Wolfe? I'm not afraid of disturbing some judge's precious sleep. In fact, I'm sure any judge in the county would be mighty interested in hearing how you run this town."

She started dialing numbers, any numbers, but Wolfe cut her short. "No need to call a judge anyway," he said. "There won't be any bail."

"That's not for you to decide. You can't hold a man without bail."

"No charges. No bail. Simple."

"No charges?" Mother said. She sounded disappointed. Arlen dropped the receiver in the cradle.

"Red Elk told me to forget it. I could do it myself. I was there. But Red Elk says to me, 'What's the point? I don't swear on the white man's Bible.' White people. White jury. White witnesses. One big Indian with a braid. One dark-skinned sheriff with a grudge. Waste of time. You want to take your man home? Fine. I'm glad to get him out of my jail. Stinks worse than any badger I ever had to shoot. I can go home. Sleep in my own bed."

Daddy cussed when we woke him. Blood from the scratch on his chin had dried to a crusty brown, and he smelled even worse than Wolfe said, urine and beer, a man who'd spilled his drink and pissed his pants. Arlen wasn't so keen on helping him now. She backed out of the cell and waited in the hallway.

"Time to go home, Dean," Mother said. She spoke fast, clipping her words. Father sat on the edge of the cot, afraid to look at her. "Now or never," she said, turning toward the door.

"I'm coming," Daddy whispered.

AFTER MY father was out of the way, Caleb Wolfe still didn't get much of a chance to sleep in his own bed that night. For days afterward he told his story to anyone who would listen, reciting the events of August third as if they were a litany. Men nodded and said it was a damn shame. The sheriff was hoping for some response that would set him free. Women whispered among themselves, saying it was a terrible thing. But no one ever thought to tell Sheriff Wolfe he wasn't to blame.

Around six-thirty the calls started. Folks were just waking up when they spotted someone skulking around their windows, a man trying to get a look at fat ladies wriggling into girdles. The sheriff could track him by the calls: Seventh to Willow; he wasn't moving fast. Wolfe took his time getting dressed and finally nabbed the suspect just past Ike's Truckstop, less than five minutes

after the fellow had exposed his most private parts to Miriam
Deets as she was setting the place up for the breakfast crowd.
Glory hallelujah, she reported him saying right after she said,
"Mornin', Myron." *Glory hallelujah.* Then he pulled his jacket
open, revealing his unzipped pants and all that dangled out of
them.

Wolfe wasn't getting off easy this time. There were going to
be charges, all right—even though the man was no stranger and
no threat, even though he apologized to Miriam and Ike and
offered to pay for the pitcher of cream Miriam had dropped on
the floor. He even offered to wipe up the spill. Ike Turner told
Caleb Wolfe to get that damn pervert out of his place. Wolfe
said, "I'll just take Myron downtown and call his mother to take
him on home, if you folks don't mind." He didn't realize that
this was the last time Myron Evans was going to get away with
his quirks in this town.

"Don't you dare," Ike thundered. "Look at this poor girl,
shaking like a rabbit, maybe scarred for life, and you want this
piece of garbage out walking the streets again tonight? Too bad
you don't have a wife, Wolfe. You'd see it different."

Caleb Wolfe leaned over and tapped Miriam's shoulder as she
scrubbed the floor. She shrank away as if a man's hand was a
terrible thing. "Ma'am?" the sheriff said. "Do you want to press
charges?"

"What?"

"Do you want Myron to go to jail, ma'am?"

She kept wiping the tiles even though the cream was gone. By
then Lanfear Deets had come in from the pumps, waving his
stump, telling Wolfe to get that scum out of there. Later people
asked each other: If Lanfear had two hands, would he have
strangled Myron, or told Miriam to forget it and just let him go?

Miriam Deets was a leaf in the wind of Lanfear's voice; she

had no choice but to blow his way. Wolfe planned on talking to her later in the day, or maybe tomorrow. She'd come to her senses and see that Myron Evans was as harmless as they come. She'd laugh at herself for getting worked up and being afraid of a man who unzips his pants and limps around town.

Sending Myron to prison would be as cruel as strapping him down in a chair and turning on the electricity. Men like him had a hard time in prison. Men like Myron had to sleep with one eye open. People who showed themselves never did anything about it. Wolfe knew that, and plenty of other things too. He'd sit Miriam down after she'd had a few hours to calm herself, a few hours for the image of Myron's *Glory hallelujah* to fade.

In the meantime he had no choice but to take Myron downtown; still he refused to use his handcuffs, not on a lame man, dammit, and he let Myron sit in the front seat, a friend, not a prisoner. The morning light over the blue mountains was something to see with all that smoke in the air. They said so, Myron Evans and Caleb Wolfe, and didn't say much else. Later Wolfe swore he had no clue, no clue at all, but he should have read the sign: he knew what was coming when the horizon turned the color of blood at dawn, and he would have paid attention except for the fact that he stopped believing the warnings in the sky when he moved to this town.

THREE THINGS happened after Myron was arrested that morning. The first was that Myron's mother refused to visit him in jail. And the second was that Sheriff Wolfe, having had a very long and tiresome night, fell asleep at his desk. That's how the third thing happened.

*

IT WAS past noon when Caleb Wolfe woke with the image of the red sun burning a hole in his skull. He was groggy from the heat and stiff from sleeping in the chair. When he looked out the window, the sun was high and white, but he still had the distinct feeling something was wrong. He splashed water on his face and fumbled down the hall to see if Myron wanted something to eat.

Myron Evans wasn't ever going to be hungry again. Myron Evans wasn't going to peep in any windows or sing out any *Glory hallelujah*'s. Myron Evans was hanging in his cell, strangled by his own shirt.

At 12:17, Dr. Ben pronounced him dead; and by 12:45, Arlen was at our door saying it could have been Daddy if we'd left him there all night by himself, as if something in the cell made Myron do it, as if it had nothing to do with the man himself. Myron left a note for his mother: *I try to be good, but sometimes I can't help myself.*

Every time I closed my eyes that night I saw Myron's thin white chest, his skin stretched so tight I could count his ribs. His face bulged above the knotted sleeve of his shirt. His eyes never closed. The last thing he'd done on this earth was kick the chair out from under his feet. When I could make every other picture disappear, I still saw his feet dangling, those heavy shoes, black and thick-soled, those neat bows, tied for the last time.

The next morning I went looking for Freda Graves. I needed her to lay hands on me so I could say the right things when I talked to God. When I thought of Him on my own, I wanted to curse Him for letting Myron hang himself. I could understand Caleb Wolfe falling asleep on the job, but God, why were His eyes closed the night Elliot Foot set the town on fire? What kept His hands so busy that morning as Myron Evans took off his shirt? All He had to do was give Caleb Wolfe a little nudge, jolt him awake, let the chair fall with a clatter. That wasn't much to ask of God.

Freda's blinds were pulled shut, just as they always were. I pounded on her door; the sound was so hollow I thought the house must be completely empty, that even the furniture and carpet had disappeared. I went back three times that day. As the last smoky light of dusk gave way to a starless night, a neighbor poked his head out his window and said, "Just missed her. She had a bag and was headed toward Main. Good riddance. Nothing but trouble that woman." I didn't wait to hear the rest; I tore after her. I ran almost a mile before I caught sight of her heading west. Her steps were slow and steady, as if she meant to walk to Idaho. A black shawl draped her head, and she plodded along, a stooped old woman trying to sneak out of town in a quiet way, moving slow so no one would see she was running.

I got close enough to touch her and almost put my hand on her bony back, but something stopped me. I kicked gravel at the heels of her shoes; she didn't turn. I said her name and still she kept on shuffling, deaf and dumb. Finally I ran ahead of her to stare her in the eye, but even that was impossible. As night filled up the valley, Freda Graves hobbled down the highway wearing a pair of mirrored sunglasses.

I said, "Myron's dead."

"Yes."

"Where're you going?"

"Away from this valley." Her voice was a scatter of stones falling on the road.

"Take off those glasses."

"I cannot."

"They're not glued to your face. Let me look at you," I said. I wasn't afraid of her anymore. Nothing mattered. Not after what Myron had done.

"I've put out my eyes."

I reached out to tear the glasses off her face, but she dodged my hand. "You're not blind," I said. "You saw me."

"I felt the air move."

I didn't believe her, but I didn't try again. Blind or not, Freda Graves couldn't help me. She had lifted us toward God in her mighty arms, but she was a coward in the end and we were farther from the Lord than we ever imagined. Freda Graves didn't care what happened to us. She wasn't going to stick around and take the blame for Myron and Elliot; she was going to let us fall alone, one by one.

I watched her for a long time, until she became a dot on the road. I thought of the bag she carried, and I wondered what she chose to take. I imagined all her little Christs jostling against one another: the smooth soapstone Jesus she would fondle when she stopped to rest; the frail, twisted man, arching off the Cross; the Jesus with the burning eyes who blamed us for our sins, who said, *I must die so that you may live*, who shouted, *Murderers, sinners*, who cried out, *Bring me water*. And if she spoke the truth, if she had blinded herself, she would run her fingers over the cool pages of her Bible, waiting for the words to rise off the paper and speak to her.

I remembered Freda Graves saying we had to watch out for ourselves because God wasn't looking down on us every second. He had the universe in His charge. Our lives were small, rags on sticks in the wind. She said that when Job cursed God, God answered from the whirlwind: *Does the rain have a father?* It made sense to me then but not now. I said, yes, yes, you are that father, you who demand so much. But God said, *Who has given to me, that I should repay him?* And I knew this was His final answer. In the end, even Jesus asked, "Father, why have you forsaken me?"

22

DADDY MADE himself sicker by the day. "He'll be fine by the time that scratch heals," said Dr. Ben, chuckling. "In a week or so people should have something else to talk about." The doctor laughed again, but Mother was not amused.

Father stayed home from work, lying on his bed like a man who expected to die. Half the people in town had seen him go after the big Indian, and the other half claimed they were there. He was a sooty-faced madman. His followers conveniently forgot how they'd cheered him on. Dean Macon was a lone fool.

Besides that, Arlen had put it in his head that he could have been the one hanging from his own shirt in that cell, and my father believed it in a way. I think Myron's death made him afraid of what could happen to a man who exposed himself to Miriam Deets. Father could never do what Myron had done, but he'd laid himself bare all the same, and the things he wanted from that girl took on a new meaning. He figured he'd better lie low and stay out of fate's path.

Mother didn't leave the house for days in a row. She sent me to the store for groceries. "Don't answer any questions," she said, "even if you think you know the answer."

As I wheeled the cart down the aisles I heard whispers, my father's name and my own. I kept my head down. If someone tried to speak to me, I gave the cart a push and jumped on the back for a quick ride.

Mom kept her hands busy that week. She defrosted the refrigerator and vacuumed every rug in the house. On Tuesday she started washing windows in the living room, and by Thursday she'd reached my bedroom in the attic.

The day of Myron's funeral I rode my bike to the cemetery and stood on the hill above the gravesite as they lowered his mahogany coffin into the ground. Mrs. Evans had spared no expense. I heard the coffin was lined with white satin, and the handles were solid brass. She was sorry now. She should have gone to see Myron that day, though she was disgusted by what he'd done. "I wouldn't have left him there all night," she'd said to Sheriff Wolfe the day Myron died. "Didn't he know? Didn't he know his mama would forgive him?"

Reverend Piggott's speech was brief. I suppose he didn't have much to say for a man who had committed the final sin of taking his own life. Less than a dozen mourners saw Myron buried. Caleb Wolfe peered over the very edge of the hole, holding his hat in his hand, watching the box shudder as it hit bottom. Bo Effinger wept like the overgrown child he was. Tiny Mrs. Evans wore a netted veil to hide her bloodshot eyes. When she threw the first clod of dirt, I saw her fury: she heaved it with all her pitiful strength, then turned and walked away, letting the men with shovels finish their job.

She sat in the hearse, waiting for the others, and I wanted to go to her. I wanted to say something kind and comforting, but I couldn't think of anything Mrs. Evans would believe. I hopped on my bike and coasted down the hill. *Myron loved his cats,* I said to myself. *That was something.* The road blurred in front of me.

I think Daddy might have forced himself to go back to work on Monday if Willis hadn't been hit with another tragedy. Bad luck comes in threes, folks said; the fire and the hanging just weren't enough. "The devil's got to have his due." I must have heard that a dozen times.

Arlen and Les and their kids were swimming at Moon Lake when the devil took his third delight. They saw the whole thing, watched the plane lose power and go into a dive, straight into Moon Lake at the deepest part, watched the waves suck it down, a tin toy in a whirlpool.

When Arlen busted through the front door to tell us about it, Mom and I were sitting in the living room in front of the fan with nothing on our minds but that hot wind. Daddy had just ventured down the stairs for the first time all week.

"You won't believe this," she said. "You will not." Her hair had dried in twisted strands and shook like a head full of water snakes. "I wouldn't believe it myself if I hadn't seen it with my own eyes." She saw Daddy standing at the bottom of the stairs, looking like his own ghost. "Mercy me, Dean, you are going to broil wearing that flannel robe in this heat."

"Mind your business, Arlen," he said.

"How dare you tell me to mind my business? I saved your life, Dean Macon, and I could have just kept to myself."

"Please," Mom said, "not again."

Daddy sat down on the last step and tightened the belt of his robe. I was glad he stayed clear of the wind of the fan. He had the weeklong smell of sickness. When I took him the breakfasts he didn't eat or the suppers he barely poked, I left the tray on the nightstand and slipped out of the room as fast as I could. Mom refused to sleep with him though he begged not to be left alone

in the dark. At first she pretended it was accidental: she fell asleep
in the chair in his room or on the couch downstairs; but now she
slept in Grandma Rose's room every night, and I didn't blame
her. Still, I believe I would have slept on the floor before I slept
in the bed where a woman died.

"I think it was a two-seater," Arlen said.

"What?" said Mom.

"The plane. I'm telling you about the plane we saw go down
in the lake. It was such a little thing, like a piece of folded paper.
It circled wide at first, real high, a kind of loop-the-loop. Then
it started spinning, tighter and tighter, heading straight for the
water. We all sat on the beach—laughing and clapping. We
thought it was a show. Any minute we expected the pilot would
pull back. But all of a sudden, there wasn't a sound. The engine
stopped dead. The wind stopped too, and the plane fell out of
the sky like a bird with a bullet in its belly. Dead duck. Hit the
water like a duck too, that flat splat. It sat on the surface for a
couple of seconds, bobbing; then it sank so fast I thought I'd had
a dream and none of it had happened."

I looked over at the stairs to see how my father was taking
it, but he was gone. This past week he'd gotten so quiet it scared
me—no more clomping or banging, no more yelling or snoring.
He was slipping out of the world, it seemed to me, and I wondered if you stopped hearing a person before he disappeared for
good.

"Well?" Mom said.

"Well, what?"

"The pilot, did he get out?"

"Now, this is the truly strange part, if you ask me. I swear on
my dear mother's grave I saw someone swimming away from the
wreck. Les and the boys just laughed at me. They said the crash
would have knocked him silly; he didn't have time to get out,

and even if he did, he'd be in no condition to swim from the middle of Moon Lake to the shore. They said I saw driftwood or a piece of the plane rocking on the waves, but don't you think I know the difference between a man and a piece of wood?" She laughed. "Well, sometimes it's harder to tell than others, but this time I'm sure: there were arms moving. There were legs kicking. Someone's alive and we should find him before he's not."

"Did you call the sheriff?"

"That worthless dog? He's barely moved all week. Won't wear his badge either. Sits in his office, panting from the heat. Broken-hearted over Myron Evans, I hear. You'd think they were sweethearts. Anyway, I tried to get Les to drive around the east shore, just to see, but he said I was on the verge of one of my hysterical fits and he was taking me home. He thinks I'm in my room, right this minute. He locked the door himself, thinks I'm sitting on the bed waiting for Dr. Ben to come give me a tranquilizer. That man could have been a fine horse doctor the way he can put a person to sleep. Whatever ails you, he thinks the best cure is to knock you out for a day or two. Never mind. You know how I escaped?" She was getting the giggles, and I began to think Uncle Les might have been right about that hysterical fit. "I climbed out the window and slid down the rain gutter. Me. Forty-eight years old. Spry as a girl. Young heart." She gave my arm a slap. "Bet you couldn't slide down no rain gutter, Lizzie."

"Don't give her ideas," Mom said.

"Anyway, somebody's alive," Arlen said. "I hope they find him in time."

I believed her at first, but as soon as she told us how she escaped from her room, I began to think my uncle Les had had a good idea calling the doctor. She thought Jesse was alive too—for days—even though we'd all seen his eyes flung open, wild with surprise. We'd all seen Nina breathing into him, the only one who thought to call him back, but it was hours too late. And we'd all seen the sheriff wrap him in a sheet after the doctor said, "Been dead since two o'clock." It was well past five. Still Arlen didn't believe it, and Les had to hold her back when Caleb Wolfe drove away with the soaked sheet making a dark spot on the backseat of his car. At the burial she wailed: *Take my baby out of that box.* Reverend Piggott waited for her moaning to stop before he said: *Ashes to ashes, dust to dust . . .* And then, raising his hands to God, *Weep not for him who is dead, nor bemoan him; but weep bitterly for him who goes away, for he shall return no more to see his native land.*

My grandmother dreamed of water the night she died. "I was caught in an eddy," she told my mother, "spinning in the cold river. My head was about to go under, but I woke before the water could suck me down for the last time, and I'm still alive."

Grandma Rose must have known how close she'd come to the rocks, that they waited for her on the other side of her closed eyelids. But my mother said, "Hush now, hush now," and pulled the knotted sheet from her crippled hands. When my grandmother slept at last, Mother slipped away.

In the morning, my mother found Daddy in Rose's room and almost scolded him for waking her. But he was on his knees, his head resting on her bed, quiet, so quiet. He had uncovered the old woman's feet and was staring at them. He caressed one, touched her toes with his fingertips, so tender, full of awe, as if he touched the feet of Jesus. "I had a dream," he said. "I saw her swirling in dark water, but I couldn't reach her, you see? I didn't get here in time."

·········· *23* ··········

EVERY NIGHT Daddy called me to his room. And every night he asked me to read the paper, the *Rovato Daily News,* just the parts about the plane crash. I did, despite the fact that Mother had forbidden it. She didn't like my going to his room at all. She said, "If we stay away, maybe he'll take a bath." That was all she had to say concerning my father.

For a week he'd barely eaten enough to keep a chicken alive; now he ate everything I brought him and asked for more: biscuits and honey, bacon and runny eggs that dribbled down his chin, pork chops and gravy and heaps of mashed potatoes. It seemed he thought it was his duty to eat enough for himself and for that boy from the plane who might be lost in the hills above Moon Lake.

Three days passed, and the divers still hadn't found a trace of the plane. This confirmed Father's old fear of Moon Lake, and his belief that there were trenches so deep a man might never be found. But on the fourth day the *Rovato Daily News* printed a strange letter that made Daddy weep until he heaved. That ended his days of feasting. He was so weak he let Mom take him to the bathroom. She didn't bother to shut the door, and I watched from the hallway as she stripped him, her kindness swift and silent. She washed his hair and scrubbed his back, brushed his teeth as if he were her child. When he stood, shivering and naked, he held a towel in front of himself and said, "Don't look at me."

Mother said, "I wiped the shit off my mother's ass for eight years. You think you can break my heart like she did, old man?"

Daddy sat down on the edge of the tub. "He killed her," he said. "He killed my girl."

This was the letter:

I am a friend of the boy who flew the plane into Moon Lake. He has asked me to write this letter so that you will understand and hopefully forgive what he done. Yes, he is alive, but a long way from here where you won't ever find him. There's a girl in that plane, Gloria Zykowski, and she is not alive but my friend says please get her out and send her home. He knows he did the wrong thing but there is no changing that so please don't think it will do any good to find him and punish him. It won't. That girl is dead. He rented a plane in Calgary and filed a flight plan going north but they made a wide circle south to Moon Lake where you saw them. He did not mean to kill her. He loved her. He wanted to marry her but she's only sixteen and her father said no, so my friend, Roger Skeba, that's his name, came up with this plan to fly the plane into the lake and swim away. No one would be looking for them way down in Montana. He figured it would be just like they disappeared. Looking back it's easy to see it was a stupid plan but he didn't mean any harm to her. They were going to get married and live in a town where her father would never find them. He said it was going to be like they was born again, that's what he said, but it didn't work out that way as you already know.

Sincerely yours,

A. Friend

Now, of course, a lot of people thought that letter was a hoax, some crazy kid playing the meanest kind of joke imaginable; but the next day the Rovato paper tracked down a story from a Calgary newspaper: a small plane, supposedly heading north, had disappeared on August 9. Sure enough, the missing people were Roger Skeba, twenty-four, and Gloria Zykowski, age sixteen.

We were still taking bets on it—somebody reading about the missing plane in Calgary and the crash in Moon Lake might have put the stories together for his own amusement. It was hard to believe anyone would down a plane in a lake on purpose, even a fool for love. Of course Arlen believed it and felt vindicated: that was no wood on the water.

Mom made me swear not to aggravate my father with this crazy speculation; but the next night when I took him supper, he begged me to read the paper and I couldn't refuse him any more than I could have refused a dying man a sip of water.

A dozen men were on the job now, trying to find the plane, but that kid must have had a good eye because he aimed straight for the deepest crevasse of Moon Lake. From the sky, he must have seen the place where waves darken, where green rolls over itself, a froth of white, then black. "I told you," Daddy said. "They might never find her." His eyes began to tear. The evening sun burning through the curtains made the room close and hot, but Daddy hugged himself and shivered, a chill in his blood as he sank to the frigid depths, stones tied to his feet.

"Fish big as men, peering in the windows, looking at her, I saw them. And she's cold, Lizzie, she's so cold. I saw her last night, right there." He pointed to the window. "She said, 'I can't see, Daddy, the water's too dark. The water's in my eyes.' But she stared at me. She saw me. She blames me."

My father believed his water dreams.

"Please," I said.

He pounded the bed with his fists. "No. I won't believe it. I won't believe she's dead till I see her face."

People were looking for that boy, but he'd vanished like a vapor off the water, leaving no tracks and no scent. Father wasn't the only one who took it personally: there was a fervor to the search, as if Roger Skeba had stolen each man's daughter. Some folks swore that Red Elk must have guided the boy over the mountains. Who else could have done it? The old hatred flared. But no one went after the big Indian. They'd seen him leap into a burning building and survive. They knew they didn't have a chance with such a man.

On the seventh day the men working the lake dropped a line and hit metal. It took all afternoon to get it hooked up, and it was almost dark by the time they dragged the plane off the bottom of the lake and hauled it to the shore.

But it wasn't too dark to see the girl slumped in her seat, still strapped tight by the belt. The men stared at her through the windows, their eyes wide as fish eyes, and they were afraid to open the door, and they were afraid to touch her and know her name.

We wouldn't have heard the news until the next day if Arlen hadn't come flying into the house, shouting her fool head off, the joyous bearer of bad tidings. Daddy jumped out of bed and started pulling on his pants while Mom stood in the doorway, arms crossed, shaking her head.

"Where do you think you're going?" she said.

"Looking for that boy," said my father. "We oughta lynch that boy for what he did." But already he was swaying, his muscles flaccid from days in bed. He had to sit down before he fell on his face.

"You're in no condition to chase after anyone. Besides, that boy's long gone."

"He killed my baby."

"No, Dean, some other girl, just a stranger."

But he didn't hear her. He rocked on the bed, clutching at his side. He looked as if someone were squeezing the breath out of him. "It hurts," he said, "here—and here."

Mom whispered to me, "Call Dr. Ben. Tell him to get here quick." She sat down next to Daddy and held him while I went downstairs to make the call. Arlen was halfway down the block already, going from house to house spreading the news about the girl and telling her own story over and over, saying she'd seen that boy swim away from the wreck, and if Les had only believed her for once in his life they might have caught him. Yes sir, he'd be in jail this very night, and if he'd lived till the trial, they might have seen some justice done. That poor girl.

Dr. Ben appeared at the door in twelve minutes flat. For once he understood there wasn't time to spare. By then Daddy had curled up on the bed with a pain that shot from his groin to his shoulder. Mom was sure he was having a heart attack, that's how his father had died, sprawled on the floor at fifty-two.

Dr. Ben pressed and poked, shook his head, poked again. I thought the worst, but all that feeling and head shaking only meant that Dr. Ben didn't have a clue. "It's not his appendix," he said, "I know that, and his heart sounds fine—to me." He put the stethoscope on Daddy's chest again. "Yes, yes, I think so, it's fine, just fast, that's all, from the pain, I suppose." The doctor didn't instill great confidence in me. I wondered if his hearing was good enough to listen to a man's heart. "I'll just give him a shot," he said, "a little something to get him through the night." I remembered Arlen calling Dr. Ben a horse doctor for the way he doled out tranquilizers.

"I'll check on him in the morning," the doctor said. "Call me if there's a problem." Daddy moaned; he didn't think he'd last till morning. Dr. Ben filled the syringe, jabbed my father's butt, patted Mom on the arm and said, "There now, he'll sleep straight through. Don't you worry."

But we weren't worried about him sleeping; we were worried about him waking up. The shot did its work: Daddy's fists uncurled. Still, I wasn't convinced Dr. Ben had done the right thing. I'd seen my father bring a hammer down with all his might and smash his thumb. I'd seen him cut his leg nearly to the bone. In times like those he swore until I thought his head would spin off, but he never let out a whimper as he did tonight, a helpless animal cry. That's how I knew this was different. And that's how I knew this was bad.

I grew up trusting this doctor. He was always old, his eyes filmy, his hands soft, his hair white and so thin the pink scalp showed. He'd taken care of me and Nina when we'd had everything from chicken pox to poison ivy. He stitched my head when I fell on the ice, and he did a pretty good job except that no hair ever grew in that one place behind my left ear. He was slow, but if you could just hold on, he'd come to your house no matter how late you called or how hard it was snowing. A child with a fever was the most important business in the world to him. But I didn't trust him now. Maybe he'd tipped into senility. How could he look at my father and not be afraid the man would die in the night?

Something else nagged at me and made me wonder about the doctor. I knew he couldn't do everything. I remembered Mother holding Nina's head on her lap. My sister cried and cried. She had just been to see Dr. Ben. She kept saying, "He won't do it, Mama. He won't do it."

And Mom said, "Maybe he can't."

"He won't," Nina said, "that's all. He says it's wrong."

"We're going to have to tell your father. He'll know soon enough."

"Wait, please, just a few more days. I have to think. Maybe Dr. Ben will change his mind."

He didn't change his mind, though, because in a few days Nina was gone. At the time, I didn't understand what the doctor had refused to do for her, but I knew now. He wasn't always right.

Even the tranquilizer wasn't strong enough to hold Daddy down for long. My mother and I watched as dreams tossed him. His eyes stayed closed, but his body raced up hills and down ravines, splashed across rivers in the dead of night. He was looking for that boy. He meant to kill him with his bare hands. Mother stayed to see him run, and I went to my room.

I opened my window wide, not wanting anything between me and God. I thought of Mrs. Graves. In times of trouble, she'd told us, we mustn't try to change things, only understand them. She'd understood why God gave her daughter a deformed baby, and I could see where it had led her. My mother was right about using your own head sometimes. I wasn't willing to trust God any more than Dr. Ben if it meant Daddy might die.

That night, I struck the second bargain of my life with God: I begged Him to take the pain from my father's body and put it into mine. I thought of Job with those sores from the top of his head to the soles of his feet; I knew how bad it could be. I took a deep breath and felt the first pinch in my own chest. I waited for more. I longed for it.

I closed the window halfway. The house was quiet. A breeze from the mountains felt almost cool and the leaves of the maples in the yard rustled like praying hands. I took this as a sign.

In the morning I felt a dull ache in my bowels, a throbbing in my head. I believed my prayers were answered, and that God in His infinite mercy was bringing my affliction on slowly so that I could bear it. I trotted down the hall to Daddy's room, expecting to see him sitting up in bed, smiling, his big hands folded in his lap. And I would sit beside him, suffering and holy. In my purity, I wouldn't stoop to reveal the reason for his recovery.

Mother looked up at me as I opened the door, her eyes puffy, bruised from lack of sleep. Daddy lay curled into himself, an unborn child, a fetus in a jar, his hands balled into pitiful fists. "Doctor's on his way," Mother said. I closed the door and ran back to my room.

God had no justice. I told Him I didn't care who He was. He was wrong to let the devil tamper with our lives, wrong to give him the key to our house. God closed His eyes but the devil followed on my heels. God minded the rain and the stars, spun the planets, filled the oceans. He was too busy to look into my heart. But the devil loved my human soul, my failure, my lack of faith. Right then I told him he could have me. As soon as I said the words I felt myself torn loose, a limb snapped in a storm. I would never talk to God again. He would never fill me with our secret words. I'd just be dead when I died. I wouldn't mount the wings of eagles with the chosen ones. I saw my own bones, buried by sand, unburied by wind, again and again.

My sister walked through the desert of my mind. My father rose to follow her. But I called him back and he heard me, and he turned and lived. My soul was a small price.

UNCLE LES and Arlen and Mom and I carried my father down the stairs on a makeshift stretcher. We loaded him on a mattress in the back of Dr. Ben's station wagon, and Arlen kissed him as if she didn't expect to see him again. It took an hour and a half to cover the fifty jolting miles to the hospital in Rovato Falls. Dr.

Ben had a hunch; we didn't even shoot for Missoula. The X ray showed a gallbladder full of stones. That was all. My father got a good dose of morphine and a day of peace. Twenty-four hours later they operated.

I sold my soul for this. Some of us go cheap.

24

FATHER SHOULD have recovered in a week, but there was something worse than gallstones inside him. He couldn't get over the fact that they never caught up with that boy who left his girlfriend in the plane. A. Friend wrote another letter to the *Rovato Daily News* saying Roger Skeba was already living in Nova Scotia under a new name. Other men in town were relieved just to know the boy was out of their county, but Daddy wanted to look him in the face. He wanted to see the eyes of a man who could leave a girl the way Roger Skeba did, a man who could swim to the surface knowing she didn't have a chance alone, leave her for fish to watch and strangers to find.

Daddy had shaken the feeling that the girl had Nina's face—just a dream; he knew and even said so. But he couldn't get over the idea that Nina was dead, that she could have been left anywhere—the way Gloria Zykowski was abandoned—without our ever knowing. Nothing was going to make him well until he knew for sure, one way or another.

Mother had loyalty I couldn't fathom, devotion deeper than my fragile faith had ever touched. Her feelings for my father were too simple for the burden of words, so she didn't bother to explain.

She knew we had one chance of finding Nina, and she was willing to humble herself, willing to crawl in mud if that was what it took. She asked me to go with her, and I couldn't say no, but I was afraid. I thought the man we had to visit would just as soon kill us as look at us. No matter how I judged the world, I wasn't ready to die.

Daddy watched from his window as we pulled out of the drive. "Does he know where we're going?" I said.

Mother shook her head. "He's just afraid to be alone."

The hot vinyl seat of the truck burned my bare legs. Dust swirled around us as we headed out of town on the old river road, filling the cab till our eyes teared. Mom pulled a handkerchief out of her purse. "Tie this around your mouth," she said, but I wouldn't. If my mother was willing to eat dirt, so was I.

In the distance, lakes wavered where there was no water, then burned to nothing before our eyes. Mom wasn't altogether sure where she was going. Caleb Wolfe had given us directions. "We'll know it when we see it," Mother said. "Just a shack with a privy out back. The sheriff said to look for a wide spot in Bear Creek."

I saw plenty of wide spots, but no shacks and no outhouses.

"Are you sure we're on the right road?" I said.

"How many roads are there, Lizzie?"

She was right, of course. There was only one road. After a half hour or so, Mother let the engine grumble to a stop. I thought she'd given up, but when the dirt settled, I saw an unpainted wooden cabin with broken windows.

"This is it," she said, "has to be."

"Nobody's home." I was ready to turn around; we weren't going to get any help from a man who lived in a hole like this.

"Hard to tell unless you knock." Mom patted my leg. "Come on, Lizzie, just get out of the truck with me."

As soon as our doors slammed, a hairless yellow mongrel tore around the side of the cabin, yipping and snarling, running back and forth across the path; he wouldn't let us near the hut.

The door of the cabin split open a crack, and a voice said, "Get on outa here. We don't want nothin' you got to sell."

"I'm not selling anything," Mother said. "I'm here to talk to Red Elk. Is he home?"

The door slammed. I heard the wood splinter on the hinges. "Guess he's not here," I whispered. Mom stood in the yard with a look that said she could wait, an hour, a hundred years, what was time to us? The hairless dog circled us, cowering but slinking closer every second, his ragged, chewed-up ears flat back on his head.

The door squeaked again and Mary Louise Furey stomped out on the porch. Her long hair was scraggly, streaked with gray. She wore a man's shirt, size extra-large, and her jeans were ripped and ragged at the knees.

"I know who you are, lady," she said. "I gotta gun. I don't got no sentimental feelings for children, either." I believed her. A woman that ugly wouldn't be burdened with any feminine softness. She jerked her head in the direction of the house, and I thought I saw the glint of a silver barrel, the gun propped in the doorway.

"You won't be needing a gun, Miz Furey," Mom said. "We're not here to stir up any more trouble. We just want to talk to your husband for a minute. Could you ask him?"

"Ain't here."

"When will he be back?"

"Next month."

The yellow dog seemed to grin, exposing his stained teeth and dark gums.

"You know how I could find him?" Mom said.

"No way to find him. He's trapping. Gone in the mountains."

Mother and I both knew he wasn't trapping in August. Animals have more skin than hair in summer. Mom coughed. "It's awful hot out here, Miz Furey. Could we just trouble you for a drink of water before we go?"

She pointed one thick finger toward Bear Creek. "There's a whole river, and I won't stop you from drinking as long as you do it downstream."

"Miz Furey," Mom said, "I don't believe Red Elk isn't here."

"You callin' me a liar?"

"No, ma'am. All I'm saying is I'd like you to let *him* decide whether or not he wants to talk to me."

"He did decide. He said, 'Get 'em off and don't take too long.' He said, 'Tell 'em the dog got bit by a rabid skunk.' And I'm saying it might be true. That dog don't look too good to me and he won't drink."

She was right. The yellow dog's tongue hung out of his mouth and his ribs jabbed at him from inside his mangy hide.

"You give him a message," Mother said. "You tell him my husband's sick and I want to find my girl. You tell him if he knows where she is, he can call me. I'll write down my number."

"We ain't got no phone and your husband can die and rot in hell for all we care."

"I'm sure that's true," Mom said, "but I'd appreciate it all the same if you'd just give Red Elk the message."

"I'll think on it."

The hairless creature crouched lower and lower till I thought his belly might scrape the ground. He looked more lizard than dog; I imagined him flicking his tail and skidding across the dirt, snapping my leg before I had a chance to unroot my feet.

"Come on, Lizzie," Mom said, "no sense in wasting the day."

I backed up all the way to the truck—that dog wasn't going to get a look at my hind end.

By the time we got the truck turned around, Mary Louise had disappeared, and I saw a hulk of a shadow in the doorway. Mom saw him too. She stopped and told me to keep my eyes on the road, not the house. We waited. I thought we'd fry in the cab of the truck with the sun beating down on us through the glass and the air still as the last breath in a closed box. Finally I felt him coming toward us. "The road, the road," Mother whispered, as if glancing his way might make him vanish, as if he were a spirit we had to charm.

He stuck his head in my window. I flattened myself against the seat. He smelled of sweet tobacco and wood fires, of the animal fat that greased his braid. "I'll look," he said, "but I won't promise. She's not with my boy."

He was already walking back to the house, stooping to pat the yellow dog, before Mother could thank him.

25

THE BIG Indian rolled up to the house two days later. He'd brought some girl. She hunched in her seat, and he had to yank her from the dusty blue Dodge. She shook off his grip, but he stayed close to her, just in case she tried to make a break. The girl was small and skinny, no match for the man; he could have snapped her in two with one hand. She wore tight jeans and a sleeveless blouse that might have been white before she made the long drive with Red Elk. Her peroxided hair frizzed, a head of yellow wire.

I stood with my nose pressed to the screen door, wondering why Red Elk was bringing a girl like that here. Maybe she knew Nina, I thought, but she wasn't the kind I expected my sister would choose as a friend.

Just then Mother pushed past me saying, "Oh God, my baby." I thought all the fuses in Mom's brain had finally blown. This girl looked less like Nina than I did. But my mother grabbed the stranger's hands and squeezed. Funny little sounds caught in her throat as if she were being poked from the inside. She tried to hug the girl, but the wire-haired stranger smirked and cocked her head. She knew my poor mother was crazy, but she had no sympathy.

Mom invited her up on the porch, real polite, keeping a proper distance. She said, "Lizzie, Lizzie honey, look who's here." Red Elk climbed back in his car, turned the key and revved a tired engine, pulled away and left the girl with us.

Mom said, "Come out here, Lizzie, say hello."

I pushed the screen door open with my forehead. I didn't like anything about the way that girl looked. She glanced my way now and then, throwing me half a grin, as if we were playing a nasty trick on my mother. Finally she said, "That really you, Lizzie, or is that some no-tongue ghost standing in your skin?" She giggled and I knew, but I was still pretending it couldn't be. I was five-eight; my shoes were nines. I had four inches on this girl who was supposed to be my big sister. She was Mom's height but scrawny in a sick way. The only curve on her body was a little pouch of a tummy, the kind you see on underfed children. Her hair was fried, all its golden light burned out. My heart knew, but my head kept saying the devil had put my sister's voice into this stranger's throat.

She lit a cigarette, and when she sucked on it, dozens of tiny lines creased around her lips. "What're you staring at?" she said to me.

"I'm not staring. I'm just looking."

"Well, you sure are looking *hard.*"

She squinted and peered at me the way I must have been eyeing her. I don't suppose she much liked what she saw either.

"Why don't you make us some iced tea, Liz?" Mom said. "Your sister must be parched after that drive." She turned to the girl she called Nina. "Unless you want to see your daddy right away."

"No," the girl said, "plenty of time for that. I'm dry from my throat to my knees. That damn Indian didn't stop once. Thought I'd make a run for it. Might have too, but here I am."

When I returned with the three glasses of iced tea on a tray, the girl was gone. I was relieved. This was all some middle-of-the-day dream brought on by the heat. Mom was going to wonder why I had three teas instead of two. But she didn't wonder. She said, "Nina went to freshen up." Then she whispered, "What's wrong with you, anyway? You've barely said a word to your sister."

"She doesn't look right to me."

"Maybe we're not just what she remembers either. People change."

I looked at my mother, at the gray strands twisting through her pretty dark hair in the places where a red sheen used to glow; I looked at her lined hands, but not too long, at her ankles swollen from the heat. "But we didn't go anywhere," I said.

I ran inside, past the girl, and pounded up the stairs. Locked in my room, I could hear their mumblings on the porch, Mom explaining my bad behavior, no doubt, and the girl chuckling, a gurgle that erupted with a rush and thrill like birds' wings, a flock in sudden flight.

But there were silences too, long and heavy, falling between them like blinding sheets of rain.

Later someone knocked, Mom wanting to comfort and scold me, I thought, so I unlocked the door. The girl stood there holding my glass of tea. "Thought you might be thirsty," she said.

I stared at the tea as if she'd offered me a cup of piss. "Ice is melted," I said, flopping back on the bed and pulling the pillow up on my lap.

She set the tea on my dresser. "Look," she said, "I don't blame you for not being altogether delighted to see me. Red Elk told me Daddy was dying. That's the only reason I came. Now Mama says he exaggerated the case, but I'm here all the same." She slouched from the hips and didn't use her hands to talk. I remembered Nina's hands were always flying, drawing pictures I could see in the air. "Anyway, I won't be staying long if that's what's eating you."

Fine, I thought, go back where you came from. But that didn't make me feel any better. She left without bothering to close my door and headed down the hall toward Daddy's room. For a skinny girl, she had a heavy walk. I followed. If my father fell out of his chair at the sight of a dead girl, I wanted to be there to pick him up. If he didn't recognize her, I wanted him to be able to look at me, his familiar daughter.

Not even a second passed when he didn't know her. He saw beyond her lined mouth, beyond her brassy hair and lightless eyes to a place where she was still shining, a place that made him shine just to look at her.

"Nina," he said, "my Nina."

Father didn't need me to catch him. And he wouldn't need me to read the *Rovato Daily News* or bring his supper on a tray. Nina was there, right in front of him. She was not lost or drowned. "Daddy," she said, "you look like a miserable old geezer sitting there with a blanket on your lap. I am about to melt, I swear, and there you are, bundled up like an old lady." Nina, the only one who could talk to Father that way. "Mama says you been laying up here for days with some nonsense in your head, and Dr. Ben says there's no reason for it—unless you're just plain lazy. I don't remember you being lazy, Daddy. You haven't gone soft on me, have you?"

He looked like a man about to choke.

"Speak up, old man," she said.

He swallowed hard several times and stroked his neck as if he wanted to rub the words out of himself. "Sit down," he said at last, "let your father look at you." His voice was hoarse and tender, one he never used with me because I had no power over him, and he did not need my pardon.

I slunk downstairs and sat in the kitchen with Mom. She didn't scold me, but she didn't comfort me, either.

Nina stayed with Daddy till it was almost dark. I couldn't imagine their talk. In my whole life, I'd never exchanged more than four sentences in a row with my father, except for those nights I'd read to him from the Rovato paper.

When Nina stood at last in the kitchen doorway, she wore a yellow dress, short and loose with tiny white buds. Her hair was damp and pulled into a tight ponytail. She looked almost pretty but not like my sister.

"What've you got to eat?" she said. Mom didn't seem to hear her, and Nina sat down and began rocking back in her chair. "Something wrong?" she said.

"Well?" said Mom.

"Well, what?"

"How were things with your father?"

"Fine."

"Fine? Just fine?"

"Yeah. Fine. What'd you expect? A frigging miracle? We made up, okay? I can't hang round here forever, you know. I've got a job."

"Just a few more days," Mom said, "please."

"What's to eat?"

"Cold chicken. Salad. Potatoes. What do you want?"

"Everything. Some of everything."

She meant it too. She ate four pieces of chicken, tearing the meat off the bone with her sharp little teeth. She licked her fingers and reached for another piece before the one on her plate was half gone. I fried two leftover potatoes and Nina smothered them with ketchup, then scooped them up with a spoon. Maybe she really was a devil masquerading as my sister, maybe this was how I had to pay for the bad deal I made. Devils were probably hungry all the time, I thought, and gluttonous besides.

She patted her stomach and I could see it was tight and hard, distended under her dress. "I'm gonna burst," she said. "I'm not used to eating so much. You can fry up the rest of those potatoes for breakfast, Lizzie. You do them just right." I nodded. We'd have to go to the store twice a day if she kept this up.

Nina lit a cigarette, and Mom said, "I wish you wouldn't smoke in here."

"Christ, I'm home half a day and you're already bitching."

"I'm not bitching. I'm just saying."

"Fine," Nina said.

"Never mind," said Mom.

"I said *fine*, didn't I? Don't use your long-suffering voice on me, Mama. I'm too old to fall for it." She grabbed her cigarettes and kicked the back door open, letting the screen door slap behind her.

"Her father's daughter," Mom said, "every inch."

Whose daughter am I, I thought, and almost said it, just to be cruel.

I LEFT Mother in the kitchen under the glare of the fluorescent lights. I was in no mood to keep her company. I blamed her for asking the Indian to bring this stranger home. When Nina went away again, I'd make it up to my mother, but not tonight.

I sat alone on the front porch. Crickets called from the grass, and I let them pull me toward them. I followed their voices across

the yard and down the street, one block and then another, until
I came to the vacant lot next to Myron Evans's house. A solitary
light burned in an upstairs room where Myron's mother must
have sat, alone forever to blame herself, to play that morning
backward a thousand times, back from the jail cell where her son
was hanging, the shirt unknotted and buttoned back over his thin
white chest, a chest too delicate for human eyes, the ribs too frail
for the arms of Caleb Wolfe as he cut Myron down. Myron's
mother would unravel that day, returning the chair to its place
against the wall, the safe and harmless chair, unkicked. And in
her mind, Myron's mother would see her own endless walk, head
held high, a hat with a veil to hide her eyes from the judgment
of her neighbors, those neighbors squinting through blinds, peering behind curtains, and Mrs. Evans still walking, clutching her
little blue purse. What does she care what they think? And now
she is paying Myron's bail, bringing him home. Home. *Make me
some tea before you go to bed, Myron dear, make some tea for your
mother; that's a good boy. Myron darling.*

I knelt in the tall grass, lifted my face to the night sky and
waited for stars to fall on my wet cheeks. The choir of crickets
kept up their song, a song that held neither joy nor sorrow, an
endless song for the endless nights of summer. I remembered a
time not long ago when I believed each star was a person who
was lost, that they watched us but could not come home. Myron
saw me now; the girl in the plane followed her lover across
Canada—her eyes on him never closed, never accused or forgave;
my cousin Jesse had the brightest eyes of all because he mocked
death with the knowledge he'd been taken before his time—death
had made a terrible mistake. They had stories to tell but no
mouths, only eyes. I used to lie on my back and pray for a star

to fall, for a lost child to come home, and dozens fell, showers of meteors in August, but none was Nina's star.

And now a girl with my sister's name sat in our kitchen, smoking cigarettes and cussing at my mother. The Nina I loved, the Nina I'd longed to see again, was not a star in this brilliant sky. She was not here, or anywhere that I might find her.

26

MY TWO oldest cousins seldom knocked at our door. Sometimes they yelled at me from the backyard; that was as friendly as they got. But when Justin and Marshall heard Nina was home, they came around the front like regular gentleman callers. I followed Nina to the door. Marshall wore a black T-shirt two sizes too small, sleeves rolled to the shoulders to reveal the bulge of his biceps. Sinewy blue ridges popped up along his forearms: he had good blood and plenty of it. Nina said, "Well, well," taking a long whistle of a breath between her teeth, "it's been a while." She eyed Marshall from his cowlicks to his cowboy boots.

Justin stood a step behind his younger brother, seeing how Nina stared at Marshall, her own cousin. I was embarrassed, thinking she was no better than any of the Fureys, that she'd risk having six-toed babies with heads too small for a normal brain. Justin counted the seconds, knowing he'd get half as much—if he was lucky—that she would not linger fondly to consider his spreading paunch or short legs. She would not study his face, though she might pause long enough to observe to herself that his ratty beard did a poor job of camouflaging the weak chin. So

Justin shook her hand and turned away first, chose the moment, gazing back over his shoulder to the western sky where the sun had sunk, leaving a rosy glow above the foothills. "Beautiful night," he said.

"Still too hot," said Nina, lifting the hair off the back of her neck.

Marshall said, "They're talkin' rain tomorrow or the next day."

Nina regarded him with such gratitude and wonder you would have thought Marshall was going to make the rain himself.

"It's gonna hit this fried earth and stink like steam off an iron," I said.

Nina turned on me as if I'd uttered something close to blasphemy. "I didn't know you were there," she said. Then she laughed that laugh that made boys think of cool water running down their backs. "My little sister's so quiet sometimes I think she's just a shadow that decided to stand up straight instead of lying on the ground."

"Your little sister's not so little anymore," said Marshall. Then they were all staring at me. My blouse felt too tight, as if a button might burst; a prickle of heat worked its way from the back of my knees up the inside of my thighs.

"Have a seat, boys," Nina said.

They both scrambled for the porch swing, thinking she'd sit with one of them; but when Justin got there first, Nina sat in one of the wicker chairs and Marshall took the other. "We were hoping you'd drive over to Alpena with us tonight," Justin said. "The Blue Moon has a live band. Good dancing music."

"This heat has me so sapped I can't even tolerate the *suggestion* of dancing," Nina said.

"It's air-conditioned," said Marshall. "We'll let you get nice and *cool* before we drag you on the floor." They seemed to already whirl in a private dance, Nina a planet slowly circling the sun, and Marshall one of her brilliant moons, revolving around her, throwing his pale light on her face. Justin and I were in separate orbits, far planets in a lonely sky.

Nina said, "That'll never do. Are the three of us going to hang on each other all night?" I knew just what she was thinking, dreading the idea of dividing herself between Justin and Marshall, all that wasted energy.

"We can find someone else," Marshall said.

"Yeah, who?" said Justin, his voice old and bitter, the voice of a thousand injustices, the voice of a man who has brought a girl home with him and known that his brother held her hand under the table while they all sat at dinner, known that she didn't swat him away even when his hand moved up her thigh, right there in front of everyone, unseen but understood. The brothers stared each other down, memories raging between them. They spun backward to a summer day, the year Marshall grew taller and stronger and pinned his big brother to the floor, held his arms down with his knees and laughed triumphant, thirteen and cruel.

"We know a lot of girls," Marshall said.

"*You* know a lot of girls," said Justin.

Nina went into a sulk, thinking about the girls Marshall knew.

Marshall looked around the porch desperately, as if he expected some plain, kind girl to materialize from the hot air, a watery mirage of amiability, a girl who would pity his brother enough to flatter him for one night.

That's when Marshall's glance caught the girl who still stood in the doorway, slightly slumped, a girl who was definitely plain enough if not altogether kind. "Lizzie can go with us," he said. "It'll be perfect."

"She's just a kid," Nina said. "They'll never let her in the Blue Moon."

"They let *anyone* in the Blue Moon," said Marshall.

"Mom won't let me go," I said, grateful to know she was such a sensible woman.

"We'll beg her," said Nina.

"Won't do any good," I said, rising to my full height, feeling my feet go suddenly light. I was filling with air; soon I'd float into the cobalt sky right before their amazed eyes.

"Won't do any harm to ask," said my pretty cousin. He jumped up and went inside to find my mother.

"You want to go with us?" Nina said. I was surprised she even thought to ask.

"No."

"Well, it doesn't matter to me one way or the other."

"I figured."

"It might be fun, though."

"I don't know how to dance."

"Nothing to dancing. The less you know the better. You just stop thinking and start moving."

"Why don't we just forget it?" Justin said. He'd lost all interest in dancing now that he saw his partner.

I'd been certain of Mother's answer, but she was charmed by Marshall's grin or lost in the violet haze of Nina's presence in the house, the misguided desire for my sister and me to have some fun together. Marshall promised Mom: "One of us will stay sober to drive."

"Nothing for Lizzie," Mom said.

"Wouldn't dream of it," said Marshall.

So I was going to the Blue Moon because if I refused now, no one would be dancing tonight. We'd sit on the porch for hours, too hot to talk, and Nina would blame me.

She transformed herself in minutes, splashed water on her face, changed into a denim miniskirt and a silky red top, dabbed color on her lips and cheeks. She glowed with the knowledge that men would watch her and feel hunger on full stomachs.

We wedged ourselves into the cab of the Munters' pickup. Justin drove. I sat next to him. Marshall had the other window, and Nina rode halfway up on his lap, perched on his thigh. The Blue Moon sat two miles out of Alpena, a square shack all alone at the crossroads. A blue moon on a wire stuck out of the roof and the doorway flashed with a ring of miniature Christmas lights. Even from the outside, the place seemed to vibrate, and I knew I wouldn't enjoy a minute of this night.

Inside, the air was clogged with smoke, the smell of beer and men from the mill who hadn't stopped at home to wash. The women were flashy but few, twenty years past their prime, stuffed into jeans that fit last year or the year before. They'd painted their faces white so they'd have fresh palettes for stripes of rose where they imagined cheekbones ought to be. Eyes smoldered, rimmed in black, smudged with gray shadows or green, mauve or icy blue; every pair of lips was full and dark: too red, too purple, too orange, overripe fruit, the limp petals of poppies sagging in the heat. Nina floated, a princess among them, young and firm, flawless and unlined in this dim light, her blond hair almost believable. Men turned as we wove our way up the bar; some leaned off their stools, slightly, touching her as she passed, brushing up close to her, accidentally, as if her skin were medicine, a salve to heal all their old wounds, as if this girl were a mystical oily fish swimming up against them. *What's your name, pretty girl?* Nina, Nina. *Pretty girl, pretty baby. Baby. Hope these are your brothers. Baby.*

We found a corner table, barely big enough for our elbows. The band twanged out a song about a man who killed his unfaithful wife. Justin hopped up to the bar to buy a round, and Marshall tugged Nina onto the center of the dance floor, under the throbbing lights where every man in the place could see her and envy him. How many pretty women were there in this county anyway? Women watched her too. I expected jealousy, hands that itched to tear her yellow hair out by the roots, but their glances were confused, their looks wavered between pity and desire, as if they knew how little time she had, as if they were almost glad to be done with all of that so there was nothing left to lose. Men never think that way. They don't worry about all the days a woman lives outside the circle of beauty. They want her in those hours of perfection. The future is of limited importance. The morning is a distant country. Even ugly men think they deserve a pretty woman; they take her as their due. But homely women know they'll never lay their hands on the bare chest of a beautiful man.

Justin returned with two beers in each hand. "I'm not drinking," I said.

"I am," he said. "I'm drinking plenty. You just set that beer in front of you till I'm ready."

Nina and Marshall rocked straight through four tunes, songs about men drinking and gambling too much, forgetting what town they were in, being saved or being drowned by a woman, lying to her either way to get free again and back on the road, lonely as it was, the only life they knew or could bear to live. There were variations, I suppose, silver-tongued devils and regret, a woman who left before the man had a chance to lie because she found the wedding ring he'd hidden in his wallet. She split with his cash and left the ring on top of the wallet so he'd understand why she took her payment. Every woman's a whore in the end; the singer belted out the moral of the song. I think Justin and I were the only ones in the place listening to the words; everyone else was having too good a time to trouble with details. Nina held on to Marshall's hands and leaned back, twirling round and round, a wild circle, a dizzy spiral.

They plopped down at the table and guzzled their beers. "Guess you didn't need time to *cool* down after all," Justin said, but Nina was blank, already forgetting that conversation on the porch, that long-ago talk more than an hour in her past. What did it matter? Now she was free, away from her parents' house. Everything there faded to a blur: her sick father, his rheumy eyes, his damp hands, his bony ribs protruding; her mother standing on the porch, twisting a Kleenex till it came apart in her hands, dropping it on the porch when she waved good-bye, stooping, slowly—much too slowly—to pick it up. Yes, all that was blotted out beneath these sallow lights. Nina pulled out a cigarette and Marshall fumbled to light it; he was a poor gentleman, unpracticed and deliberate, but Nina eased his awkwardness by steadying his hand with her own as he held the match.

Marshall shoved his way to the bar for a second round. He brought four beers, then made a second trip to fetch three shots of Jack Daniel's.

"Which one of you is going to stay sober to drive?" I said, and they all laughed.

Marshall said, "Lizzie's not having a good time, are you, Liz?" He flashed that grin but did not enchant me. His teeth were crooked, too big for his mouth; his gums were stained from chewing tobacco.

Nina said, "My sister's never had a good time."

I thought, How would you know what I've done in my life? Where have you been for the past five years? And I hated her for the way she meant it, and for the ways she might be right.

Marshall asked me to dance, but I couldn't. I said my shoes were nailed to the floor, and he chuckled as if I'd made a joke.

Justin tried to fondle my leg, drawing circles on my skin with one finger. I stamped on his toes.

"Bitch," he hissed. Then he moved close enough to spit words in my ear that Nina and Marshall wouldn't hear. "You're too homely to be choosy," he said.

I knew that was true, but I figured even an ordinary girl has the right to choose nothing at all.

Justin talked Nina into giving him one chance. I saw how she suffered. Her legs had turned sluggish. Her head rolled back, tired, tired, the longest song she'd ever heard. She made believe she was all alone out there, eyes closed, swaying in her own dark room. A big man with a red beard cut in on Justin and he had to sit down, but Nina didn't like this partner either. She headed back to the table as soon as the music stopped.

There was a third round and a fourth, whiskey and beer, always one extra draft for Justin. He'd stopped asking Nina to dance: when he wanted her, he yanked her to her feet. After the fourth round, she didn't look as if she cared whether she danced with Justin or Marshall or some stubby cowboy. One brother was as good as the other, and strangers were no worse. All of them had rank breath, all of them whispered obscenities. If they pressed their hips into hers, she let them; if they put their hands too low on her back and their fingers inched toward her butt, she let them do that too. But she stopped giggling and she stopped smiling. She lit up a new cigarette before the last one was snubbed out. She tossed back her whiskey in one gulp, wincing as she slammed the shot glass on the table. Marshall quit drinking and looked around the room for a woman who was less drunk than Nina and not too ugly. He was tired of my sister, her cigarettes and sloppy talk. Men stopped cruising our corner. Justin torched a pack of matches and didn't drop it in the ashtray till the flames reached his fingers.

The band wailed on: a preacher man got carried away with a choir girl and had to leave town when she got big and her daddy went crazy; a woman in Wyoming went looking for her husband and found him four years later in Tennessee, with a new wife and three kids.

"YOU DRIVE," Justin said to Marshall as we careened out of the Blue Moon. Marshall was a long ways from being sober but he was downright holy in comparison with his brother. Justin clung to Nina and lurched toward a truck that wasn't his, wasn't even the right color.

Marshall steered him in the right direction. "Yeah, I'll drive," he said, his tone more self-righteous than a man in his condition deserved to use on anyone. Nina sat between the boys and I sat smashed against the door. Marshall rammed the truck into reverse, lifting his foot off the clutch before we'd slipped into gear; we might have been jolted off the seat if we hadn't been crammed in so tight.

Once we hit the main road and Nina's drunkenness was a private matter, Marshall seemed to like her well enough again. We plowed through the thick night. As soon as he jerked us into fourth, Marshall put his free hand on Nina's thigh. He didn't bother being sneaky, starting at the knee and working up: he clawed at her skirt and grabbed the inside of her leg barely an inch from her crotch. A skunk had just been hit. The smell filled the cab and stayed with us all the way home. Justin pawed Nina from the other side and sucked at her neck. I heard a slurping noise, bits of flesh being pulled into his mouth. I wondered how he felt, pawing this drunken woman, this Nina who was once a girl he would not dare to touch, remembering the days when putting his tongue to her flesh would have been sacred or profane.

Surely this was not how he envisioned it in those dark hours of dreaming, those bleak early mornings when he woke, his sheets damp, his belly sticky. Surely in those dreams she kissed him back, tenderly or viciously, even fury was better than this numb response, these closed eyes, this slack mouth, like Jesse's mouth, watery and full of death. Surely her legs opened slowly, waves opening and closing around him, enveloping his body, lapping his thighs, warm, not the lake, not like that at all, a pool up the shore, water trapped behind a rock where the sun beat down on it all day till it was almost hot. But now, in the truck, the girl's legs twitched where he touched her, neither welcoming nor forbidding, the twitch of a drugged animal, a dog on its way down, a sick pig, his favorite one.

IT WAS well past midnight when we turned into my cousins' drive. The truck was still a truck and the footmen hadn't turned to mice. But the beautiful girl was in tatters. Our bodies seemed to expand as soon as I opened the door of the truck, and suddenly there was no room for me on the seat. I nearly fell on my butt but caught the handle in time.

The boys pulled Nina out. I wanted to run inside, but I was afraid they wouldn't walk my sister to the door. She might sleep where she fell—in the gravel of their driveway or the pricker plants in their unmowed lawn.

Justin kept kissing her, sucking her mouth into his. Marshall took his turn too, and their hands never stopped moving, up and down her body; they rolled her between them, and I watched, too dumb to speak, too scared to take her hand and lead her away. I thought of Lewis Champeaux, how I'd watched the other boys steal his pants. I could have helped him sooner, spared him his humiliation. But I didn't speak—not then, not now. I told myself this was different. The Indian boy was afraid. But Nina didn't care.

I like to think I would have stopped my cousins eventually. But I can't be certain. I might have turned my back on my sister, marched across the yard, and climbed the stairs of my dark house. I might have pulled the covers over my head and hidden in the hot tent of my bed, where I could pretend I didn't know what the boys had planned. I'd tell myself they wouldn't fling her into the truck bed. I'd hum louder and louder, drowning her muffled cries, blotting out the image of their dirty hands over her mouth.

But I didn't have to face my own cowardice. Nina saved herself. Her limp body stiffened; her back arched. She whirled. Vomit sprayed against the truck, splattering yellow bile on the three of them. Marshall and Justin were too stunned to miss the first heave; but by the time she arched again, they were halfway to the house. Nina and I squatted in the drive, and I held her from behind while this night and countless others like it were torn out of her. She spewed them out on the sharp stones that cut into her knees. She retched herself dry and still she heaved till she was too weak to stand. I made her drape one arm over my shoulder and clutched her wrist tight. I wrapped my other arm around her waist and lugged her home.

She collapsed on the couch and drew her knees up to her chest. I wiped the vomit from the corners of her mouth, washed the dirt from her legs, and covered her with a sheet. As I climbed the stairs, I felt her weight still on my shoulders.

27

I WOKE to the smell. My fingers revealed me: mute witness, betraying sister. Just once, I wanted to believe in something enough to risk my life; I wanted to be as brave as Red Elk, ready to leap into flames to save the life of a foolish boy. The big Indian's faith in himself kept him alive. I wanted to love someone enough to plunge a plane into a lake. But I would not leave her. I would swim down and down into the dark trench and free her.

I was afraid to face Nina, to see her on the couch, her red silk blouse encrusted with spittle, her glance an accusation I deserved. And later her steady stare would demand the whole truth. Perhaps some small piece of the night had lodged in her brain, a shard of glass; she would recall my silence, the way I inched backward, ready to turn and flee. When she saw me today, the glass might splinter in her skull, and the night would pierce her a hundred times.

But Nina was not twisted in the sheet. She sat in the kitchen, smoking. "I've been waiting for you," she said. "I thought you might fry up some more of those fine potatoes." She was a devil to be hungry after last night. She'd washed and changed her clothes. Even Nina couldn't have ignored the bitter taste in her mouth, but perhaps she was more accustomed to it than I imagined.

My shame boiled up and turned to rage. What if I had left her? What difference would it make to a girl who could forget anything—a girl who could leave home for five years and not weep or plead for our forgiveness? She cut her own head from our photographs. She left us to imagine her death day after day. And still she was not sorry.

NINA COULDN'T be satisfied. For breakfast she had three scrambled eggs, four slices of toast and the rest of those potatoes swimming in ketchup. She was ready for lunch at eleven and dinner at four. That gave her time for an extra meal at the end of the day. After each meal she fell asleep: on the porch swing, on the couch, in the bathroom, at the kitchen table. But she refused to lie down on a bed.

Somehow she managed to get Daddy out of his chair, and she walked him up and down the hall twenty times or more. By evening she had persuaded him to come downstairs. She brought him out on the porch to trim his hair. It was the only time in his life I'd known him to let someone else take a pair of scissors to his head. Their chatter rolled in through the screen door, mumbling through the living room. Nina said, "I never noticed what big ears you have." And Father answered, "The better to hear you." Their laughter bubbled into the kitchen, where Mother and I peeled vegetables in silence.

I saw Nina as a child of twelve, standing on Daddy's feet as he waltzed her around the room. They bumped into chairs, shook the cabinet of china. I had to dodge them, and Mother ran from the kitchen with a spatula still in her hand. She slapped at the air

and told them to stop that nonsense before they broke her teacups.
But they didn't stop. They giggled just as they did now.
Everything amused them today. "Oh dear," Nina said, "I nicked
you, Daddy." And he laughed. I will never understand why.
Then they whispered. Who knows what they said.

"It's hot today."

"Yes."

"You have such coarse hair, Daddy."

"Not like yours."

"Mine's so dry it breaks off when I brush it."

"You used to have such pretty hair."

"Yes."

"Bound to break sooner or later."

"My hair?"

"The weather."

Perhaps that was all they said. But why, why did they have
to whisper?

IT WAS on the fourth day that Nina had another visitor, "another
gentleman caller," Mom said as she and Nina and I sat on the
porch, and I thought of my gentleman cousins.

At first I believed the boy in the yellow Volkswagen across
the street was Coe Carson, and I sat smug, thinking how surprised
they'd be when they realized a boy was calling on me, not Nina.
But this was a foolish thought. No boy had ever knocked on my
door. No lover had thrown gravel at my window or sung to me
in the dark.

My mistake was simple enough. The boy in the car was Rafe
Carson, Coe's older brother, one of those boys in the trees during
the long summer before Nina ran away, the boy in the woodshed
with his hand stuck down Nina's bra, one of the dozen or so she

left behind to pine for her, to imagine her golden hair in a hundred damp and hopeless dreams.

Rafe was almost as skinny as Coe, saved only by the fact that he wasn't as tall. His red hair was cropped close to his skull. His cheek and chin showed a sparse fuzz, a futile attempt to grow a beard. He wore a white T-shirt, yellowed at the pits, and faded jeans.

Mom tried to scoot me inside, but I sat on the porch swing, smack in the middle, staring at the two wicker chairs. If at some later time Rafe and Nina decided they wanted to sit together, they'd have to ask me to move my ass. Nina shot me a look, an old look that spun through the years to a time when I would have done anything to please her—would have stood on my head in a corner till my face turned the color of a ripe tomato if it would make her happy. That look had sent me scuttling to my room night after night so she could be alone with some boy or another, but this time I just looked back at her with the blank eyes of a cow.

"Hey there," said Rafe, putting his foot on the bottom step and waiting for an invitation.

"Hi yourself," said Nina. She twisted a brassy curl around her finger.

"I heard you were back," Rafe said, shading his face with his hand.

"Yeah, I'm back."

"How long you staying?"

"Long as I want."

"Mind if I get out of the sun?"

"I don't mind," she said.

He took the chair to Nina's right, giving her a quick, sideways glance.

She rubbed her bare arms, and Rafe stared, his longing simple:

he wanted nothing more than to touch those arms. Nina said, "Lizzie, honey, I'm about to drop from this heat. Be a sweet girl and get me a cool rag."

I knew her, but how could I refuse?

When I returned with the damp cloth, it was just as I expected: Nina had moved to the swing. But Rafe still sat rigid in his chair.

Nina reached for the rag and read my mind, moving one leg onto the swing so I couldn't plop down with her. I had to take the chair next to Rafe, bound like him to watch Nina wash her throat and the back of her neck. She dabbed at her arms. Rafe Carson had to sit on his hands to keep himself from begging her to let him wash her knees. She made each part of her body precious, then closed her eyes, oblivious to the suffering she caused this boy.

"I can't remember a time I was ever this hot," she said. "It wasn't this hot when we were growing up, was it, Rafe?"

"No, ma'am," he said, "it wasn't."

"Ma'am? Ma'am? What am I, your mama? Or some old woman on the street?" She leaned forward and the neck of her dress gaped, exposing a smooth white place the sun hadn't touched.

"I didn't mean that. I didn't mean that at all. You're still the prettiest girl who ever lived in this town."

"That's not saying much."

"In this county."

"Thanks again. I feel like I've just been crowned Hog Queen at the state fair."

Rafe Carson squirmed, thinking through his short list of compliments, tortured by his lack of words. "You know what I'm trying to say."

"I'm tired of guessing what boys mean." She stretched out on the porch swing; her eyes were slats. I wanted to warn Rafe that he'd better keep talking because Nina was apt to fall asleep the minute she got comfortable.

"I'm no good at talking to girls."

"Well, it's time you learned."

"I haven't had much practice."

"What have you been doing for five years, living in a hole?"

"Something like that."

"A monastery?"

"Not exactly."

"Join the Army?"

"They wouldn't take me."

Nina sat up straight, truly looking at Rafe Carson for the first time. "They let anybody in the Army. Unless he's some kind of cripple. Are you deformed, boy?" Something in her tone made me think she liked the idea and wouldn't mind seeing a humpback or a clubfoot for herself.

"I've been in prison."

"You mean that boys' school, that country club for delinquents? That was ages ago. I didn't think they even put stuff like that on your record."

"They didn't. I've been in a real prison. Over in Washington. Three years for armed robbery."

"Three years? That's all?"

"Well, the gun wasn't loaded. Actually it wasn't even a real gun, but the kid thought it was, crapped his pants, literally, said so in court. That's why they gave me three years if you want to know the truth, three years for scaring the shit out of some pimple-faced kid."

"Another gas station?"

"Seven-Eleven."

"How much you get?"

"Nothing. Damn fool wouldn't open the register. He was

gonna die for minimum wage. How do you find a kid like that? Fifty lousy bucks, that's all I wanted."

"What for?"

"I was trying to get across the border before anybody got the bright idea of drafting me."

"Why'd you go to Washington? You could have *walked* to Canada from here."

"I had to throw my father off my trail. He wanted me to enlist. He would have tracked me all the way to the Northwest Territories if he knew how yellow I was. He'd rather kill me with his own hands than have people in this town call one of his boys a coward."

"He'd rather have a convict than a coward?"

"Yeah, he would—as long as I don't let on I didn't have a real gun."

"Well, you got out of it," Nina said. "You didn't have to go to Canada or Vietnam."

"What a lucky guy."

"I'd say so."

"I missed a lot. I'm still missing it." He stood up and paced. His face was dry and red, and he couldn't look at Nina. "I feel like I got my arms cut off. You don't know what it's like, being locked up, looking at men every minute, never seeing a woman, never being alone. And then one day you're staring at yourself in the mirror and you see there's some guy behind you, and he's watching you too because you're skinny and the youngest one on the block, and he knows he can have you. He puts his hand on your shoulder, moves it down your spine. And you let him."

Mom stood behind the screen door with a pitcher of lemonade and three glasses on a tray. Rafe yelled at her through the screen, "Do you know what I'm telling you?"

Mom said, "How about some nice lemonade?"

"No," Rafe said, collecting himself, remembering his manners, "no, thank you, ma'am."

"This heat can make a person crazy if you don't get enough to drink."

Rafe shook his head. This had nothing to do with the heat. As he walked away I imagined his shirt sleeves hung empty, flapping in the hot wind.

"That poor boy," Mom said, pouring the lemonade. "I had no idea."

Nina grunted and slumped down on the swing. She leaned back. Before I'd finished my drink, her lips fluttered and she snored like an old man.

"It's all those cigarettes," Mom said. "I don't think that girl can breathe right anymore."

I didn't care if she could breathe or not. I thought there was something more seriously wrong with her than too much smoke if she could fall asleep after a man told her he felt as if he had no arms. A man with no arms can't hold a woman. A man with no arms can't break his fall.

THAT NIGHT Daddy came downstairs for dinner—the first meal he'd had at the table since the night of the fire. He even dressed himself, but his pants had grown baggy and he had to cinch his belt up two notches. His blond hair was beautiful, combed back, trimmed perfectly over his big ears, delicately curved on the neck. Mother set an extra place for him and acted as if this were nothing unusual. Nina sat beside Daddy. She let him hold her hand while he said grace, the old grace that he hadn't said since we were children: "Father, we thank thee for these mercies. . . ."

Arlen showed up just as we finished supper. "Well, I'll be damned," she said. "Lazarus has risen. A walking miracle. No, I stand corrected, a *sitting* miracle." She cackled, and I thought this might send my father skittering back up the stairs to hide in his room for another three weeks, but Nina truly had worked a miracle.

"How are you, Arlen?" Dad said, as if he'd seen her just yesterday.

"Better than you. You look like a starved rat."

"How're Les and the kids?" Dad said, not taking the bait.

"Fine, they're fine." For once Arlen was short on words.

Nina said, "What have you got there, Arlen?"

"Oh, this. I almost forgot. I made pies today, apple. Thought you might like one."

"Course we would," said Nina.

I could see it now. Nina would wolf down half the pie and fall asleep with her head on the kitchen table.

That's just how it happened too, except that she didn't eat quite half the pie because Daddy was chewing even faster than she could. Later he shuffled out to the porch. Weeks in bed had made him lame; he'd spend a month shaking old age out of his legs. He said he smelled the wind changing. We were in for a cool night. But in the kitchen where Mom and I cleared dishes around the sleeping girl, the air was close and hot.

I heard the lone coo of an owl. It reminded me of the old days when there were always boys whistling in the grass. But tonight's cries went unanswered; the girl slept, the food in her stomach heavy as a drug, a drug that kept her safe from the story a boy with no arms wanted to tell.

28

MOM AND I sat on the back steps in the dark. My father was right: the wind was changing, blowing the stars out of the night, leaving the sky heavy with yellow fog. In the kitchen, Nina cried out. I ran inside and flicked on the light. She jerked straight up in her seat as if to pretend she hadn't been out cold for the past three hours. We heard Daddy limping up the stairs, on his way to bed.

"I guess he's better," Nina said.

Mom was right behind me. "Because of you," she said.

"All I did was be alive."

"That's no small thing."

Nina stretched her arms over her head. "Is there any more of that pie?"

"Your father finished it." Mom reached for Nina's hand, but Nina stood up to shake off sleep and the dream that had made her yell.

"I hope you can forgive him," Mom said.

"For eating the pie?"

"For what he did before."

"You mean for telling me he never wanted to see my face again? You mean for nearly breaking my jaw? You mean for calling me a piece of trash and a worthless slut and no daughter of his from that day forward?"

Mom nodded, ashamed, as if they were her words, not my father's.

"Hell," Nina said, "that was nothing. I don't blame him. I could have let him cool down for a month or two and shown up on your doorstep. With my belly the way it was, he never would have hit me. I chose my life. Nobody ruined me and nobody's gonna save me, either. Shit, I bet Rafe Carson blames his father for wrecking his life, making him run away. But Rafe didn't have to steal no fifty dollars. He could have earned it in a week. He was looking for an easy way and you can see where it got him."

"What did happen after you left here?" Mom said.

Nina hummed a snatch of song. "I think it's cooler tonight," she said. "Smells like rain." She twirled on her toes. "Wouldn't that be something? Rain. Now, *that* would be a miracle."

"Please," Mom said, "tell me."

Nina leaned against the stove, sighing like a girl who'd been dancing all night. "Don't make me think of all that now."

"But you'll leave—"

"Yes, in the morning."

"—and I won't know anything about you. You've been wandering around in my head for five years, Nina, like some dead girl who can't rest."

Nina fell into her chair. "I'm not dead, Mama, but sometimes I'm afraid to lie down. I can't sleep in a bed without it getting narrow in my dreams, without a lid slamming shut on me. I can't hear a sound—my ears are full of water. I see Jesse. Remember how white he was? Like he didn't have any blood." She held out her hands, exposing the underside of her forearms. "Look at me," she said. "Look how pale I am." And it was true. That skin was as white as the underside of a fish.

The girl in the airplane pressed her face up to the glass, stunned and silent, awed by her own death. Even Myron Evans who chose his time must have been startled when it finally happened. He didn't know death would be a hard slap, a boot in the back, knocking him off the chair—no, he was hoping death had arms to hold him, fingers to smooth his hair, lips to kiss his eyes closed, good-night for the last time.

Nina put her head down on the table. "No," Mom said, shaking her, "you can't sleep now. You have to tell me."

"Tell you what?" She sounded groggy already. She was afraid of her dreams, and still she longed for them.

"What happened to Billy? What happened to the baby?"

"Oh *that,* that was so long ago." She looked around the room as if she expected someone to walk in the door and tell the story for her. "Lizzie," she said, "could you make your old sister some tea?" I nodded and she smiled at me as if I'd just done her a great kindness. Her gratitude mocked me. All these days I'd been wishing she would go away and leave me with my visions of my sister, and the only thing she wanted from me was a cup of tea.

"Why did you go with that boy?"

"He touched me right."

"That's no reason."

"It was to me. The boys before Billy made me feel like a heap of damp ground. They couldn't wait to get their hands under my clothes, but I could have been anybody in the dark—I could have been a pig tied down tight for all they cared. Not Billy. He had a way with his hands. Once a wild canary landed in his palm, and his fingers closed around her so slow that she was stunned and didn't try to fly away. He called me his yellow bird. He said my heart whispered to his hand. He said if I left with him, he'd fill my house with birds—owls to coo us to sleep, peacocks to parade in the yard, a rooster to wake us at dawn. But I woke one day and realized a house of birds has walls of feathers that fly away the first time the wind blows. I woke up on the reservation and saw my house just as it was: a plywood shack with a roof of corrugated tin where the birds never landed, where the sound of rain on metal could make you go mad. Nobody sang to me, but my whole body was awake with sound, and the sound was my baby's cry. I heard it so deep I thought my bones were sobbing.

"Billy rubbed my breast with his callused fingers, telling me, 'Amos is awake,' as if I didn't know. He poked at me, using a touch he'd learned somewhere else with a woman who liked it hard and fast, good-night. Those fingers had forgotten how to tempt birds. That palm could have rested flat on my chest without feeling the beat of my heart. He was bored with me. He'd already found some dark-skinned lady who made him laugh and didn't expect too much. This was February, the first year. I already saw myself leaving."

The teapot whistled and I leaped out of my chair. Nina snorted. "Everybody has to answer to something," she said. I put the pot and the cups on the table, and Nina kept talking. "I told Billy I couldn't stand that filthy crook in the road they called a town, that rathole he called a house. I wanted curtains to hang in my windows instead of sheets. I wanted a car that ran instead of a rusty pickup with no tires, sunk in the mud of our yard. I wanted to live where people painted their houses white and yellow and gray instead of turquoise and flaming pink. I never wanted to see another trailer turned into a house again. I said we were moving to Missoula to live like decent people. 'Like white people,' he said, 'isn't that what you mean?' And I said, 'Yeah, what's wrong with that?' And he said, 'You'll see.'

"So we did move, stayed almost a year, but Billy couldn't keep a job. He said folks didn't trust Indians; I said he made his own misery expecting people to treat him wrong.

"One night I was doing the dishes. Billy patted me on the butt and said, 'I'm goin' out for cigarettes—you need anything?' 'Milk,' I said, 'for Amos.' He was gone an hour and I started to wonder. Sometimes the neighborhood kids waited in the alley and ran at him with sticks.

"There was only one other explanation. I'll tell you the truth: I wanted to believe he'd been beaten more than I wanted to believe he'd left me that way, with a pat and a lie. Things weren't too bad by then. He'd had the same job for two months. We'd saved nearly fifty dollars. He didn't like heaving garbage, but nobody gave him a bad time. 'All garbage men look dirty,' he said, 'so they don't notice me. And there's nothing to steal.'

"By midnight, I knew Billy was on his way back to the reservation. I planned to go after him in the morning, drag him home by his hair if I had to, but a storm whipped through the night and the snow piled up all the next day. Frozen waves blew across the road. The wind found every crack in the apartment. I thought I'd just lie down and let the bed fill up with snow. Amos and I crawled under the blankets, made a tent for ourselves and waited. I needed the damn milk. All I had was a cup of powder; it wouldn't last long, and Amos didn't like it. At least Billy could have brought the milk before he split."

Nina looked at the screen door; a cool breeze filled the room. "There it is," she said, "the rain." It took me longer to hear it. At first it was no louder than leaves rubbing together in the dark, as hard to hear as your own heart. But in a flash the sky heaved and broke and poured out all the rain held back through the long hot days of August. Rain pummeled the side of the house with a thousand furious fists, and Nina said, "At last."

"So you didn't go after him," Mom said.

"As soon as the blizzard died down, Billy's boss was looking for him. We didn't have a phone, so he called Mrs. Clate, the landlady. That fat bitch came banging. She said, 'I know your husband's gone—if he is your husband—and I say good riddance, but don't get the idea I'm running some kind of charity home here. You pay the rent like everybody else or you're out on your ass. I rented to you against my better judgment, but don't think there aren't limits to my kindness.' Amos sat in the middle of the floor. He was barely a year old, but he burst into a full-bellied scream just like he understood every word, just like he saw the two of us on our butts in the snow. Mrs. Clate poked her head inside and said, 'I'm sick of his squallin'. You keep him quiet or you're out whether you have the rent or not.' I slammed the door so fast I almost caught her nose. 'Against her better judgment.'

"We stashed our money in a tin under the tea bags. I'd been afraid to look. Now I prayed he hadn't left me dry. We paid Mrs. Clate by the week: on Monday, I'd need twenty dollars. I bolted the door and walked to the cupboard, picking Amos up on the way and bouncing him on my hip. I was in no hurry. The money was there or it wasn't. Running and digging weren't going to change anything. I dumped the tin on the table. Billy had left me nine tea bags and forty-seven dollars. 'Look, Amos,' I said, waving a five-dollar bill in front of his nose, 'we've got two weeks, as long as we don't eat much.' Something about that struck me funny and I started giggling. I got cackling and rocking so hard I couldn't stop. Then all of a sudden I was crying and Amos was crying too and we sat there for a long time, rocking ourselves and wailing at the ceiling.

"I thought, I don't know how to do a damn thing. Best job I could get would be slapping mayonnaise on buns in a burger joint. By the time I paid somebody to watch Amos, I might as well stay home. So I paid the rent early and told Mrs. Clate I'd be back in a couple of days. She took my money, but she didn't believe me.

"I strapped Amos to my chest under my coat and hitched down to the reservation. Billy wasn't hard to find. I knew he'd be with a woman. I asked around. When I knocked on his door, he acted like he'd been expecting me. He told me the woman's name was Rowena and she was his cousin, and I said, 'Yeah, I know,' like I believed him. She was twice my size and didn't try to hide it. She wore a down vest over a flannel shirt. The woman looked old enough to be Billy's mama. I figured that's what he saw in her, some kind of mama love I couldn't touch. I knew there was no sense in begging. How could I compete with a six-foot-tall Indian with a punched-in nose and a barrel chest? I was a wild canary and she was a buffalo. A man has to choose. I told him, 'You wanna live down here, fine with me, but you're gonna have to take Amos because there's no way I can make it on my own with some kid hanging on my rear end.' Amos was already on the floor, playing with Rowena's boys. She had three of her own plus one that belonged to her fifteen-year-old daughter. Billy looked from me to Rowena and back again, thinking I'd put a wire cage over his head. But Rowena set us all free. She laid her hand on my shoulder. Her touch surprised me—something flowed through that hand, some kind of healing in the heat of her blood, and I knew why Billy loved her. She said, 'He can stay.' With three words, a woman I didn't know gave my life back to me."

"You left him?" Mother said. The rain streamed down the windowpanes in thick rivulets. "You left your baby?"

"Maybe it would have been different if I'd found Billy right away. The snow blinded me. But when the wind died down, I saw what I had to do. We never did get around to getting married, so all I had to do was shake hands and leave."

"But Amos—you can't shake hands over a child's life."

"Oh I've heard all this," Nina snapped. "I'm some kind of unnatural mother, some kind of monster who's deformed on the inside. Listen, I was nineteen years old; I had twenty-seven dollars and no job. I tell you, women with warm houses and cupboards full of soup and beans, women with husbands who come home at the end of every week with a paycheck, women like that, like you, Mama, have the luxury of loving their children in a *natural* way. Women like me aren't so lucky. Love to us is leftover scraps, bits of rags, other people's garbage. How much love do you think a woman has when there's no money and no food, when the baby's howling his head off and the landlady is banging a broom on her floor so hard your ceiling rattles?"

"We would have taken him—our own grandchild."

Nina pounded her fists on the table. "No, Mama. Can't you see? Look in the mirror some night and see how tired my life has made you already. If I'd brought Amos here, I would have had to stay too. What kind of life would that be for any of us?"

"What kind of life do you have now?" My mother's voice was cool and hard as a polished stone.

"My own life," Nina said. "My own life." And her voice turned to water, fast and clear, rolling over every rock in her way. "I don't mean to offend you by talking this way, Mama, but I can't live my life the way you lived yours—doing things for Daddy, doing things for us, never taking one sweet breath that was just for you. When I hear about women who run away and leave their families, I'm not surprised. You know what surprises me? It surprises me when any woman stays. I look at

you, Mama, and I wonder why you don't hate us all. What did
any of us do for you that was half what you did for us?"

The rain beat out a steady answer: nothing.

Mother cradled her head in her hands. "I have hated you," she
said, "all of you. But it goes away if you can just wait." Her voice
was so low I had to look at her to be sure her lips moved.

"How many years?" Nina said. "How many years do you have
to wait, Mama?"

I closed my eyes. Nina threw a merciless light on us. I couldn't
bear to see our faces in that glare. I thought of the reservation
and the dark highway, a dead dog in the ditch. I saw my mother
pressed up against the sweaty body of a stranger, the trucker who
listened, and I knew how badly she wanted to keep driving north.

The sky tore above us. A rip of thunder exploded in the
distance. Already it seemed the rain had fallen forever, that the
words in this room had made it unstoppable.

My mother spoke from the hollow box of her years. "Tell me
about this life you call your own, Nina."

"I live in a basement, two rooms, fifteen a week. I don't mind
the dark. I tend bar down the street. It's better than waitressing.
I did that for a while. When you're behind the bar, some guy
can grab your hand but he can't grab your ass. It's just temporary,
fast money till I find something better. Rowena said the problem
with me is that I can't imagine my life. She says I only saw three
choices in this town: get married quick, sling slop out at the truck
stop, or sell lipstick at the five-and-dime. Rowena thought up her
whole life and then made it happen. She left the oldest girl with
her mama and went to college. Now she's back on the reservation
teaching school. She says she got tired of white women full of
their own good deeds coming to the reservation and running
away after the first hard winter, after the first drunken suitor
banged on her door. She said those kids needed someone to

admire, someone who looked like them, someone they'd see around town. She says she always dreamed of knowing things worth telling other people and now she does. I never dreamed anything like that for myself. I let my life fall on me. Everything I've ever done was an accident. Did you imagine your life, Mama?"

"No."

"I didn't think so."

"My mother got sick and my father was long gone. I had to take a job. Like you say, a girl in this town doesn't have a lot of options. So I filed papers at the mill. I met your father. He was the only man in town willing to take me and Mother both, so I figured I could learn to love him. Your grandmother did love him. She begged me to marry him. She wanted to know somebody was going to be there to look after me when she was gone. 'Put your old mother's mind at ease,' she said. I married him because a dying woman wanted it. She forgave his transgressions easier than I did. If he came home stumbling, my door was locked, but hers was always open. Lots of mornings I'd find him asleep in a chair in her room. She told me, 'Drinking's no crime as long as a man comes home at the end of the night. Your own daddy didn't touch a drop, that holy man. Just look what he did for us, Evelyn.' "

"Did you learn to love him, Mama?"

"Well enough, I suppose." My mother's hands lay on the table, pale and limp, the knuckles already beginning to knot with arthritis, like her own mother's hands. I wondered how long it would be before I sat beside her in Grandmother's room, how long before the bad dreams came and I had to pull the covers from her gnarled claws.

I thought she'd tell Nina how she wanted to go to Canada with that truck driver. I saw them crossing the border, humming along with Patsy Cline. But she spared my sister that knowledge. What difference did it make? Nina was already gone by then. She wasn't the one our mother wanted to leave. She wasn't the one who would have sat by the window day after day, afraid to move, afraid to breathe. She wasn't the one who would have had to watch our father drink himself blind. No, Nina would not have heard the windowpane shatter, would not have picked the slivers of glass from his bloody fist or bandaged his hand while he wept.

Somehow day had come without its ever getting light. The rain had spent itself and given way to a gray drizzle. It rolled off the roof with the weary sound of a child who has cried herself to sleep and still sobs in her dreams.

Nina said, "I'll just pack my bag and wait for Daddy to wake up so I can say good-bye."

I couldn't stay in the kitchen alone with my mother, hearing things about her life I never wanted to know, hearing there were times she hated us, knowing we deserved nothing better for the way we'd stolen her life away from her before she had the chance to dream it. I stood, and Mother said, "Turn out the light before you go."

LEAVES HUNG heavy with rain and tree trunks stood slick and black against the sky. The rain had come too late to save the yellow grass. Nina rustled upstairs, running water in the bathroom, whispering to Daddy. And all I could think, after my years of longing, was how glad I would be to see her go: glad to have her makeup off the bathroom counter, glad not to hear her words to my mother, those words that Nina would leave behind and I would live with. And I would be glad when she could not keep secrets with my father. He would get better or worse, but he would have to depend on us again either way.

I went back to the kitchen, where Mother still sat at the kitchen table, staring at her own hands. "Shall I make coffee?" I said. She was deaf to my question. I made it anyway and put some in front of her, but she never drank it.

Nina clamored down the stairs, her startling heavy steps smacking the wood. In the hallway she made a phone call, her voice hushed and sweet, a demand and a plea. "Thanks, baby," I heard her say. "I knew I could count on you."

She stood in the kitchen doorway wearing her denim skirt and denim jacket, leaning against the frame, Nina, a glimmer of her old self, always leaning up against something, the porch railing, a window, and the boys watching, always, their bodies saying, *Lean against me.* But she was not that girl. She had her bag in one hand and a cigarette in the other. I remembered the silky curtain of her golden hair falling across one eye; now it sprang from her head, curly and wild, that weird unbelievable blond.

"Daddy promised me he'd go back to work," she said. Mom cleared her throat, her eyes still fixed on her own hands. "Mama, I'm sorry if I hurt you," Nina said, as if more words could change the ones that the walls of this room had heard and taken as their own. She scuffed to the sink and poured cold water over her cigarette, then flicked it in the trash.

"No need to be sorry for speaking the truth."

"Then look at me, Mama, please, because I have to go."

Finally my mother raised her head. Her eyes caught no more light than dust on the road. "There now," she said, "I'm looking."

Nina kissed the top of her head and said, "Oh, Mama," into her hair.

"How're you getting back?"

"Hitching down to Rovato Falls. I'll catch a bus from there."

Mother didn't make any offer to drive her or fuss about the hitching because all three of us knew this was one of Nina's small lies. And I believe my mother didn't want to know for sure, didn't want to be told straight out that Nina had called a boy, that for all her talk about having her own life, she was wrapping some kind of rope around her neck again.

I said, "I'll walk you to the highway." I don't know why I said it. Maybe I wanted to be alone with her. Maybe I just needed to get out of that house full of all the words that could be spoken only at night. But I was thinking at that moment that I wanted to make damn sure she really left town.

I carried her bag and we didn't talk. The drizzle touched my cheeks like tiny fingers, tender and probing; I was a leaf bud they wanted to open, and I lifted my face but my heart remained stubborn, a fist in my chest, forever closed.

Rafe Carson was parked on Main Street, right in front of Elliot Foot's burned-out bar. Rafe, the only boy left in Willis for Nina to call. Rafe, the boy who would never hurt her because he knew the sorrow of being forced to his knees. I thought of the day they raised the sign above this bar; I had a vision of the gutted building being fixed up again, and everything starting all over. Rafe's yellow Volkswagen gleamed, glazed with rain, the only bright spot on the gray street.

Nina trotted now, fast and sure. With her escape in sight, she couldn't get out of Willis soon enough. She said, "You won't tell Mama," her words a statement, not a plea.

She tugged her bag out of my hand and tossed it into Rafe's car. "Fancy meeting you here," he said. And she answered, "Yes, just imagine."

Nina turned and hugged me quick, so I didn't have time to hug her back or pull away. "How'd my baby get so tall?" she said, then climbed in the bug and rolled down the window. "Take care of them for me, Lizzie."

I have been, I thought, all this time—for you, because of you.

I stood and watched the Volkswagen buzz down Main. The fine rain fell through the open roof of the Last Chance Bar, fell on the steps of the Lutheran church and on the street in between, that street like a river, carrying my sister away again.

I thought, At the end of the day the rain will still be falling. My father will stand alone at his bedroom window. My mother will sit at the kitchen table. All the lights will be off when dusk comes, and dark. And the doors will be open, and the wind will blow through our house.

The little yellow car disappeared. I wondered how far Rafe Carson would drive her. I wondered if he would be able to leave her at that dingy bus station in Rovato Falls, or if somewhere along the way he'd say, "I might as well drive you to Missoula; I'm not doing anything else today." And I wondered if he'd stay the night or the week, a year or half a life. How strange that she'd chosen him, a boy she'd taunted back in the days when she was a beautiful girl. But they'd grown alike somehow, both of them living on the borderline, trying not to step across. They might hold on to each other for a while and be safe; maybe the best kind of man for Nina was one who couldn't afford to judge her.

I thought she was brave in a way, taking all the credit and all the blame for her own life. I didn't know whom to admire— Nina who cut herself free or my mother who took her life just as it was. I only knew that I wanted my own life someday. I wasn't going to wait on the road for some trucker to take me north. I wasn't going to settle for some redheaded boy whose misery and humiliation matched mine. Someday I was going to leave this town. But when I did, I was leaving by myself, and I was going to decide where I was headed before I got there. Standing on Main Street in the rain, my own life was the only thing that seemed worth having.

Epilogue

YOU COULD play the days of August forward or back and it made no difference: in the beginning Nina was gone and in the end too.

Father did return to work, just as he'd promised her. He didn't talk much about Nina. You could see he held her clutched inside him, in a place no one else could touch. The snake that had curled in his chest for so many years finally disappeared, leaving only its own skin behind. Nina's forgiveness freed him.

Seeing my father step so close to death had made me fear him less. When he yelled at me for skipping school or threatened to slap me for talking fresh, I wasn't afraid. I was too big to paddle, too fast to catch. This knowledge disappointed me in a way, and I felt strangely alone. Neither he nor God watched over my life. Neither could punish or protect me.

So my father and I accepted each other in our silent, uneasy way. He never looked at me as he had looked at Nina or Miriam Deets, eyes opened wide, hands trembling. I was just as glad. I didn't think I could bear to have him need that much from me.

I can't say Mother was happier, but I believe she was less sad. She started painting on her eyebrows again, and the high, thin arches made her look more like her old self: bemused and wise. Sometimes I caught her at the window, staring at nothing in particular. I turned quickly, careful not to startle her, wanting to allow her this small illusion of privacy. I stopped being afraid of her wish to leave us. She had had her chance and she'd stayed. In my selfish heart, I was grateful.

Mother no longer wondered if she could have changed Nina's life with some magic words. Nina had chosen her own life, just as she said. For all of us, it was better to imagine her pulling drafts in a noisy bar, to see her sleeping in a dank basement room, than it was to envision her lost in the desert, blinded by wind-blown sand, or to see her face wavering behind glass at the bottom of a lake.

People asked what else could go wrong in Willis. It's not that so much happens in a small town. Very little happens really. It's just that everything touches someone you know. The quiet fall settled into a still, long winter and the days of August became a legend, a myth about the devil visiting our town, hiding smoldering coals in dirty rags and setting fire to Main Street, sucking a plane down in Moon Lake, tying a knotted shirt around a man's neck and kicking the chair out from under him. In death, Myron Evans was finally accepted. I suspect he would have laughed to hear folks speak of his small kindnesses, and that laugh would have been bitter and full of blame.

Elliot Foot was never accused of arson. He and Joanna returned to the Lutheran church, to bland sermons and calming prayers. Elliot talked about building a café where the Last Chance Bar had been. I don't know if Joanna let him stuff his shoes under her bed or not. I don't know if he cared.

Lyla Leona got back to business. When her neighbors reported that Bo Effinger was her best customer, I was sorry for both of them. I'd expected their promises to be more permanent. I no longer admired Lyla's independence. She relied on men after all. She was a wife three times a night. She had to smile when her head was splitting and remember not to talk too much about herself.

Minnie Hathaway fell off the wagon fast and hard. Most days she was drunk by noon and the oaths spewed from her lips with new force; all those months of holding back gave her renewed energy. Children teased her on the street, just as I had when I was young. Once I saw a pack of them prancing in a circle around her. She spun so fast, looking from one to another, that she fell to her knees. The hooligans scattered and I ran to help her; she cursed me as I lifted her to her feet. Her whiskey breath hit my face, and she called me a string of names, mistaking me for one of the cruel children. Her crippled fingers pinched my arms, and I saw her white gloves were soiled from her fall. I offered to walk her home, but she only snarled. I was relieved, to tell the truth; I could endure her rebukes but not the sight of those dirty gloves.

Lanfear and Miriam Deets left town after Myron hanged himself. I was glad to see them go, though I knew Miriam had no hold on my father now. Still, I didn't wish to pass her on the street and see her look at my mother with pity. She knew nothing of our lives, not really, but Daddy's gifts had entitled her to indulge in this false intimacy, this superior sense of mercy.

Caleb Wolfe left too; every morning when he woke, he saw Myron Evans in his jail. The dead man accused him for falling asleep, or so Caleb Wolfe believed, and I thought how strange it was that the only person who had shown Myron kindness in the last hours of his life should be the one to bear the guilt.

In late November the *Rovato Daily News* reported a story about a blind woman preacher in Idaho who had led her followers to a secluded valley, a valley of darkness, to wait for the second coming of Christ, which, according to her, was due any day. She had seen the signs: fire and drought, men and animals going mad. They built shacks and stashed a store of rifles for the great battles that would come in the final days. They claimed to grow their own food and hunt, but farmers in the area reported stolen chickens and sheep, missing bushels of potatoes, and too many footprints in the yard. Arlen, of course, knew someone who knew someone else who had a daughter who joined the group and later escaped. The preacher woman she described—six feet tall and bony as a starved mule—could not have been anyone but Freda Graves. She was still wearing mirrored sunglasses and telling the story of how the wickedness she'd seen made her put out her own eyes; that is how deeply she grieved for those she knew had fallen away. I knew now she had not blinded herself. I knew there was no daughter, no misshapen grandchild.

Red Elk stayed at the mill for a few months and had no trouble with my father. Daddy knew the big Indian had brought his Nina home, and he knew that a different kind of man might have killed him the night of the fire. After Caleb Wolfe left town, some folks urged Red Elk to run for sheriff, but he refused: he wanted no part of our law.

I thought about the big Indian a lot. He had saved our family three times. He saved my father by keeping Lanfear Deets alive, and he spared me from damnation when he rescued Zachary Holler. He gave us all a second chance the day he found Nina. This man whom Father once chased from our town did not weigh good and evil. He did not live by the laws of our God: an eye for an eye, a tooth for a tooth. He did what he thought was right, and never stopped to ask himself if we deserved his mercy.

I wanted to live by his code, but I had enough trouble just trying to be good, keeping myself from saying nasty things to Marlene Grosswilder, or leaving surprises in her locker. I made

an effort not to speculate on exactly what Eula and Luella Lockwood did in their tub for four hours every day, but it was
difficult to keep my mind from wandering and stop my tongue
from flapping. I kept seeing Myron gripping the pencil, writing:
I try to be good, but sometimes I can't help myself.

Of course I knew that my bargain with the devil was nonbind-
ing. He was never going to knock on my door, looking to collect
his due. The devil didn't want me, and God hadn't even noticed
my father's passing illness. He hadn't heard the frenzy of my pleas
and confessions. If it was true that the devil who loved attention
went after only the best souls, he probably recognized me as one
very much like himself. My soul was not prime territory. I was
no saint, no martyr. I never had the gift of speaking in a tongue
only God could understand. I babbled worthless gibberish. I
wasn't one of the chosen any more than Myron Evans or Minnie
Hathaway was. We were hungry. That was what we shared. It
was only the depth of that hunger that set us apart for a time.
We weren't marked for goodness, but we weren't lucky enough
to be extraordinarily bad, either.

I was alone, all of us were. God had created the world and
let it spin. The Father of the rain took no notice of our daily
struggles. I finally accepted my mother's god, the god with no
mouth to whisper answers in the night, the god with no ears to
hear the cries of the living or the drowned, the god with no hands
to raise me up or beat me down.

If I managed to do something right in my life, it would be
small and have entirely earthly dimensions. I was bound to make
a lot of mistakes and cause grief to others, probably those I loved
best. And when I did, no great hand would strike my head in
retribution, not my father's, not the Lord's.

*

ONE MORE person left Willis that summer: Ruby Holler disappeared before Zachary's hands healed. As Nina said, it wasn't surprising when women ran away, it was only surprising that so many stayed.

At school I looked for Gwen. I thought I might say something kind to her and she might say something back. But she didn't come to school that fall, and I thought maybe she'd gone after her mother. *If she screws, I'll be right behind her,* she said that summer night so long ago when we'd slept in her trailer. I got up the nerve to ask Zack, but I couldn't find him at school either. So it was Coe Carson I cornered in the schoolyard one blustery afternoon in mid-December. He didn't have a hat and his ears burned a brilliant red. I said, "Hey, Coe," and he looked at me as he always did, blank as ice, not knowing me from one month to the next. "Lizzie Macon," I said, "Gwen's friend."

"Oh, yeah," he said, kicking the snow, "I remember."

"I'm looking for Zack."

"You won't find him."

"Actually I'm looking for Gwen."

"Won't find her either." He thrust his bare hands in his pockets and hunched against the wind. It was only four o'clock but almost dark.

"They leave town?"

"Not exactly."

"Well what—exactly?"

"I can't tell you," he said, backing away. I grabbed his coat sleeve and he jerked free, spinning and sprinting across the crusty snow. I broke out after him; he was long-legged but I was strong. If I caught him, I meant to tackle him and hold him down till he talked.

But Coe couldn't keep running in the cold. He stopped and turned, panting, his breath a white cloud in front of his face.

"They don't want to see you," he said. "They don't want to see anyone. They won't answer the door. They won't even answer the phone."

He'd told me all I needed to know. Gwen was still in town. I jogged toward the Hollers' house. At the very least, I was determined to look at her, to see if there was still anything between us. I knew her house as well as my own; all I had to do was get inside. The back door was locked, and I wasn't bold enough to try the front—I thought I'd have to take her by surprise. I walked around the house a dozen times, looking up at every window, hoping to find one cracked open, but there were no open windows in Willis in the middle of December.

Finally I did see a woman's shape behind the blinds of the upstairs bathroom, but it couldn't have been Gwen. I figured Gwen's father already had some big lady living with him, some ugly woman grateful enough to mend his jeans and wash his pants, some poor widow with a nasty disposition who made Gwen ashamed to come to school and answer people's questions about her mother leaving town.

The wind died down and left the clear sky whirling with stars. My stomach growled. I decided to come back and try the next day and the day after that and the day after, until one day a careless hand left the back door unlocked. Then I remembered the door inside the garage that led to a back hallway. I had one last chance.

I stumbled in the dark, through the clutter of bikes and boxes until I held the cold knob in my hand. It gave and I ducked inside, safe and terrified. I flattened myself against the wall and listened. There was no pounding on the stairs, no shouts or slamming doors.

I darted through the living room, where the air hung thick with dusk. Any minute I imagined all the lights would blaze and

I would stand like a fool, blinking and blind, staring down the barrel of some tough boy's rifle with no way to explain myself. But I made it to the other side of the house and up the stairs without Zack or Gwen or the swaybacked lady in the bathroom hearing me. Now I stood at Gwen's door, my hands flat on the smooth wood, knowing I had no right to enter or even knock, knowing she might spit in my face; I was nothing more than an intruder, a burglar with only a girl's privacy to steal.

I tapped, lightly, thinking she might not hear me and I'd be free to go. Maybe that lady would come galloping after me, her flesh quivering, and run me out of the house. If she stopped to ask Gwen who I was, Gwen would deny she knew me and the woman would boot me down the stairs.

But Gwen did hear my knuckles on her door, and she didn't ask, "Who is it?" Instead, softly, she said, "Come in," expecting no strangers, no former friends.

She looked up as I opened the door, and I was the one too stunned to speak. I squeezed my eyes shut; but when I opened them, the girl on the bed still looked the same. The fat lady in the bathroom was Gwen, and here she sat, her belly bulging, her face swollen, her stringy hair unwashed and uncombed.

"Close your mouth before you catch flies," she said. "It's me." I stared at her bare feet; even they were fat. "None of my shoes fit," she said. "Dr. Ben says that some of the things that make the baby grow make parts of me grow too. Look at my hands." She spread her fingers under the little lamp near her bed. The lampshade had dancing teddy bears and red rocking horses. I inched closer to study her hands. She said, "Don't be afraid. You can't catch it, not from me."

Then I knelt beside her and took her hands in my hands, lightly, running my fingertips along her palms, feeling the knobby joints of her thick fingers, one by one.

"What took you so long?" she said. I looked at her eyes, or tried to; they were dark slats behind puffy lids. I didn't understand. "To visit," she said, "what took you so long to visit?"

I took off my coat and let it drop in a heap on the floor. "I didn't know where you were."

"Well, there aren't too many places for a girl like me to go."

"You told me once you'd be right on your mother's tail if she ever split."

She patted her stomach where the thin cloth of an old flowered housedress pulled at the buttons. "I couldn't run fast enough to catch her. Besides, she left on account of me. All these years I thought it was just Zack and my dad she couldn't stand, but you should have seen her when I told her I was pregnant—held her breath so long I thought she'd go blue and faint. Called me a little bitch in heat and said didn't I know how to control myself? Said I should get married and be a burden on some stupid boy instead of her. I told her no way. I told her I didn't even like the boy anymore, and he didn't like me. 'Who gives a damn?' she said. 'Just tell your daddy who he is. He'll take care of it.' I told her to forget it. I wasn't going to do it. I told her I'd give the baby up for adoption, and she said, 'Oh fine. And I'm supposed to stick around and listen to people talk and hold on to you while you puke every morning? No thanks. I've been sick enough mornings of my life without looking after you.' I guess I gave her that push she needed. Zack wasn't out of the hospital yet. She didn't even say good-bye to him."

She smoothed out the blue comforter next to her. The old spread was splattered with faded dusty roses. "Sit down beside me," she said. "No one sits beside me. I know I'm not too pretty, but my father treats me like a leper."

I sat close, our shoulders and thighs touching, and I thought of the girl I'd kissed in the tree house, how her lips frightened me, her mouth as fragile as butterfly wings, and mine dangerous as the clumsy, clutching fingers of a child. I stroked her matted hair and said, "You should take care of yourself, you'd feel better."

She leaned against me, her head resting on my chest, so there was nothing I could do but put both arms around her and hold her tight. "I knew you'd come," she said. "I knew you'd be the only one."

I said, "You shouldn't stay cooped up in here. You need to walk. You need fresh air."

"My father won't let me out of the house. That's the deal. He says I can stay here but I can't disgrace him. He feeds me. He pays Dr. Ben. I have to follow the rules, but I wish he didn't spit every time he sees me. There's nothing unnatural about it, you know. No reason to be afraid of people seeing me. What could they say? 'Gwen Holler's having a baby'? Then they'd be done with it. And what's so terrible about that? I'm not the first. He doesn't even let me come downstairs when he's in the house. Zack brings me breakfast and supper."

I found this difficult to imagine: Zachary Holler acting as nursemaid, carrying a tray up the stairs to his sister, fetching it later and doing the dishes. Gwen said, "You wouldn't know him. He's not so proud, not since the fire. His hands are scarred and the left side of his face got burned too—it's speckled pink and still peels. He thinks he's even worse to look at than I am. He's ashamed. He told me something else too. Remember that night when Myron Evans offered him five bucks?" I nodded. "That night Zack snatched one of Myron's cats and choked it; broke its neck with his own hands. Just like what Myron did to himself. Zack has this crazy idea that he was the one to put the thought in Myron's head."

"That was more than a year ago," I said.

"Yeah, but something else happened later, just before the fire. Zack took his money. You know what I'm saying? He took his money and he didn't run with it. He let Myron do what he wanted, right out there in the vacant lot—my brother and Myron Evans."

I didn't tell her that I already knew. I remembered standing next to Myron, how he grinned when Zachary was inside the burning bar. I saw him piss on Freda Graves's window and heard the words: *That boy took my money and God didn't stop him.*

"He acts like he killed Myron just like he killed that cat," Gwen said. "He's afraid someone will find out; he thinks someone might have seen them together. He never wants to go outside again. I told him that if anyone's responsible for Myron Evans hanging himself it's that little fool Miriam Deets, making a big deal out of nothing, like she'd never seen a guy's dick before. Maybe ol' Lanfear only did it in the dark."

I said, "We're all to blame for Myron, you and me too, chasing him, making his life a misery."

A door slammed downstairs. "The warden's home," Gwen said. "You'll have to fly out this window or pay Zack to sneak you out of here." She giggled. "No, better not offer Zack money."

I held her hand tight. I didn't feel much like talking. I was thinking about all that had happened to us, to everyone in this town.

I saw a man slip five dollars in a boy's pocket, and I saw that man's white-footed cat lying limp in his arms. Now the man huddled over a tiny pad of paper, scratching out his last words.

In a hot room, a bony woman pulled another man's hands toward the flame of a candle. And the flame exploded and torched all our lives in a single summer night.

They hauled Jesse from the lake on a windless summer day.

Nina leaned over him, put her mouth on his with the fervor of a lover; her hair brushed his face, and she wept and pleaded, but he was far beyond the cry of human voices, and his open eyes mocked her.

Years we spent learning not to fear that lake until the day one more boy heard the irresistible call of water and aimed his plane toward the blue surface. Looking for freedom, he found death. Bubbles poured from his lips as the plane plunged deeper and deeper along the rocky ledges of a trench. On his lover's forehead, a purple bruise the size of an egg would tell her story to the men who dragged her body to shore and stood around her, each one praying that his own daughter might be spared the wrath of love.

In a dream my father had, the girl behind glass at the bottom of Moon Lake had my sister's face. And this might be true because the girl who came home looked nothing like my Nina. But in my dreams I saw her in a burning building, her golden hair aflame. I stood mute, too scared to grab her hand or even call her name.

My father and I, for all our love, could not bring Nina back. Only my mother was brave enough to face a yapping yellow dog and a white woman with a gun; only she had enough faith to trust the big Indian my father hated. Daddy had to pretend Nina was unchanged, and I swore she'd never come home. But Mother allowed her to be who she was; Mother sat in the terrible light of the kitchen while Nina's words fell across her neck and shoulders, hard as hailstones dropping from the summer sky.

"Will you do something for me?" I heard my sister's voice but knew it was Gwen who spoke.

"Anything," I answered.

"It's hard for me to wash my hair," she said. "I can't lean over far enough in the tub to get my head under the faucet. Do you think . . . ?"

"Of course."

"I won't repulse you?"

"I don't know."

"You can close your eyes."

"Yes, I can close my eyes."

She waddled down the hall in front of me, her back arched, her bare feet slapping the wood, her hips swaying with the weight of her belly. I carried the towels.

When she stripped, I kept my eyes open and gazed at her full and drooping breasts, wondered at the suddenness of age, the white lines under the skin where flesh had stretched too fast; I touched her hard stomach and jumped back when the baby kicked my hand, then laid my hands on her again, amazed.

"Look at my arms," she said. "I've grown all this extra hair—everywhere." She lifted one leg to show me the dark hairs sprouting along her shins. "It's weird. I feel like I'm living in someone else's body. Dr. Ben says it will go away when the baby comes. I'm going to shed." She smirked, disgusted and amused.

We ran the water till the tub nearly overflowed. I poured pitcher after pitcher over her head, scrubbed her hair three times with shampoo, soaped her back and between each toe, all the places she couldn't reach. Then I dried her too, and wrapped her head in a towel so she stood, naked, like some great-bellied princess in a turban. I dried her thick ankles and her dimpled knees; the coltish legs of the girl were bloated beyond recognition—her limbs had filled like bags of water. I rubbed her thighs with the rough towel, patted her dry in the soft triangle where droplets beaded in dark curls. I followed the knotty joints of her spine, neck to buttocks; even her back was covered with an unfamiliar downy fuzz, the soft growth of hair that made her feel her body had bloomed in strange, unwelcome ways. I brushed the towel lightly along the high ridge of her stomach, making small circles, then bigger and bigger, until I traced the whole great globe of her yeasty, risen loaf. I rubbed her like a magic bottle till she shook, weak with laughter, wobbling on her watery knees.

She was clean and sweet-smelling despite the rage of hormones, sweet and grassy as she was when we stood at the crest of the gully where she kissed me, the first time.

She had a woman's hands now; I told her so as I dried each finger. "Hands to tell stories," I said.

Hands to hold a child if you change your mind, I thought, but I dared not whisper these words.

She said, "Will you come see me again?" And I said yes. The dirty housedress was the only thing she had that still fit, so I told her I'd bring something the next time I visited. "Tomorrow?" she said, and made me promise: *Yes, tomorrow.* "I'll tell Zack. He'll let you in."

"He won't be embarrassed?"

"He has to let someone look at him sooner or later. It might as well be you."

Yes, I thought, it might as well be me. And if I could see the wonder of Gwen's misshapen body, then surely Zack's scarred hands and peeling face would not startle me or make me turn away. I knew now that this was how Jesus healed the lepers, by not being afraid to look at their ravaged flesh, by sitting down beside them. Yes, at last I understood one small thing in this world, that to look at people as they were, without fear or shame, was a kind of healing, sometimes the only kind that mattered.

But I wasn't ready to face Zack tonight. Tomorrow was soon enough.

I don't know why I changed my mind. It seemed I was always turning my back on someone. What had I learned from Red Elk? What had I learned from my mother? I was still running, leaving Nina in the truck with my drunken cousins, moving too slowly to stop Drew Grosswilder's pals from yanking the pants off the Indian boy. I was afraid of Joshua Holler; I was afraid to look at Zack. But I wondered how Gwen could stand even one more night locked in her room.

So I turned around, knocked on her door again. I said, "Come on, we're going to my house," and she didn't argue. She found a pair of heavy wool socks.

"Shoes," she said, "I don't have any shoes."

"We'll take your dad's galoshes."

Josh Holler tried to stop us at the door. "Where the hell do you think you're going?" he said.

"Outside," I told him. He barred the door with his thick body. "There's more than one door to this house," I said. "You'll have to knock us both flat to keep us from leaving." He lurched forward to threaten me, but I didn't budge. Zack watched from the hallway, half hidden in shadow. I thought his loss of beauty would free me from desire; but no, scars or not, he was unchanged, and I longed to touch his face, to say: *It doesn't matter now, none of it matters.* I felt a strange, exhilarating power, knowing I was strong enough to forgive. He grinned at me, glad to see someone stand up to his father, and I grinned back, trusting Zack Holler for the first time.

Joshua moved away from the door. He wasn't going to hit a pregnant girl or another man's daughter; he wasn't going to chase us from the front of the house to the back. "I want you home at nine," he said, and Gwen nodded, generous enough to let him still believe he had some hold on her.

I knew my parents would be surprised to see Gwen Holler this way, her body swollen, her skin dull. They were already in the kitchen. My father's ears reddened when he looked at Gwen, but he said, "Have a seat," and he tried to smile. Mother touched Gwen's shoulder, lightly, just as a mother would touch her own child. Gwen said, "It smells good in here. It's been so long since I smelled real food. Zack only knows how to cook scrambled eggs and chipped beef with creamed peas on toast."

We laughed, though it wasn't funny. I could see Daddy's struggle as he looked at the pregnant girl. I imagined he was wishing he had let Nina stay all those years ago, let her sit at his table, let her pat her huge stomach in her distracted, absent way. But the best a man can do is to make the right choice when he gets a second chance. We sat down together and joined hands. My father bowed his head. "Father, we thank thee," he said, "for these mercies. . . ."

I was proud of my mother and father just then. Until that night, I had never said those words to myself. Gwen scraped her plate clean, and Mom gave her more macaroni and cheese, another heap of green beans. "You need your vegetables," Mom said. I saw what a mother's concern meant to Gwen. She rubbed her eyes with her napkin. And I was thankful to my friend, realizing how much more difficult it is to accept kindness than it is to offer it. After dinner, Daddy went out on the porch to smoke a cigarette in the dark. I washed the dishes while Mother sat with Gwen, drinking pale tea.

JUST BEFORE nine, I walked Gwen to her house, kissed her cheek and promised I'd bring her oranges and chocolate when I came tomorrow. I turned and ran down the block. Night had broken clear and cold. A touch might have shattered the frozen sky if human arms could reach that far. Above me the thick stars of the

Milky Way spun in the blue-black air, all the eyes of lost children, of those missing and those dead. My eyes on them mur-
mured a prayer that had no words. Soon there would be one more
child in this world, a child Gwen meant to give away before she
could be tugged and bound by love. And this child too would
disappear from our lives and become a star to watch over us
without pity or judgment. This child, his eyes locked in Heaven,
would see us night after night but would not ever find a path
to lead him home.

ABOUT THE AUTHOR

MELANIE RAE THON was born in Kalispell, Montana, and now lives in Boston, Massachusetts.